"Your reputation is precious to you, Sarah," he said, reaching up for her. "I doona wish to cause you any trouble."

He lifted her down, taking his time, relishing the caress of her body as he brought her to the ground.

"We should not be here alone," she said.

"Who will know?"

He felt her swallow, but she protested no more, nor did she pull away from him.

"You're trembling." Brogan lifted her chin, but she avoided looking at him. "Are you afraid of me, lass?"

She shook her head, then spoke quietly. "I must be beyond reproach."

He lowered his head. "One kiss does no' a harlot make."

Other **AVON ROMANCES**

A DANGEROUS BEAUTY *by Sophia Nash*
THE DEVIL'S TEMPTATION *by Kimberly Logan*
THE HIGHLANDER'S BRIDE *by Donna Fletcher*
MISTRESS OF SCANDAL *by Sara Bennett*
THE TEMPLAR'S SEDUCTION *by Mary Reed McCall*
WHEN SEDUCING A SPY *by Sari Robins*
WILD SWEET LOVE *by Beverly Jenkins*

Coming Soon

TEMPTED AT EVERY TURN *by Robyn DeHart*
WHAT ISABELLA DESIRES *by Anne Mallory*

And Don't Miss These
AVON ROMANTIC TREASURES
from Avon Books

BEWITCHING THE HIGHLANDER *by Lois Greiman*
HOW TO ENGAGE AN EARL *by Kathryn Caskie*
THE VISCOUNT IN HER BEDROOM *by Gayle Callen*

Margo Maguire

A Warrior's Taking

AVON BOOKS

An Imprint of HarperCollinsPublishers

AVON BOOKS
An Imprint of HarperCollins*Publishers*
10 East 53rd Street
New York, New York 10022-5299

Copyright © 2007 by Margo Wider
ISBN: 978-0-06-125626-4
ISBN-10: 0-06-125626-9
www.avonromance.com

First Avon Books paperback printing: July 2007

Avon Trademark Reg. U.S. Pat. Off. and in Other Countries,
Marca Registrada, Hecho en U.S.A.
HarperCollins® is a registered trademark of HarperCollins Publishers.

Printed in the U.S.A.

10 9 8 7 6 5 4 3 2 1

This book is dedicated to my husband, Mike, the man who brought magic to my life. And keeps it there.

A
WARRIOR'S
TAKING

Chapter 1

The Western Sea off the Isle of Coruain, 981

Ana took hold of her cousin's powerful arm. "Wait, Brogan! You are too brash by half!"

A muscle in his jaw tightened. "As I understand it, we've no time to waste, lass." He secured the strap of his satchel to his back and stepped up to the edge of the chieftain's magnificent ship, ignoring the chill of the air on his bare skin as they sailed toward the portal that would propel him through time. "While my brother placates the elders with tales of blood stones, I will begin my quest."

"But Brogan, you must take more time to confer with Merrick! There is so much for him to teach you about—"

"My brother has told me all that is necessary. I am to use no magic, but find the stone. By tomorrow, I will have the prize and return to Coruain House."

"Brogan, it will no' be so simple! You must listen to what Merrick can tell—"

He did not wait to hear the rest. He'd listened until he was sick of his brother's voice, and burning to take action. To avenge the death of his father, Kieran, high chieftain of all the Druzai. They had never anticipated that the evil sorceress, Eilinora, would escape her bonds and come to Coruain.

Never dreamed Kieran would be vulnerable to attack.

"Brogan, wait!"

"Eilinora took my father's scepter of power," he said. "She could return to our isles at any time."

Tears welled in Ana's eyes. Brogan knew she grieved deeply for her uncle, the most powerful and beloved of all the Druzai chieftains. But Kieran's brutal murder compelled him to action now.

"If you and Merrick are correct," he said, "our only chance against the witch is with the *brìgha*-stones. And you say they were hidden in time."

Ana nodded as Brogan climbed to the prow of the ship. "Brogan, I couldna *see* what force released Eilinora from her bonds. She is not our only worry!"

"Do you think she is aided by some mighty sorcerer who wishes to disrupt Coruain?"

Ana touched her cousin's arm. "I doona know, Brogan. Mayhap 'tis not Druzai . . . it might have powers beyond our own. You must take special care—"

"Wish me Godspeed, cousin," he said, anxious to act. "If I survive the Astar Columns, I promise to return the blood stone to Coruain on the morrow. A few days at most."

Brogan made his dive into the depths of the sea, calling forth the charms that would protect him until he reached the Astar Columns. Once he was through them, his survival would depend on his physical strength and endurance.

And his ability to function nearly nine hundred years in the future, without alerting Eilinora and the Odhar to his presence.

The rugged North Cumbria coast, late summer, 1813

Lost in thought, Sarah Granger followed Margaret and Jane Barstow across the beach, picking up all the cockles they could find, placing them in heavy canvas sacks, then carrying the sacks to their rickety pony cart. So preoccupied was she with the news she'd received from Captain Barstow's solicitor in nearby Craggleton, she scarcely noticed the children or their gamboling cat, Brownie.

She'd had a strong premonition of changes to come, but never this.

"Miss Granger, look!" cried Jane, a year younger than her sister at age six. She pointed to a bit of indigo color caught in the surf near the rocks ahead.

"'Tis naught but a clump of rags, Jane," Sarah replied absently, but the child scampered ahead, roused by the possibility of treasure to be found.

"Look at her," Margaret added, "with her torn stockings and her tangled hair."

It was true; no matter how clean and well-dressed the child was at breakfast, she managed to look like a homeless urchin by noon. But Margaret was the picture of good breeding, with her tidy clothes and neat braids. If not for their similar features and pale blond hair, no one would guess they were sisters.

Sarah rarely took Jane into Craggleton, for she did not wish to subject the child to the same kind of ridicule Sarah had felt after the death of her own father. Her peers had been cruel, mocking her for her father's descent into drunkenness, his failure to earn a decent living, and the charity on which Sarah had been dependent after his death. She'd moved from household to household in the parish after his death, working for her keep, lamenting the futility of all her dreams.

She hadn't ever belonged anywhere, not until Captain Barstow had brought her to Ravenfield.

How she loved the place.

"What does Jane think?" Margaret scoffed. "That she'll find something of value on this empty beach?" The child's sober view of life was anything but childlike and had only gotten worse since they'd received news of Captain Barstow's death in battle.

"Ah, but we know Jane, don't we?" Sarah said fondly as she caressed Margaret's head. "She probably hopes a ship was wrecked out at sea and there will be—"

"She dreams such rot," Margaret interjected, cynical beyond her years. She needed much more loving attention than her sister, and Sarah was happy to provide it. Sarah and their housekeeper, Maud, were the only family the girls had.

Except for Charles Ridley, the distant cousin Sarah had just learned of.

Jane screamed suddenly, her cries loud above the crash of the surf on the rocks. "Miss Granger! Margaret! Come quickly!"

Sarah dropped her sack of cockles, shouting as she ran. "Don't go into the water, Jane!" But the girl ignored her, stepping into the waves.

When Sarah saw what it was, she, too, wasted no time, and dashed into the sea to get to him. It was a man, waterlogged and unconscious, perhaps even dead.

"Go back to the shore!" Sarah ordered Jane, taking hold of the man's arms.

Jane scampered out of the water while Sarah struggled to drag the man out of the sea. She hardly noticed that he was naked, or nearly so, with only a shimmering violet cloth covering his buttocks.

They could drag him no farther than the sand, and when he started to cough and choke, his wide shoulders flexing and contracting as he struggled for breath, Sarah sank to her knees beside him and pressed her hands soundly against his back.

"That's it," she said under her breath. "Breathe."

"Is he a Persian pasha?" asked Jane, pointing to the wide copper torque that encircled the thick muscle of his upper arm.

"Don't be stupid, Jane," said Margaret. She turned to Sarah. "Is he?"

Sarah had never before seen a man with long, raven-black hair, or cloth such as the indigo scrap that covered his private parts. She could not imagine who he was or how he happened to wash up on their shore.

"Girls, go back to the pony cart and wait for me there."

"But Miss Granger," Jane whined, "I'm the one who—"

"No arguments, love. Go." She spoke the words without taking her eyes from the young man who lay so still and pale, so beautiful with his hair slicked back from his face. He lay prone with his head turned to the side, so all Sarah could see of his face was his strong profile, his dark brows and the thick black lashes that curved over his cheek. He was definitely a stranger to the parish, and Sarah wondered if there *had* been a shipwreck overnight. Maud had mentioned seeing some strange lights the night before . . .

She quickly discounted that thought, for there would be much more debris on the beach, and Maud's eyesight was failing. The man must have fallen overboard, or been caught unaware by the tide. Gingerly, she placed the backs of her fingers on his cheek, and found his skin icy cold.

Ignoring her sodden clothes and ruined shoes, Sarah ran her hands down his tapering torso, then back up, vigorously rubbing his bronzed skin, warming him as much as she was able. "Wake up! You must awaken, sir!"

"Look, Miss Granger!" cried Jane with excitement. In true form, the child had strayed from the cart and was clambering among the rocks nearby while Margaret stood dutifully beside the pony cart. "A satchel! It matches his . . . his . . . *drawers.*"

Caught in the rocks was a pack constructed of the same violet material that was draped about his hips. "Put it in the cart," Sarah said, without letting up her efforts to revive the man. "Then run home and get Maud, both of you."

The girls quickly turned to do her bidding.

"And bring blankets!" Sarah called after them.

The young man coughed again, sputtering enough sea water to drown two men. Coming to awareness, he pushed himself onto his hands and shook his head, tossing droplets of water from his hair, just as a wild animal might do. The bulging muscles in his arms gave Sarah pause, and her heart fluttered a bit faster in her chest. The air seemed to shimmer around him, and she was certain she'd seen no English farmer who possessed such raw masculine beauty. And she'd certainly never seen so much exposed male flesh.

Maybe he *was* some foreign potentate.

He turned and fell onto his back, then raised one arm to cover his eyes, unaware of Sarah's presence. Sarah was astonished and fascinated by the whorls of dark hair that covered his chest and arrowed down the rippled plain of his belly to disappear beneath the cloth that covered him.

His groans startled Sarah's attention back to his face.

"Hello?" she said. It was only right to alert him to her presence.

He dropped his arm and looked sharply at her, his eyes the same startling color as the cloth that covered him.

"You, uh . . ." She gestured toward the water, feeling unsettled by his gaze. "You seem to have washed ashore, sir. What happened to you?"

Hardly acknowledging her presence, the man turned to glance at the sea while Sarah averted her eyes from the virile expanse of his body. Even his legs were densely muscled, and she wondered at the physical power that must be leashed within him. While she knelt shivering in the sand from the cold of the water, he did not even recoil when the surf washed up to drench him again.

"Wha' place is this?" he demanded, his voice deep and raspy, his accent distinctly different from any she'd ever heard before.

He seemed barely civilized, the absolute opposite of Squire John Crowell, the handsome gentleman who'd owned Sarah's heart ever since she'd first seen him in Craggleton, a youth not much older than herself. On the few occasions when they'd crossed paths, he'd given her a polite nod and gone on his way, never making her feel like the misfit she was.

Sarah had entertained any number of foolish fantasies about the squire since then, but knew he'd never really noticed her, a destitute orphan who was compelled to work in Craggleton's better homes for her survival. Besides, there were any number of beautiful, dowered young ladies in Craggleton who were far above Sarah's station.

Sarah turned her attention to the stranger. Now was not the time to dwell on her impractical dreams of the unattainable Squire Crowell. If nothing else, Sarah had learned to be a practical woman. "Are you a Scot, sir?"

He shuddered and pushed himself onto his elbows, ignoring her question. "I am weaker than I anticipated. Move aside, lass."

Scot or not, he was arrogant, if not outright rude. He would soon learn she was no one's lass. She was twenty-two years old and held a position of some responsibility as nurse and governess to the daughters of the late Captain Barstow. She had managed the house and estate without help in the months since they'd learned of his death.

The man glanced around. "My satchel. Did ye see it?"

"The children took it when they left to get help," she replied. "Who are you, sir?"

Without answering the question, he levered himself up from the sand and came to his feet. "I need no further help," he said in a condescending manner, his unsteadiness belying his words.

"I think you do, sir. Wait. Let me—"

He started to fall. Sarah moved to support him, but their arms tangled and they both fell to the ground.

* * *

Brogan twisted his body to take the brunt of the fall, landing with the heavily-dressed Tuath woman atop him. Breathing heavily, she lay perfectly still against him, her face mere inches from his, her mossy green eyes stunned.

They lay still in their intimate position, both of them hardly breathing, but he could feel the rapid beat of her heart against his chest. She was soft and feminine, her scent foreign and enticing. Primitive.

In one swift maneuver, he changed their positions, shifting the lass to the sand beneath him. Her lips were full and pink, and he could think of naught but tasting them. Feeling raw and fundamentally male, he slipped one of his thighs between her legs and pressed upward until he heard her take a sharp breath.

He was no longer a powerful Druzai warrior, but just a man, inexorably drawn to that mouth in spite of her being Tuath. He lowered his head until he was a breath away from tasting her. Her lashes fluttered closed, and he knew 'twould take but one slick move to dispense with her skirts and slide into her—

"No!" He jerked away abruptly, moving off her, wondering what sorcery she'd used to beguile him. He had heard no tales of Tuath magic, yet this lass had nearly bewitched him.

Even as the odd intensity of their physical encounter burned through his veins, Brogan resolved to interact no more than absolutely necessary with anyone in this time and place. Finding the *brìgha*-stone was his only reason for coming to this inferior world. With the information Ana had given him, he was certain 'twould be a simple task to find the stone and return to Coruain. He had only to find the site called Ravenfield and collect the stone.

He shook his head to clear it of the staggering disorientation resulting from his passage through the Astar Columns, as well as the fierce arousal the lass had managed to kindle. If he weren't so weak, he would use his hunting skills to determine whether she'd actually used magic. But as it was, he could not even stand unaided.

He frowned when he noted her scampering away from him as though he had fangs and was covered by black scales. He was no pesky sìthean.

And she was but a Tuath.

Still, she was an uncommon beauty with dark russet hair falling in loose tangles 'round her narrow shoulders, and a light dusting of freckles across her nose and high cheekbones. When her cheeks blushed pink and she avoided meeting his eyes, Brogan recalled something of Merrick's warnings about Tuath etiquette. The woman was undoubtedly embarrassed by their intimate contact.

Which suited him just as well. He intended to leave no lasting impression on her or anyone else when he went through the Astar Columns again to return home.

Despite his persistent dizziness, Brogan sat up in the sand and rubbed his face. He could still smell the woman's intriguing scent, and he felt impossibly drawn by the warmth of her body against his skin.

'Twas ridiculous to be so enthralled. He was sure there was no magic on earth that could seep so insidiously inside him.

She got to her feet and stood over him. "Wh-what happened to you, sir? How did you . . ." A small crease appeared between her delicately arched brows, and she gave a slight shake of her head. The sun caught the red of her hair, and it shone like the copper of the Mac Lochlainn torque on his arm.

He growled with disgust at such a nonsensical thought and turned away from her pleasingly disheveled form, and the spark of intelligence in her sea-green eyes. He had to get his bearings and start his search, not waste time ogling a common Tuath wench.

"'Tis not often that strange men wash up on our beach," she said pointedly. "In fact, never."

"I'm no' strange, lass," he said irritably as a burst of pain shot through his skull and down his back.

He glanced 'round the desolate beach with its high cliffs and scattered rocks, then back at the woman. She'd soaked her gown pulling him from the water, and it hugged her so well that it left very few details of her figure to his imagination.

Yet when she quirked her brow and threw a stern expression his way, she reminded him of a mighty Druid priestess, one of the very people Eilinora had nearly ruined. They were the very reason the Druzai had created their own kingdom and retreated to it, never to cross paths with the Tuath again.

But Brogan was going to need her assistance.

He muttered a quiet curse and wished he'd paid closer attention to Merrick's advice about the people of this place and time. He could not allow her to suspect he was anything but one of her kind. Having fought against interaction with the Tuath for so many years, he was not going to compromise his principles now.

Nor would he succumb to the ridiculous tug of attraction he felt for the Tuath woman. She was not of his class, and such a temptation would only interfere with his purpose here.

He considered whether he could risk using a spell of his own to counteract her appeal. Ana and

Merrick had warned against using sorcery, certain
that Eilinora's cronies would be able to hunt him
if he made any use of his magic. But he'd never
felt a tug of power like the one this Tuath used
against him.

"Sir?"

"I must have fallen overboard," he finally said,
deliberately turning away from the sight of her
unattractive gown and the way it hugged her
breasts so snugly. He wondered if their tips were
smooth and light pink like her lips, or hardened
coral peaks.

"From what ship?" she demanded with quiet
authority.

He snapped his mouth closed and redirected his
thoughts, belatedly understanding that he had to
fabricate a story for her. "Ship?" He'd never been
so muddle-headed before, and his lack of clarity
irked him.

The lass stalked away, but only a few paces. Her
posture was stiff and forbidding, her attitude as
haughty as a royal Druzai daughter. Yet no sorceress had ever spoken so condescendingly to him.

He scowled at her next words. "This is *my*
beach, sir, and you are an intruder. One without a
name. When I notify the magistrate—"

"No magistrate." *Mo oirg*, this was becoming
complicated. "I simply . . . fell from my boat when
a wave swelled over me."

"Hmmpf."

Affronted by the skeptical sound she made, Brogan nonetheless realized he was not as convincing as he needed to be.

He ignored the suspicious gleam in her eyes, and resisted the ridiculous urge to take her down to the sand again and remove layer after layer of her preposterous clothing. He would demonstrate the superiority of a Druzai man over any Tuath lover she'd ever known.

"Really?" Her sarcasm interrupted his sensual fantasy. "Then what happened to your clothes?"

Chapter 2

The Scot did not frighten Sarah, not as the callous boys in Craggleton had done before she'd come to Ravenfield. But she felt certain he was lying. He didn't want the magistrate called, and somehow he'd lost all his clothes, except for the strange cloth that covered his, er . . .

Sarah turned away quickly, before she could embarrass herself any further. She'd already sprawled over him and under him, and had come perilously close to doing the unthinkable—kissing him! She could not imagine what had possessed her.

Unless it had been the way they'd fallen positioned so intimately that she'd forgotten herself; or the way he'd gazed at her mouth, as if he wanted to devour her. That was certainly a novelty. No man in the parish had looked twice at her in the years since the death of her father.

She was anything but a good catch, with no

property, and no particular lineage. She'd been known as a charity case, the whelp of a drunkard. No one cared that she'd been well-educated and respectable before her father's decline. She was as capable and intelligent as any young woman in Craggleton, and living off the charity of the parish had not changed any of her abilities.

If anything, she'd become more independent, and a good deal more cautious in her dealings with the world. She'd learned to become invisible to those who would torment her, to the mean boys who cornered her and tried to molest her, to the spiteful housewives who used any excuse to give her a vicious slap, and to the husbands who thought to make illicit visits to her chamber during the night.

Invisible or not, Sarah still did not enjoy going into town, knowing that she was remembered as Paul Granger's whelp. Soon she would have to change that. With the news she'd received from Captain Barstow's solicitor, she was going to have no choice but to face those same heartless people every day.

"What have we here?" cried Maud from the shrubs that lined the path to the house. Sarah was exceedingly glad to see Ravenfield's housekeeper.

Maud's well-worn apron was tied about her waist, her sleeves rolled to her elbows, and she was flanked by one little blond-haired girl on each side. Catching Sarah's glance, she approached, just as curious as the children. "Oh my dear saints! The girls told me they'd found a drowned man!"

Maud had worked for the Barstow family much longer than Sarah, doing the cooking and cleaning, and helping to care for Margaret before Mrs. Barstow's death in childbirth. Sarah didn't know what she would have done without the round, robust little woman with her pewter-gray hair and warm, mother's heart. Still, she knew Maud wanted to retire and go down to Ulverston to live with her widowed sister. She'd stayed at Ravenfield only to help Sarah after Captain Barstow's death.

"I'm no' drowned, as you can verra well see," growled the stranger.

It was the most he'd said yet, and Sarah was struck again by the unusual cadence of his speech.

He pushed up to his feet, grimacing in pain. This time, he did not reject Sarah's assistance. For such a well-muscled man, he was as wobbly and feeble as a newly walking child.

"Oh dear, dear, dear," Maud said as the stranger stood up to his full height.

Sarah was unsure where she should take hold of him. Surely every rule she'd ever learned was being broken now, but what choice was there? The man had no clothes, and they needed to get him back to the house, to get warm and dry. It was no time to stand on ceremony.

Taking hold of the arm with the burnished torque, she draped it over her shoulders, then wrapped her own arm around his waist. Maud came to his opposite side and did the same.

"You'll ride in the pony cart," Sarah said.

"I'll walk," he protested, as though he did not quite grasp how weak he was.

"Not all the way home," Sarah countered. "'Tis too far for a man in your state."

"What happened to your clothes?" Maud asked, squinting her eyes to see him more clearly.

Sarah waited to hear if the man would answer, or ignore the question once again.

"As they were, ah . . . pullin' me down in the water, I discarded them."

"I see. Well, 'tis no matter now. We'll find you something suitable at Ravenfield."

"Ravenfield?"

"Aye. Our home," Maud said, raising her brow at the emphasis he placed on the word. "You know of it?"

Sarah was entirely taken aback when the Scot let out a harsh growl and suddenly doubled over. His legs buckled under him and she could not hold him up, even with Maud's help. They eased him back down to the sand, where he lay unconscious and gray-faced once again.

Sarah crouched down, alarmed by the stranger's deathly pallor. "Maud, what do you think is wrong with him?"

"I don't know, but for certain we won't be able to help him until we get him into a bed and call for the doctor," said Maud. "Go get the cart, girls."

"You'll never lift him into the cart," said Margaret.

"Aye, we will. He'll rouse enough to get himself in."

"But how—?"

Maud removed her apron and hurried down to the sea, bending to the surf to soak the cloth in the cold water. When she returned, the woman wrung it out over the man's face.

Roused by the splash of cold water, the man coughed and sputtered nearly as much as before. He muttered a word Sarah did not understand, then looked up at Maud. "What in holy Hades—"

"Watch your language, if you please, sir," Maud said, and the girls drew the cart closer. "Come now, you'll have to help us." Somehow, they managed to wrestle him into it, then took him all the way up to the house while Jane chattered happily about the Scotsman's good luck, and Margaret made the occasional dire prediction.

He roused himself enough to help them get

him inside. He remained pale and weak, and nearly insensible when they put him in Captain Barstow's too-short bed in the room on the first floor of the house.

"He's got to be over six foot," said Maud. "And such a comely one!"

"Maybe so, but he is terse and overbearing. And his manners leave much to be desired." A gentleman would never have pulled her down with him . . . Nor, once down, would he have insinuated his leg between hers. And rolling her to a position beneath him was utterly indecent. She was a respectable woman, certainly no pauper to be indecently used as the well-heeled men in town would have done.

"Ah well, he did help us to get him into the captain's room, didn't he?" asked Maud.

"Just barely," Sarah said, shivering away the odd tingle that coursed down her spine. She took the violet satchel from Margaret and once again noted the strange cloth. Besides its unusual color, it looked as smooth as glass and seemed to be holding its own heat, which begged the very question Sarah had been struggling to avoid.

"I wonder if his wreck was what I saw over the cliffs last night," said Maud.

Sarah held her tongue. There was no point in mentioning the possibility that her eyes had played tricks on her. Maud was worried enough about her failing eyes.

"What's that in his drawers?" Jane asked.

Sarah's face heated, suddenly afraid she'd voiced her own inappropriate question aloud. She'd felt it—the long, hard, masculine ridge that had created a storm of sensation when he'd pressed against her. Her reaction was surprisingly different from her revulsion when the boys in town had pushed themselves against her and tried to touch her breasts.

"Never you mind, young lady," Maud admonished as Sarah quickly pulled the blanket over the man's large frame. "'Tis no concern for the likes of you."

Or for Sarah, either, she reminded herself.

"He'll probably die," Margaret said. "And we'll have to bury him at St. Edward's, behind the fence. His stone will read, 'Here Lies the Drowned Scotsman.'"

"He is so lovely," said Jane, her voice wistful. "I surely hope he doesn't die."

"Nay, you never call a man lovely, Jane," said Maud. "Handsome is what you'd say."

The girls' talk of death shook Sarah. "Shall I go into Craggleton for the doctor?" she asked, without considering that they had no money to pay for his services. "Or summon Squire Crowell?"

Maud shook her head. "His color is better

now that we've got him home. No doubt a good night's sleep will cure whatever ails him. It works for most every ill I know of. Come on now, girls, time to get your tea."

Maud herded the little ones to the door, then turned back to Sarah. "I expect we'll find out all about this one in time. No need for the magistrate, at least not yet."

Sarah nodded. She put the satchel on the floor beside the bed and tucked the blanket around him before quitting the room behind the others.

Brogan snapped awake, struggling for breath, thrashing against the weight of the water holding him down. He'd been secure enough for his descent through the deep sea waters to the Astar Columns, but his passage through time had jolted every muscle and nerve in his body, and rattled his mind. He must have lost consciousness for a time, because he had no idea how he'd survived the ordeal and passed to the other side of the columns. He could remember naught.

The ancient elders must not have anticipated a need for passing through time without any spells to protect the traveler. In ancient times, they'd buried the columns at the bottom of the Coruain Sea with full confidence that any Druzai who had sufficient need to use them would also use the necessary magic to arrive and pass through safely.

They had never anticipated Eilinora's escape and subsequent attack.

Brogan had a deep awareness of barely having survived. Even now, his body and mind staggered with the trauma of his passage. His disorientation persisted, and he rolled from his resting place to land on his feet, feeling raw and ready for battle. Then he remembered why he had come, and a wave of grief hit him just as hard as the agony that had struck when the Tuath women helped him into the cart.

His father had been brutally killed by Eilinora and her Odhar, and no magic could return him to this life. Merrick, Ana, and Brogan had sent Kieran off in a funereal swirl of light and thunder, the magnificence of which had never been seen on Coruain. It had been a fitting funeral, yet hardly grand enough for the high chieftain of all the Druzai islands.

As he sat down on the bed to combat a wave of dizziness, he felt a moment's regret that Merrick had not presented any grandchildren to their father. Kieran had always said that his sons' lack of heirs was the one imperfection in his life.

Brogan had never felt compelled to wed for the purpose of supplying royal offspring for his father. He would settle for no less than a *céile* mate, one woman whom he was destined to bond with forever. But he was well past the age when Druzai men found *sòlas* with their one true mate. 'Twas not likely to happen at this late date.

He flexed his muscles and stretched. His body felt as though it had taken a beating, and his memory of entering this chamber was hazy. The pain in his belly had subsided, but he felt ravenously hungry. His head ached and his legs still felt weak, hard-pressed to hold him up.

Brogan had heard Merrick's warnings about the perils of moving through time, but he'd been so anxious to take action that he'd barely heeded them. Merrick always moved too damned slowly for Brogan's liking, carefully deliberating every possible consequence to his actions. Brogan knew one thing: Coruain was doomed to suffer further assaults by Eilinora if they did not find the blood stones and return to the isles quickly.

Setting aside his grief and his impatience with his brother, Brogan took stock of his surroundings. 'Twas certain the comely Tuath woman did not sleep here, for the room was cramped and cluttered, and smelled stale, as if it had been closed up and unused for some time. He wondered if he had heard right, that this place was Ravenfield. If so, 'twas going to be an easy task to find the *brìgha*-stone—even without using magic. Anxious to begin, he rose to his feet again and made a quick search of the room. But he found naught of interest.

Though he should not have expected immediate success, his failure to locate the stone quickly was frustrating. He could not help but wonder if Ana had *seen* correctly. Standing nine hundred years in the future, he felt far removed from Druzai magic and Ana's abilities. What if she was wrong?

He pulled open the door and stepped into yet another room illuminated by an oil lamp, startling the young woman who'd helped him earlier. She stood abruptly, dropping a large piece of cloth to the floor. "You're awake!"

She'd changed clothes, but the plain gray gown was hardly better than the one that had gotten soaked when she'd pulled him from the sea. Brogan could not help but think she would be well-suited wearing the soft gauzes and colorful silks favored by Druzai women.

He glanced 'round the room. It was poorly lit by the lamp on the table next to her chair, but he could see that the rest of the furnishings were sparse as well as shabby. With its threadbare rug and narrow, curtain-covered windows, the room was clean and tidy, but had seen better days.

There were two more chairs, a sofa, and a large wooden case that appeared to be a musical instrument. 'Twas unlike anything he'd ever seen on Coruain.

Brogan returned his attention to the woman. "We're alone?" he asked.

"Of course not!" she snapped. In an instant, her eyes changed color from soft green to fawn brown, and he sensed a change in her from unease to indignation. "Maud is here . . ." She half turned toward another door that led to a dark hallway. "Well, she's gone to bed," she amended, "and so have the children. But they're—"

"Not here, are they?"

He knew he should not goad her. The rapidity of the pulse at the base of her neck was proof of her nervousness, and Brogan supposed he should reassure her, for he might need her assistance.

He took a step closer and could not help but think how well those soft curves would be displayed in a Druzai tunic. Her scent beckoned him even closer.

"I willna harm you, if that's your concern." He only wanted the stone and a quick exit from this world and his strange reaction to the Tuath woman. He wondered if he could risk asking her for it, then thought better of it.

"My concern is your lack of clothing, sir. Must you display yourself in such an uncivilized manner?"

Her words caught him up short. She thought *he* was uncivilized? "Woman, I nearly drowned in your cursed sea!"

"But you did not, sir," she retorted. "And I left clothing for you on the chair beside the bed. Please go and—"

He put his hands on his hips and braced his feet firmly on the floor. Her ridiculous demands were not going to divert him from his purpose. "What is this place?"

In spite of his stern question, she crossed her arms and began to tap her foot.

No woman on Coruain, except mayhap Ana, would ever presume to take such a high-and-mighty attitude with him. Brogan was the son—now brother—of the high chieftain, and commander of all Druzai warriors. If she were not Tuath and he could divulge his identity to her, she would kneel to him and thank him for the honor of his presence in her humble house.

Folding his own arms, he glowered at her, but she did not relent. With a resolute expression, she surprised him by taking hold of his arm, turning him, and starting to propel him toward the bedchamber.

"I do not know how things are done in Scotland," she said, her cheeks flushing with color, "but it is highly improper for you to appear outside the bedchamber unclothed, sir. Get dressed while I prepare a meal for you. Then we'll talk."

He could easily have stopped her, but the firm touch of her hand and her obstinate manner interfered with his good judgment. He'd never been treated in such a way by any woman. In any case, if the lass's tongue would be loosened by his donning the clothes he'd brought, then he was willing to comply with her command. He let her take him back to the small, musty room, and did not once regret having embarrassed her.

Not when her blushes were so enchanting.

Removing his clothes from the satchel, he could not explain what it was about this thorny Tuath lass that made him lose track of his priorities.

Sarah leaned back against the closed the door of Captain Barstow's room and took a deep breath as she tried to erase the sight of the Scotsman's bare body from her mind. She knew she should call Maud to come down, but the poor woman had been so worn out after supper that Sarah didn't have the heart to wake her.

She had to deal with the pompous Scot herself. For all his size and strength, Sarah believed he meant her no harm, just as he'd said. He was obviously a stranger to Cumbria, seeming almost as though he'd come from another world. She guessed much of his peculiarity was due to his near drowning. It would likely take some time to recover from such a shock.

Yet his arrogance grated on her. He was little better than a half-drowned dog, washed up on their shore, yet he behaved as if his presence at Ravenfield honored her in some way. He was as bad as the philanderers in Craggleton.

In the kitchen, she added wood to the stove, then went outside to collect a couple of eggs. When she returned, she cut two slices of bread and spread jam on them, keeping her attention solely on the tasks at hand, and not on the solid wall of muscle she had just prodded into the bedroom. She did not know where she'd gotten the nerve to touch his bare skin now that he was fully awake.

That scrap of fabric that hung from his hips was unlike any of the linens Maud had ever washed and hung on the line for Captain Barstow. Sarah felt her face heat at the very thought of the inadequate purple garment and what must lie beneath. Quickly, she turned her thoughts elsewhere.

The man could not possibly have *fallen* into the sea, not unless he was wholly incompetent, and he did not strike her thus. There'd been no storms for at least a week, which meant something had happened to incapacitate him. Or he'd been pushed.

Sarah shuddered at the thought of foul play.

Perhaps Squire Crowell really should be summoned. After all, he was the magistrate, and if someone had intended to harm the Scot, there should be an inquiry.

Her inclination to call upon the squire had nothing to do with wanting to reinstate him in her mind as the most handsome of men. The interlude with the drowned Scot had merely shaken her sensibilities, causing a brief deviation from what she'd always known to be true . . . that John Crowell was the kindest and most attractive of men. She had only to think of him to remember it.

The big Scotsman soon came out of Captain Barstow's bedroom, fully dressed in a well-pressed woolen suit with a silk cravat awkwardly tied about his neck, and his top boots neatly folded. His black hair fell nearly to his shoulders, and the shadow of a beard darkened his angular jaw. For all the civility of his clothing, he still looked a bit wild, like a primitive warrior king from some unexplored country.

"Where did you find that suit?" she asked, annoyed by the breathless quality of her voice. The man was an arrogant and barbaric foreigner, and she had every intention of sending him on his way. Tomorrow, in fact.

She had no time to deal with a stranger, not after hearing what Captain Barstow's solicitor had to say.

The Scotsman glanced down at himself, and for the first time since she'd pulled him out of the water, the haughty man showed a glimmer of uncertainty. His moment of doubt tugged at an unwelcome cord of sympathy somewhere deep inside Sarah.

"What's wrong with it?" he asked.

She could not soften toward this man. She would feed him, let him sleep in Captain Barstow's bed, then send him on his way. "'Tis not the suit I set out for you."

Turning a fierce scowl toward her, he straightened and resumed his superior air. His uncertainty disappeared so quickly, Sarah wondered if she'd imagined it. "This one belongs to me, lass."

He entered the kitchen and took a seat at the table without waiting for her to sit, or even asking if she'd care to join him.

Warrior king, indeed.

"You need a valet," she remarked, glancing pointedly at the cravat, the only aspect of his appearance that was not perfect.

He grumbled unintelligibly while Sarah wondered how his suit could possibly have survived its bout with the sea. The wool was perfectly pressed, and his linen shirt had not a wrinkle in it. And his boots—how had they fit inside his small satchel? How had everything stayed dry?

She eyed him thoughtfully and passed him his bread and jam. Obviously, the clothes *had* fit, and they *were* dry, so it was useless to wonder about them. Especially since there were more pressing questions at the moment. "You never gave me your name, sir."

He ignored her, gazing at the bread as pensively as she had looked at him. Instead of answering her question, he took a bite.

His features changed as he chewed and swallowed.

Sarah eased into a chair across from him and watched the frown lines in his brow disappear and the taut line of his mouth soften. With his features so transformed, he was even more comely than before.

Sarah pressed her hands to the tabletop and reminded herself to remain firm. The man was a stranger in their house, and she needed to know more about him. "Your name, sir?"

He looked down at the second piece of bread. "What do you call this red substance?"

She could not believe his cheek. "I will not be diverted. You are a stranger to us, and I insist that you give me your name."

He swallowed again, then looked at her, resuming his stern expression. "You may call me Brendan Locke." He said his own name as though he were unaccustomed to it, somewhat in the same manner as he had looked down at his clothes. As if they were foreign to him.

Deciding it was just a quirk in his manner, she let out a long breath, glad they were finally getting somewhere. "I am Sarah Granger, and this house belongs . . . belonged to Captain Barstow."

He tipped his head at her introduction and finished the last bit of bread. "I've never tasted such good . . ."

Sarah waved off the compliment. Her jams were highly regarded in Craggleton and provided a small income for their household. It was beside the point.

She leaned forward. "Mr. Locke, I find it difficult to believe you fell from your boat. The weather has been good—"

He shrugged. "A clumsy moment."

"You do not strike me as a clumsy man."

Brogan had no intention of fabricating a more complex story, not while that amazing tart-sweet taste still tingled on his tongue. They had no such concoction on Coruain, where they used butter and honey to sweeten their bread. For all their backward ways, this Tuath mixture was . . . magical . . . as was the hard glitter in Sarah Granger's pretty eyes.

He took her combative gleam as a challenge. "This place is Ravenfield?"

Abruptly, she rose from the table, crossing to the stove, where she cracked eggs into a bowl. At least there would be no surprise as to how those would taste. Eggs were a favorite on Coruain.

"You are far from home, are you not?" she asked.

"You have no idea." Far enough that the charms of his most recent mistress eluded him. Far enough that he had to remind himself repeatedly of his purpose here.

His mind was filled with only this woman, in spite of her stiff manner and hideous clothes. Even her hands bespoke hard times, with roughened skin and reddened knuckles. She was a Tuath with primitive skills and no knowledge of the Druzai world that existed only a few leagues from her shore.

He should not feel the slightest attraction. But he spied a stray curl brushing the skin above her collar and felt a burning urge to approach her and inhale the enticing scent that had teased him ever since they'd fallen together on the beach.

He moved quietly, unable to resist touching that bit of coppery hair at her nape, forgetting, for the moment, that she was not Druzai, and would not hear his approach. His touch startled her, and she jumped, fumbling with the bowl of eggs. Brogan caught it as it slipped from her hands, averting a disaster. She pressed a hand to her breast as if to slow the reaction of her heart, drawing his attention to the full swell of feminine flesh hidden beneath her gown.

He should have taken no notice of the thick

lashes framing her expressive eyes, or the way she pulled her lower lip through her even, white teeth. They might be backward, but the Tuath did not lack beauty.

"You may stay the night here, Mr. Locke, but then you'll need to find lodgings elsewhere."

Not even her harsh tone dispelled the sensual haze that came over him as he gazed at her. The urge to taste her was nearly overpowering. "Where I come from, lass, a grand house always offers its hospitality to strangers."

"Which is why I'll allow you to stay, but only this one night," she retorted, clasping her hands at her waist. She took a deep breath as if to bolster her resolve. "I'm sure there are lodgings to be had in Craggleton if you wish to remain in the neighborhood."

He had to remind himself that she was not Druzai. But neither was she the dull, dim-witted descendant of the ancient Druids who'd been tutored by his race. Instead, he'd found something altogether different.

He gave a nod in the direction of the room where he'd slept. "This chamber suits me well enough."

"But it doesn't suit *me*, Mr. Locke. Upon the morrow, you can go into town with Maud when she does the marketing, and find a room."

Returning to his seat at the table, he hoped he

would not have to stay so long. As soon as she retired for the night, he was going to search the house and the grounds. With luck, he would be on his way back to the Astar Columns by the time the sun rose.

"Are you always so prickly, lass?" he found himself asking. "Or is it *me* that you object to?"

She blushed again. "I certainly am not prickly. But I have a family to look after, and it is entirely unsuitable for a single man to lodge here with us." She sat down across from him and gave him a sidelong glance. "*Are* you a single man, Mr. Locke?"

He grinned, curiously pleased to know that his marital state interested her. "Aye."

She stood again. "Well. 'Tis of no concern to me. But our neighbors—"

"Willna even know I'm here." He dug into his eggs. "I like it here." And he intended to stay until he found the blood stone, even if it took longer than one night's search.

"Mr. Locke—"

"So, am I to understand you have no husband, either, lass? There is no master here?"

Her cheeks colored bright pink, and Brogan searched his memory to determine what protocol he'd breached to reap such a reaction. He recalled Merrick mentioning that men held all the power in this age. That women were subject to the will of their husbands and masters. Somehow, he could not imagine Sarah Granger subservient to anyone.

She returned to her place at the table, but did not sit. "Captain Barstow was killed some months ago in Salamanca. We have been looking after ourselves ever since, Mr. Locke, and doing a fair job of it, too."

An unfamiliar sentiment lodged in Brogan's chest. He cast a glance to the wood that had been stacked neatly beside the stove, and the two heavy buckets of water standing near the back door. She should have a husband. A man to take care of her . . .

One who would loosen that tight knot of hair at her nape and kiss her sweet skin, a man who would please her as a woman should be pleased.

"Do you know, Sarah Granger, that your face goes bright pink when you doona like my questions?"

"You are impertinent, sir." She snatched up his empty bowl and placed it in a metal pan full of soapy water. "And I'm seriously considering putting you out for the night."

He doubted that, for he had sensed her interest even before taking note of the way her nipples peaked against her dress just as she turned 'round.

Brogan's own body surged with arousal as he

watched her wash the bowl, then dry it and put it on a shelf. 'Twas a burning awareness of her scent, of every freckle dancing across her nose, of the thick russet lashes that framed her enthralling green eyes.

He took a deep breath and turned away, reminding himself that his only purpose here was to search the premises for the Druzai blood stone and get it back to Coruain. There was no point in wasting any more time with this thorny Tuath miss.

Once he found the stone, he would be gone.

And Sarah Granger would barely remember him in the morning, but for the coins he would leave in exchange for the prize she probably didn't even know she had.

Chapter 3

Sarah doubted she'd be able to sleep. Not when her body tingled in places she hadn't known existed. Her nipples rubbed uncomfortably against her chemise, and a worrisome sensation crept up her spine.

It felt suspiciously like yearning.

Which was utter rubbish. If there was any man in Cumbria who had ever caused her heart to flutter, it was John Crowell. He was the epitome of culture and breeding in a gentleman, with his fair features and noble manners.

Clearly, the Scotsman was no gentleman at all.

She refused even to think of the incident on the beach when Mr. Locke had actually pinned her beneath him. He'd been weak and confused, so there was no need for her to flush with embarrassment now. He probably didn't even remember what had happened . . . that he'd nearly kissed her.

But to her complete embarrassment, Sarah certainly remembered. And was mortified to admit she'd thought of it several times since then—the press of his muscled frame against her, the heated gaze of his unusual, dark blue eyes, his obnoxious reminder of her propensity for blushing, as if it weren't embarrassing enough.

She stopped at the top of the stairs and smoothed her skirts. Straightening the prim collar at her neck, she pressed the loose wisps of hair back into her topknot.

Then she caught one hand against her chest and wished it had been Squire Crowell who had made her heart pound and her body ache for his touch. She could not possibly have reacted so wantonly with a complete stranger.

Could she? He was obnoxious and impertinent, and clearly excessively impressed with himself. He exuded a superior attitude from his very pores, and Sarah took offense at his disdainful perusal of her home, her beloved Ravenfield.

Well, he'd be gone in the morning. Maud could show him the way to Craggleton, and that was all there was to it. There was no place for such a person as Mr. Locke at Ravenfield. Mrs. Pruitt, the worst gossip in the district, would make much of his presence in a household of females.

No, he certainly could not remain here.

Sarah proceeded into the nursery and looked

in on the girls. She moved Brownie to the foot of Jane's bed, then carefully tucked both girls in. Pressing a gentle kiss to each of their foreheads, she tried to quell the unrest within her.

What a day.

Not the least of her worries was having to break the news given her by their father's solicitor. Ravenfield was entailed, and possession of the estate had reverted to Captain Barstow's closest male relative, a distant cousin named Charles Ridley. He was already considered the master of Ravenfield, making Margaret and Jane trespassers, along with Maud and Sarah. She'd kept the bad news to herself, not even telling Maud, until she knew what they were going to do. She could not just tell the children that they were to be cast out, without some plan for their future.

The uncertainty would be devastating. Sarah remembered how it felt to be left alone, reliant on the pity of the parish. She would never allow Margaret and Jane to feel such mortification. Somehow, Sarah was going to provide a home for them, and allow all of them to preserve their dignity.

She would figure out some solution.

Leaving Jane and Margaret fast asleep, Sarah returned to the hall and stood perfectly still, listening for any indication that their visitor was up and about. But all was quiet below. The only sound in the house was that of Maud's soft snores in the room at the end of the hall.

She went into her own bedchamber and undressed, weary after her eventful day. Her meeting with the solicitor had been momentous enough, then followed by Jane's discovery of Mr. Locke, nearly drowned in their sea. Sarah hoped she'd done the right thing by allowing him to stay the night.

For all the man's imperious looks, Sarah truly believed he meant them no harm. On the contrary, she could not doubt that he would prefer to be miles away from their humble dwelling. He'd practically sneered at the worn-out furniture in the sitting room, and definitely looked down his nose at the meager stores on their sagging kitchen shelves. She was almost surprised that he'd deigned to eat the humble fare she'd provided him.

Ravenfield had not been prosperous for several years, though there had always been enough with the money Captain Barstow sent them. Now that he was gone, Sarah had had to scrape for every penny. There were no extras at Ravenfield.

Sarah gazed at her reflection in the mirror and sighed. Even her nightgown was in poor condition. Like everything else at Ravenfield, it was clean, but had been repaired once too many times. And it would be a long, long time before she would be able to buy cloth to make another.

She took the pins from her hair and started to brush it the same way her mother had done so many years before, in the days of happiness and good health. Though Sarah resembled her mother, she'd inherited her father's freckled complexion and his curly auburn hair. Her eyes were her best feature, but her figure was not the willowy perfection of the stylish ladies in Craggleton. She'd never been anything special. On the contrary, she'd been the object of scorn in the parish, ever since her father had drunk himself into an early grave.

It seemed as if she'd always been alone, at least until she'd come here.

Captain Barstow had given her a home at Ravenfield. She'd *belonged* here, and the least she could do was to make a home for the captain's daughters when Mr. Ridley told them to leave.

She vowed they would never feel the same isolation and shame of poverty that had dominated her own life before coming to Ravenfield.

Brogan heard the floor creaking above him and realized he was hearing Miss Granger moving around upstairs, preparing for bed. She was a feisty lass, surprisingly different from the obsequious Druzai women whose deference to his family might have become a wee bit tiresome.

Sarah Granger knew naught of his lineage, so her treatment of him was entirely honest and unpracticed. 'Twas oddly refreshing.

He imagined her unfastening the row of small white buttons that trailed from her waist to her neck, then slipping the gown off her shoulders and letting it fall to the floor. His arousal at the thought of her standing in her underclothes should not have surprised him. It seemed to take only the merest flash of her bright eyes to make him desire her.

A Tuath lass.

He leaned against the door and focused, perplexed by the lust coursing through his veins. It should have been grief. Hatred. Vengeance. It was a worthless son who forgot the pain and suffering of his father.

He straightened and decided he could not let it happen again. The battle for Coruain loomed ahead, and he needed to keep his attention on his priorities and not on a spirited Tuath maiden.

As soon as the house became still, he went to work. 'Twould be so simple to create light by extracting energy from the air around him, but doing so might attract Eilinora's Odhar. He lit an oil lamp instead and left his chamber, first searching through the drawing room where he'd found Miss Granger. He looked in every drawer and every little nook where the dull red blood stone might have been stored and forgotten.

It was unlikely the stone would be perceived as a valuable item. According to legend, it had no luster, and no particular outward beauty. It was egg-shaped and rough-surfaced, and small enough to fit in a child's hand.

Merrick had warned him to avoid any mention of the stone to Ravenfield's occupants, for they might suspect it had some hidden value, and try to prevent him from taking it.

Brogan had doubted they'd be so astute, but after his exchange with Sarah Granger, he was not so sure. He continued his search in the shabby little kitchen and looked through cupboards and shelves. Finding naught but a glass jar containing the sweet paste that Sarah had spread on his bread, he wondered why they had no such food on Coruain. He'd always believed the ancient elders had brought everything of value to Coruain when the Druzai had left Tuath. Yet clearly they'd missed this.

Retracing his steps, he returned to the drawing room and went into the adjoining chamber. 'Twas a library with a massive desk and walls lined with shelves full of books. Once again, Brogan resisted the urge to cast a spell that would remove every book from every shelf. He spent the next hour physically moving ancient tomes and more recent works from their places, looking behind every book for some secret place where the stone might be hidden.

He found not one speck of dust, nor did he discover the one thing he sought.

Brogan took a seat at the desk and searched through each drawer, finding three sets of papers tied with black ribbons. He also found a plain gold ring in the center drawer, and a miniature painting of a fair-haired man in a military uniform. No doubt it was the hapless Captain Barstow.

Brogan sat back in his chair and pondered going up the stairs to continue his search. Visiting Miss Granger in her bedchamber had some appeal, but he was not to be distracted. Besides, she'd made it clear that she found him rude and uncivilized.

He shook his head at her misconception. If only she could see how he lived on Coruain, she would understand how barbaric her life was at Ravenfield.

Brogan stood abruptly and shook off the notion of showing Coruain to Miss Granger. Druzai and Tuath did not, *should* not, mix. The disasters of the previous millennia had proved that beyond a doubt. Eilinora's crime had been her great pleasure in instigating the bloody Druid wars and causing untold damage to the clans.

The power of the Druzai made interference much too tempting. The disasters of the past could

easily happen again. 'Twas the reason the elders
had created Coruain and commanded all the Druzai to retire there. Brogan agreed with them, yet
Merrick and their father had not. Brogan even
suspected that Merrick had made other visits to
the Tuath world, violating Druzai law.

He finished searching the lower levels of the
house, then returned to the kitchen and let himself
out the back door into a courtyard. By the light of
the moon, he could see that Ravenfield's grounds
were overgrown and in need of attention. There
was a fountain at the midpoint of the garden, but
it was dry. The center statuary was nearly as tall
as Brogan, and bore the shape of a human warrior
with wings. His head was mostly concealed by a
warrior's helmet.

"Dragheen?" Brogan asked quietly, though he
had no hope of finding an ally here. He was thoroughly astounded when the guardian answered
and stepped away from his perch in the fountain,
moving slowly in typical fashion for a dragheen.

"By Téadóir's beard!" said the deep, gravelly
voice. "'Tis many a long year since I've seen one
of yer kind, Druzai man."

"Keep your voice down," Brogan said. "Who
do you guard?"

"All who dwell at Ravenfield, of course."

"There are Druzai here?" It seemed inconceiv-
able. Yet there was much Druzai history that had

been obscured by time. 'Twas possible that a sorcerer had remained in the Tuath world to protect the *brìgha*-stone.

Brogan shuddered at the thought of being marooned here.

"Who be ye to ask such a question?"

Brogan could not see the dragheen's facial expression, but he was right to ask. Brogan's queries would have to wait until the guardian was satisfied. "I am Brogan Mac Lochlainn of Coruain, son of Kieran, Druzai high chieftain."

"Ach, aye. Kieran's fame has been whispered on the winds for many years. I be Colm, of the Abarach Contingent."

"Salutations, Colm."

"Ye be far from the isle, in years and in distance," he said in the guardians' canny way. Somehow, Eilinora had disabled all the dragheen who guarded Kieran at Coruain House. She could do the same to Colm. "What business brings you to Ravenfield?"

"Eilinora has escaped."

The dragheen made a noise that sounded like stones dragging across gravel. "Truly, ye say?"

"Aye. She and her clan murdered my father and stole the chieftain's scepter."

"Ah, then. So yer after the Druzai *brìgha*-stone."

At the dragheen's words, Brogan's chest filled

with relief. "Aye. If you'll just tell me where it's hidden, I'll take it and go."

There were more sounds of rock grating on rock. "I have no idea where it is, lad. I doona guard it, nor was I ever privy to such knowledge."

The moment's elation drained from Brogan. "You must know something."

"Little." The dragheen turned away from Brogan and gestured toward the house. "The house is new . . . has only been standing two hundred years. Mayhap three."

Dragheen moved very slowly and lived for centuries. They reckoned time quite differently from most other beings.

"Then the stone is not here," Brogan said. "My information—"

"Likely relates to old Ravenfield. The castle."

"*Mo oirg*," said Brogan, rubbing a new ache from his forehead. "I might have known this quest would not be so easy."

"Ravenfield Castle—yonder—is in ruins."

Brogan turned to view the jagged silhouette of a fortress beyond the garden, not far from the house. It looked massive. He dragged one hand across his face in frustration at the daunting task before him. "Is there naught you can tell me? Who were the Druzai who dwelled here?"

"Ah, 'twas eons ago. Lord Dubhán Ó Coileáin bade me to remain with him to keep watch over his family when the Druzai departed. But he and his issue have long since perished."

"And you've been standing quiescent in all these centuries since then?" Brogan had never heard of any Druzai remaining here, or dragheen, either.

"Of course not. There is still a family here . . . one whose fortunes have been poor of late."

"And what do you do for them?"

"I can still whisper a thought that needs thinking."

The dragheen had powers and talents independent of the Druzai. They were ruled by none but themselves, and fortunately, they were benign creatures by nature. They were capable of making suggestions to unwary minds, thoughts that would never be detected as coming from another being. These ideas would fade after a few days or weeks, sometimes leaving the recipient feeling vaguely puzzled, sometimes unsettled. Even Brogan, a powerful sorcerer-warrior, might be subject to a dragheen's suggestion. 'Twas why Coruain law forbade dragheen guardians to whisper thoughts to anyone, unless they be warnings of impending trouble. The guardians seemed always to have the best of intentions, yet their whispered ideas had the real potential of going askew.

Here in the Tuath world, there was no one to gainsay the dragheen's interference. Brogan gave

Colm a sidelong glance. "What thoughts have you whispered?"

"Ah well, 'tis my concern, now, isn't it?"

"I warn you, dragheen . . . think naught in my direction while I'm here."

"I would not dream of it, m'lord," Colm replied, his gravelly voice sounding offended at such a suggestion.

"Are there others? More dragheen nearby?"

"Aye, m'lord. A few, also Abarach. You will meet Seana on an overlook not far from the castle. Geilis resides a few miles away."

"Will you stand sentry while I'm here?"

Colm's stone wings crackled.

"I canna allow Eilinora or her minions to find me before I locate the *brìgha*-stone," Brogan said.

"I will keep watch, m'lord," Colm replied, "though I have no extraordinary powers of recognition. The witch might have already come, and I would not have known her."

Brogan clenched his jaw. "Let me know if you take note of anything out of the ordinary, then."

The dragheen gave a quick nod. Brogan was glad of the dragheen's assistance, yet well-aware that Kieran's dragheen guardians had been rendered useless during Eilinora's attack. The same could happen to Colm, or worse.

"M'lord . . ."

"What is it?"

"The young lady of the house ... Miss Granger."

"Aye? What of her?" Brogan asked.

"This be a different world than that of the Druzai."

"I've noticed."

"'Twill be fair damaging to the lass if anyone hereabouts learns you're a stranger here, sleeping under her roof."

"I'll bear it in mind, dragheen."

"One last thing, m'lord." Colm stepped up to his pedestal. "Beware of the sìthean."

"They're no trouble to me."

"Take care just the same, m'lord," said Colm. "The sìths who went to Coruain were mild compared to the little demons who stayed here to plague the Tuath."

Brogan did not know how that was possible, for the nasty sprites managed to do plenty of damage to the unwary on Coruain.

He gave a quick nod to the dragheen and left him, returning to his room to sleep until dawn. He awoke before the rest of the house, used Captain Barstow's razor to shave instead of eliminating his whiskers by his usual method, then dressed and went to the castle ruins at daybreak.

The sight of the decayed building hit him with a wave of grief so powerful that he was compelled to sit down on a decayed step. The stone shell of the castle was the ultimate symbol of Kieran's life. Once a proud and majestic man, his father was dust now, even less substantial than the rubble surrounding Brogan now.

His chest hurt.

His eyes burned.

He had not sufficiently appreciated Kieran while he was alive.

They'd been at odds for the past few years, Kieran arguing that it was time for Druzai and Tuath to intermingle. He believed it was the duty of the Druzai to enlighten the Tuath and ease their lives with the ancient knowledge they possessed as they'd once done with the Tuath Druids. Brogan had disagreed, vehemently. Their peoples had mingled eons ago, with disastrous results.

In the centuries since then, the Druzai had been a content, peaceful people, their warriors trained in mind and body to keep their world safe from intrusions by the rogue forces of the world. Yet Brogan had failed. He alone bore the responsibility for his father's death, for failing to anticipate Eilinora's escape from her ancient prison.

Brogan would not falter again. His mind and body were strong, giving him the power to succeed in his quest without the use of magic. Once he and Merrick returned to Coruain with the blood stones, they would call on all their considerable powers to destroy Eilinora once and for all.

Then they would deal with the powerful entity that had freed her.

Brogan stood, jabbing his fingers through his hair at the thought of the monumental search before him. With all due respect to his father's ideas, he had no intention of mixing any more than absolutely necessary with the plain folk here.

He familiarized himself with the castle and the surrounding area, noting that it had once been a huge and formidable fortress, its stone walls situated on the edge of a high cliff. He wandered inside and looked out one of the lower window openings, noting that the entire space below the castle was riddled with caves.

Brogan assessed the structure and realized his search might take a few days, time when Coruain was virtually unprotected. With Merrick and Brogan gone, and Kieran's scepter missing, Coruain was vulnerable to attack from the Odhar. And there was no way, at least none that Brogan knew, to stop time on the isle until he returned with the stone. His homecoming would occur after the exact number of hours or days he'd been gone.

For the time being, it was up to Ana and the elders to hold a shielding swathe 'round the isles to keep them hidden from Eilinora. Brogan prayed they'd be successful until he and his brother returned with the stones.

He intercepted the housekeeper when she came

out carrying her marketing basket, and spoke to her about keeping his room at Ravenfield. As opposed to the way Miss Granger would react to his proposal, Maud was pleased to take one of Brogan's "guineas" for the use of the chamber he'd slept in the night before. He promised more coins for the run of the castle over the next few days, gratified that he'd packed a veritable fortune in his charmed satchel.

Sarah did not sleep well at all. She'd had too many strange dreams that left her feeling unsettled and discontented. They felt like premonitions, but were much too vague to interpret.

"You're wearing your best dress today, Miss Granger," said Margaret. "'Tis not even Sunday."

"If you remember, I went into the sea wearing my everyday dress, Margaret. I must give it a wash today," Sarah replied, wishing her young charge was not quite so observant. 'Twas no one's concern that she wanted to appear anything but a ragamuffin when she encountered Mr. Locke today.

"But what about your gray gown, the one you changed into last—"

"May I have more jam, Miss Granger?" asked Jane, who sat at the kitchen table beside her sister.

"Of course, love," Sarah replied, glad for the

diversion. Mr. Locke's bedroom door was still closed, leaving Sarah to believe he must be sleeping late, still recovering from the previous day's ordeal.

She wondered if he slept in that small violet garment that had barely covered his—

"We'll run out of jam before winter, Jane," little Margaret scolded. "You must not use so much."

"A bit more won't hurt, love," Sarah interjected. "We'll put up lots more this summer."

"But then we must sell it in Craggleton, mustn't we?"

The squeak of the door caught their attention. "'Tis a dark view you take of things, lass," said Mr. Locke, looking dour and rather formidable himself.

He wore the same staid and proper suit he'd put on the night before, yet he looked anything but a staid and proper gentleman. Sarah recalled the primitive torque that had encircled his thick, muscular arm. He looked as dangerous as a pirate with his hair tied in a thick queue at the back of his head. All he needed was a gold tooth and an earring, and perhaps a sword in a colorful sash to complete the picture.

He came into the room, and Sarah pressed a hand to her chest as his presence seemed to pull the air from her lungs and make her heart beat a bit faster.

She found her voice. "Will you join us for breakfast, Mr. Locke? 'Tis a fair walk to Craggleton, and you'll want some nourishment before you leave."

He accepted her offer and came to the table. Sarah made the introductions, and her young charges stood and curtsied politely, giving Sarah a moment to collect herself. Appalled by her lack of proper discipline where Mr. Locke was concerned, she stepped away from the table and poured him a cup of tea. He had not even looked at her. "Have you decided what to do about your boat?"

"How will you get home?" Margaret asked.

"Are you really a Scotsman?" asked Jane.

He took a seat. "Do you interrogate all your guests thus?" Though his expression was dark and forbidding, his tone was not harsh.

Margaret had the grace to look abashed, but Jane continued to gaze up at him, expecting a reply. Sarah bristled when the man did not answer.

"My charges are young, sir," she said. "They are naturally curious."

"Well then," he remarked as his attitude lightened. "As it happens, I came to your shores in search of ancient ruins to explore. Your castle—"

Jane clapped her hands with excitement. "You want to stay and visit our castle?"

Sarah gave him an inquisitive glance, but

found his expression shuttered. Ravenfield Castle attracted a few visitors every summer, but Sarah could not help but wonder at his interest. Neither Mr. Locke's appearance nor his bearing resembled that of any scholar who had ever visited before. Nor had any of those old professors asked for lodgings at Ravenfield.

"I'm sorry. That will not be possible, Mr. Locke. We are a household of females. As I said last night, we cannot afford to host a gentleman in our . . . i-in our . . ."

Her words trailed off when he reached into his pocket and removed two gold coins, which he placed on the table beside the butter. "I'll be here only a few days."

"I've already spoken to Maud," Brogan said. "And we've come to an agreement." He took perverse pleasure in the discomfited expression on Sarah Granger's overly proud face.

"So much money!" declared the serious child, Margaret. Her features were dominated by a penetrating scowl, an incongruous expression for someone of her tender years.

"Miss Granger," asked Jane, the cheery one. "How many jars of jam would it take—"

"Hush, girls," said Sarah.

She took a deep breath, chewing her lower lip as she was wont to do when she was perplexed. Brogan slid a finger under his cravat, which seemed suddenly much too tight for his neck.

Her well-fitted green gown was a vast improvement over yesterday's attire, its neckline cut a few inches below her collarbone and trimmed in white lace. The waist was gently gathered just below her breasts, and the sleeves reached only to her elbows, showing the smooth skin of her arms. He wondered if he could raise goose bumps on that delicate surface by sliding his fingers along it.

"Well, then." She eyed the coins. "If Maud agreed . . ."

"Tell me about the castle," he said, forcing his attention to the matter at hand—the only question of importance. "Have you ever found any treasures there?"

"Oh yes!" Jane cried. "I have!"

Brogan steeled himself against showing too much interest. "Wha' did you find, lass?" he asked.

"Mouse bones!"

In frustration, he clasped his hands 'round his teacup. "Naught but mouse bones?"

Both girls shook their heads, and Miss Granger shrugged. "What treasures would you expect in a thousand-year-old ruin? Everything of value has crumbled away."

"'Tis a thousand years old?" Brogan asked, trying another tack.

"No one knows exactly how old it is. 'Tis said the castle's origins are not mentioned in the parish records."

Brogan knew that any ancient records of Ravenfield and its Druzai lord would certainly not be obvious. "What about tales? Are there any legends about Ravenfield?"

Jane clapped her hands with excitement. "Miss Granger knows the stories! She can tell you about the Luck and the—"

"Jane, I'm sure Mr. Locke is uninterested in our children's tales."

"On the contrary—"

"Are you going to look for treasure?" Jane bounced in her chair, clearly excited by the prospect.

Brogan shook his head, resolved to learn more about Sarah's stories. They were likely mere myths that had little truth, but there might be a seed of something useful in them.

"There will be no treasure at this late date," he said to the child. "But if I find anything of interest, I will be certain to show you."

Miss Granger pocketed the coins and gathered the children to her, her expression one of care and worry. For half a second, Brogan let himself wonder what troubled her, then stopped, turning his attention to his sole reason for being here.

* * *

Sarah took the girls into the next room, where Margaret went to a cupboard and took out their reading primers, setting them on the table. Sarah picked up the books and set them aside. "We're going to have a holiday today, girls."

Jane and Margaret gave her incredulous looks, and Sarah realized it had been the wrong thing to say. The last time she'd unexpectedly announced a holiday had been the day she'd given them news of their father's death. Her news today was not nearly as bad, but certainly bad enough.

"Not a complete holiday," Sarah amended. "But I want to talk to you."

"What is it, Miss Granger? What's happened?"

They went into the drawing room, and Sarah bade them to sit down on the sofa, one on either side of her. "I saw Mr. Merton when I went into Craggleton yesterday."

"Papa's solicitor?" Margaret asked.

"Yes. The very one." Sarah held out her hands, and each of the girls placed one of her own in hers. This was going to be so difficult, she hardly knew where to begin. "Well. Mr. Merton had some news . . . some not-so-very-good news, I'm afraid."

"I knew it," Margaret said before Sarah could even begin to tell the girls what Mr. Merton had told her.

"'Tis not good news, but neither is it the end

of the world," she informed them. "We will make do."

"What is the news, Miss Granger?" asked Jane, squeezing Sarah's hand tightly.

"Well . . . your papa had a cousin . . . a Mr. Ridley . . . who has inherited Ravenfield."

Now even Jane looked up at Sarah with a guarded expression in her eyes. "Inherited? What does that mean?"

Sarah tamped down her own emotions, but could do no better than give a halting explanation to the girls. "It means th-that Mr. Ridley . . . is now master of Ravenfield."

"But Papa . . ." Jane's voice was plaintive.

"Papa is dead!" cried Margaret.

Sarah hugged Margaret close and squeezed Jane's hand. "The solicitor believes Mr. Ridley will soon come to Ravenfield and take up residence."

Margaret started to sob. She covered her mouth with her hands and laid her head in Sarah's lap. "Will he turn us out? Where shall we go?"

Sarah swallowed the lump in her throat and stroked Margaret's blond braids. "I do not know, but Mr. Locke just gave us a grand sum of money. We'll be able to let some fine lodgings in Craggleton—"

"Leave Papa's house?" Jane cried. "We cannot go away!"

"Jane, we'll soon have no choice. 'Tis the law,

love. We must honor whatever Mr. Ridley decides."

With Mr. Locke's money, Sarah would be able to find decent lodgings in town. Maud could go and live with her sister, and Sarah would find a way to support herself and the girls. She'd been decently educated before her father's illness and death, and knew she could manage somehow.

She would have to.

Brogan overheard just enough to make him wonder what kind of world he found himself in. He was disgusted to think that Tuath law would allow a stranger to come here and evict these women—these *unprotected* women and children—from their home. It only reinforced his aversion to these primitive people, making him even more anxious to get the blood stone and return to Coruain, where society was civilized.

The children left the house in distress, and Sarah wisely let them go. Brogan finished his toast and jam and noticed that the house was empty. Maud was working in the garden, and Sarah had left the house carrying a large basket of laundry. It was his chance to search the upper levels of the house.

Feeling like a lowly prowler, he climbed the steps and started with the housekeeper's bedroom first. Finding naught of interest, he made his way down the hall, going inside every room and searching thoroughly, until he reached Sarah's chamber. He glanced at her meager belongings, and touched the thin nightdress hanging on the back of her door. She would not be able to conceal her feminine curves from him while wearing her frayed and threadbare night rail.

He brought himself up short. Sarah Granger's curves were not his concern. The only female who warranted his attention was Eilinora.

Starting with the bed, he knelt to search under it, but stopped when he came upon a pair of wet leather shoes. They had once been sturdy, but there was a hole in the sole of one, and the other had nearly worn through. He had no doubt that Sarah had been wearing these when she'd jumped into the surf to save him.

A Druzai woman would have lifted him from the surf with just a wave of her hand and the few muttered words of a spell. Sarah had had no such abilities, but she hadn't been stopped by the consequences of running into the sea for him, fully aware that she had no resources to replace the shoes or other clothes she ruined by doing so. She was far too impetuous for her own good, and certainly nothing like the sophisticated, reserved noblewomen of his acquaintance.

Brogan turned his attention to the cool wooden floor under the bed, looking for anything that might be stowed there, or a flaw in the floor where a trapdoor might be concealed.

When he found naught, he examined the window and the walls, then went to the trunk at the foot of the bed. Inside were two pairs of woolen stockings, both mended. There were under-clothes—a plain, white chemise that would hug her breasts and drape her body down to her hips, and another garment that appeared to be used as an underskirt.

As plain as they were, her underclothes were surprisingly sensual, and the thought of Sarah in them was enough to cause Brogan a stunning erection. He wasn't sure he'd be able to look at her again without thinking of these fragile, threadbare garments that kissed her bare skin. A lover would have to be very careful when he removed her linens, to prevent shredding them in his haste.

Swallowing thickly, he set her intimate clothing aside and got on with his search. At the bottom of the trunk was a piece of yellowed parchment, folded into a square. When Brogan peeled it open and looked inside, he found two locks of hair, each bound separately. Next to the envelope was a small tin box with a cracked top and some markings that had been worn nearly smooth. The top was jammed so Brogan was unable to open it, but it seemed to have little value, other than being a keepsake like the locks of hair.

He quickly replaced everything as it was and left the room, aware that he must turn his full attention now to the castle ruins. As ancient as it was, this had always been the more likely site for the stone to have been hidden.

But what if Sarah was right and everything of value was long gone?

Now that he considered it, Brogan was not certain the stone had been placed here by the elders in ancient Tuath times. Mayhap it had only recently appeared at Ravenfield.

He discounted that possibility. There was a reason the Druzai lord had remained here, and 'twas likely for the purpose of protecting the stone and other Druzai treasures Brogan had never heard of. He was on the right track, he was certain of it.

He went out to the castle and started down a long stone staircase, ending in a cave at the bottom. A small amount of light emanated from fissures in the wall, but Brogan found a torch lying on the stone floor. He lit it, then checked the walls for signs of a hiding place.

When he found none, he took the torch and squeezed his body through a narrow passageway into the next chamber. This, too, had been swept of all litter and debris, but the walls bore signs of ancient Druzai runes. Beside the runes were *crìoch-fàile* patterns, circles nested within each other, with small holes and narrow lines carved beside them. *Crìoch-fàile* were favorite Druzai puzzles, and notoriously difficult to decipher. Brogan had never been one for such games.

The runes had been carved into the walls, but time had worn many of them smooth. Lifting the torch high, Brogan tried to read them, but he could only make out a few of the words . . .

Shimmering light . . .

The next symbols had rubbed away, so he moved down to the next section.

Seek ye daughters . . .

Farther in, another set of runes read, *Hide from all . . .*

None of the carvings was in good condition, and Brogan could easily have misinterpreted what he read. The runes gave him hope that he would eventually find a clue to the location of the blood stone, but none of these hinted of it.

He continued examining the walls, making a cursory search for cracks and fissures that might be hiding places.

But he saw naught.

The next chamber was more of the same, but instead of it being a dead end, Brogan found another set of steps carved into the floor, leading down to another small cavern that opened out to the cliff beyond. From where Brogan stood, the opening seemed large enough for a man to fit through, but the ground must be at least thirty to forty feet below. 'Twould be a fatal drop for the unwary.

On a quick glance, he saw no runes, or any secret hiding places. And since the small chamber was going to be dangerous to explore without a securing rope to prevent an accidental fall, he decided to search aboveground first.

He climbed back to the surface and spied an old wooden shed near a broken-down barn. Thinking there might be shovels and ropes inside, he tried the door, but found it locked. He resisted disengaging it with a few magical words and a quick touch, and walked 'round to the house.

"Mrs. Maud has the key," said the dragheen in a low voice when he passed.

Brogan muttered his thanks and brushed the dust from his clothes, passing through the rear door of the house once again.

Sarah Granger was in the kitchen, using a long, wooden roller to press what looked like bread dough into a flat, round circle. She wore a plain white apron tied 'round her trim waist to protect her clothes. Her hair was pinned tightly in her usual fashion, but loose, curly tendrils had escaped their bonds. When she blew the moist curls out of her eyes, Brogan's breath caught in his throat. Even the smear of flour on her chin and the light dusting of the same white powder on her arms beguiled him.

"What are you doing?" he asked.

"Have you never seen anyone roll out pie dough, Mr. Locke?"

He shook his head. "Er, I've no' spent much time in the kitchen."

"Typical man, I suppose." She eased the fragile dough into a baking pan, then cut away the excess 'round the edge, leaving a neatly lined shell. A moment later, she spooned a shiny, fruity mass into it. It was seasoned somehow, and smelled heavenly . . . like Sarah.

Unable to stop himself, Brogan picked up a spoon and helped himself to a taste. Sarah quickly admonished him with a nimble blow to his hand. "I'll save a bit of filling for you later, Mr. Locke. But these pies are meant for sale in Craggleton."

He could well imagine Sarah's pies earning a fair amount of money in town. He put a gold sovereign on the table. "This one is mine."

Chapter 4

Brogan spent the rest of the day in the caves, restraining the urge to use magic as he searched. He translated a good many more runes, but none gave him any clues to the location of the blood stone, nor did he find any more *crìoch-fàile*.

Returning to the house after dark, Brogan found his way to the kitchen by the light of a lamp someone had left in the window. The room was empty and the house quiet.

His pie rested in the center of the table, a plate and fork lying right beside it.

Brogan pulled out a chair and sat down just as Sarah came through the kitchen door, carrying a small bundle of cloth. She put it down on the far end of the table and left again through the cellar door, soon emerging with a small crock of milk and an iron pan.

She poured some milk into a saucer for a little brown cat, then filled a glass for him. "Would you like to have supper before your pie, Mr. Locke?"

"Doona go to any trouble for me, lass."

"You've paid well for my trouble, Mr. Locke," she replied, taking a bowl of food from the larder. "Else I'd have retired some time ago."

"Then you are missing sleep for naught, Miss Granger," he said irritably. She might be a simple Tuath woman, but he had not intended to turn her into his servant. "I doona expect—"

"Your payment was far beyond fair." She filled the pan with a concoction of potatoes and ham, then added wood to the stove. The tantalizing aroma of the dish caused his mouth to water.

"Then a wee bite would not be amiss, lass."

Her offense at the money he'd given her was perplexing. He certainly did not expect her to toil on his account, and the household was clearly in need of funds. He did not understand the problem.

On Coruain, he would just mutter a few words and draw on the energy necessary to produce a meal. Some cheese and bread, a few slices of meat would suffice. Here, he had to rely on the kindness of Miss Granger and Ravenfield's housekeeper to keep him fed.

And their skill. Brogan could see 'twas no easy accomplishment to sustain life without magic. He had never before considered all the Tuath needed to do in order to keep themselves fed and dressed, sheltered and warm. His own people had no such challenges.

In spite of Sarah's long day of unending chores and her sharp tone, she looked softer somehow. Mayhap 'twas the glow of the lamp that made her seem less bristly this eve, for her hair was still tightly bound.

Or 'twas fatigue.

She stirred the food as it heated, then slid it onto a plate and placed it before him. "You are quite diligent in your explorations of the ruins, Mr. Locke."

"Aye . . . old castles are of great interest to me," he replied. Since it was clear that his quest was going to take more than one day, he had no choice but to give some explanation for his apparent fascination with the ruins.

"Are you affiliated with a university, then?"

"Ah . . . no." Had he said aye, she would ask which one, and he had no idea about universities. Nor did he know what reason he could give her for his particular interest in Ravenfield. "'Tis just an idle diversion, Miss Granger."

Her expression was skeptical. Taking a seat across from him, she picked up the cloth she'd discarded, and Brogan saw 'twas no random piece of fabric, but an article of children's clothing. She used a metal needle to pull thread through a hole in the dress.

He watched with fascination as she repaired the sleeve, making a ruined garment usable again. Her hands were small but capable. Hard work had reddened her knuckles, but they did not lack grace. She was as agile as any Druzai maiden, but . . . different.

He could not imagine any woman of his acquaintance putting such effort into the tasks that had kept Sarah Granger occupied all day.

"We've had a number of academicians come to study our castle," she remarked. "But they soon move on to Fullingham Castle."

"Fullingham is of greater interest?" he asked idly. He cared not a whit about any other property in the Tuath world, nor would he even be here if not for Merrick's feeble-brained scheme to find the blood stones before engaging the witch who'd killed his father.

Brogan had a legion of well-trained warriors who could challenge Eilinora and her followers, weapon for weapon, spell for spell. Even with Kieran's scepter in her possession, Brogan doubted she would be able to overcome his Druzai fighters.

But Merrick and Ana lacked his conviction, so now he found himself in this strange world, making conversation with a Tuath lass.

"Fullingham Castle is not so old, so it's actually intact," she remarked. "'Tis much more interesting to scholars."

Brogan recognized her insinuation. She wanted him to leave.

'Twas laughable. He was a Druzai prince and she a lowly Tuath with no magic at all.

Yet her mouth intrigued him. 'Twas full and pink, and moist from her tongue. He had decided there was no strange Tuath sorcery at work, but could not think what force could possibly make him want to taste her with such an intensity.

"Is your meal acceptable, Mr. Locke?"

He realized he had yet to touch the savory mass that she'd put on his plate. "Oh aye. I'm sure 'twill be perfect."

Mr. Locke's gaze disconcerted Sarah. No doubt he was accustomed to better fare, but they'd been lucky to have a few slices of ham for their hash. Sarah was still astonished that the man had bought her entire pie. And for a sovereign!

To compensate for his exorbitant payment, Sarah had suggested that Maud prepare more elaborate meals while Mr. Locke was their guest. For the few days he stayed with them, Maud would not go to Craggleton to sell pies and cockles. Instead, she would visit the butcher for fresh meat and the greengrocer for whatever vegetables their own garden could not provide.

For a change, they could keep more of their own eggs for cooking, and purchase wine or ale for the table Mr. Locke had so brazenly bought. They might be poor, but they were not destitute. At least, not yet.

He was obviously a rich man, one who had no qualms about flaunting his wealth. She could not fathom why he'd want to stay in their modest home.

And wished he would leave before the girls formed an attachment to him. Though Sarah herself had not been affected, the children were much too susceptible to a kind word from a stranger, and those gold pieces had made their eyes brighten unrealistically.

Sarah cut a generous piece of pie and slid it onto a plate, then put her finger in her mouth to lick off a bit of sweet filling. When she passed the plate to Mr. Locke, she found him looking intently at her. His throat moved when she closed her lips around her finger, and he made a quiet sound, something like a low growl.

Every sensitive part of her body prickled, from her nipples to her womb, and her limbs felt heavy.

She swallowed. "I-I'll just take my leave now . . ."

In her haste to leave the room, she forgot her mending, but would not go back for it now. She didn't know what had come over her, or why Mr. Locke's gaze should discomfit her so. But she knew nothing good could come of it, not with a wealthy stranger from faraway lands.

Heading for the stairs, she sought the quiet of her own bedchamber, and the solace of her mother's old tin Luck at the bottom of her trunk.

The torch Brogan had left in the cave was missing. He was certain he'd placed it in one of the stone sconces, yet it was gone.

He considered whether one of the children might have taken it the night before, but knew it was unlikely. The sconce was well above the level of their shoulders. They could never have reached it.

It was ominous.

He'd seen no sign of any Odhar, yet who else would have an interest in Ravenfield's caves? He intended to speak to the dragheens after dark, and ask if they'd seen any strangers lurking about the property. In the meantime, he decided to see if the Tuath women had noticed anything odd.

And when he encountered Miss Granger, he intended to guard against the way he'd reacted to her last night. No Tuath woman could possibly rouse him with such a puny gesture . . . licking her finger . . .

He entered the house through the kitchen door, but heard female voices in the drawing room. Following the sound, he discovered Sarah, sitting across from an elaborately-dressed woman he'd never seen before. She had a large, absurd hat perched on her head and a small, delicate teacup balanced upon her knee. She could easily have been an attractive woman, but there were frown lines on her forehead and beside her mouth, making her appear quite harsh.

"Well, you certainly look fine in your Sunday best, Miss Granger. I wouldn't think a woman in your position could risk damaging your best clothes."

Sarah said naught in response, but Brogan did not care for the woman's belittling tone. Still, he felt an absurd rush of pleasure to know that Sarah had dressed in her best clothes, obviously for him. He had not considered that her drab gowns would be considered work clothes . . . Merrick had not mentioned that Tuath women saved their best attire for special occasions.

"But on to the reason for my visit," the woman said. "You must take a firmer hand with those girls, Miss Granger. That younger one is a wild little baggage."

"She's just a spirited girl, Mrs. Pruitt. I would hate to—"

"I need not tell you what happens to wayward girls, Miss Granger. Captain Barstow's girls would be much better off in the parish school."

"No!" Sarah's voice crackled with emotion, but she remained sitting, her hands clasped so tightly in her lap that her knuckles had gone white. "We will make do."

Brogan wondered about the parish school and why the mention of it would upset her so.

"You must know you cannot remain here at Ravenfield indefinitely, Miss Granger." The woman sipped her tea as though she did not notice Sarah's distress. "You are an unmarried woman with no prospects. How will you provide for the three of you? Selling cockles and pies?"

Sarah stood abruptly, her hands in fists at her sides. "No, I—"

"And a *man* on your property! Of all things!" Mrs. Pruitt hardly took a breath between sentences. Brogan wondered how she knew about him. "The parish warden will certainly—"

"But it was only—"

"Don't try to tell me it was Andrew Ferris, my dear. The man I saw looked nothing like the other." She mouthed the endearment, but it was clear she did not think of Sarah as her "dear" at all. "I saw him with my own eyes when I walked along the eastern path this morning. As clear as day, I saw him going into the ruins."

Brogan cleared his throat and entered the room, forcing himself to remember everything Merrick had told him about correct behavior in Tuath society.

And never considered why he bothered.

* * *

Sarah's heart tripped when Mr. Locke came into the parlor, looking handsome and rugged all at once. She did not need this added complication. Had he remained absent, she might have been able to convince Mrs. Pruitt that she'd truly seen poor Andy Ferris, the town's wandering simpleton. But not now.

The parish warden was sure to come and ask questions about Mrs. Pruitt's story.

"Have you a cup for me, Miss Granger?" he asked Sarah, though his gaze did not leave Mrs. Pruitt's face.

"O-of course," she answered, glad she would not have to go to the kitchen for a cup, leaving him alone with the dragon lady, as the girls called her. There was no telling what he might say since he seemed not to care about the usual social conventions. She did not want him speaking too frankly to her neighbor.

He took Mrs. Pruitt's hand in his, then bowed over it, causing her to blush and flutter. Sarah puzzled over the woman's reaction to Mr. Locke's touch, then realized it was fascination. She was experiencing pure, feminine attraction.

It could not be half what Sarah had felt the night before, when Mr. Locke had pinned her with his deep blue gaze. She'd fled to her room, feeling as though she could melt into a puddle of tension. She'd hardly known what to think of it . . .

Remembering herself, Sarah introduced her two guests. "Mrs. Pruitt, may I present Mr. Locke. Of Scotland."

"I'm an old friend of Captain Barstow."

Sarah gave a slight shake of her head, unsure that she'd heard him correctly. He'd actually lied to assure that Sarah kept her reputation intact.

Or perhaps he'd actually known the captain, but had neglected to mention it until now.

His voice was deep and rough, and when he spoke, his heavy brogue captivated Mrs. Pruitt, judging by the rapt attention she focused upon him. Sarah had never seen the woman appear so pleasant. With her face drawn in a perpetually disapproving frown, she always appeared much older than the twelve-year difference in their ages.

Mrs. Pruitt had never approved of Sarah's arriving at Ravenfield a poor, orphaned relation of Captain Barstow's wife. Fortunately, the captain had been happy enough to have her services after the death of his wife, and hadn't listened to Mrs. Pruitt's disparaging warnings about entrusting his children to the daughter of a drunkard. For the first time in years—since her mother's death when her father had turned to drink—Sarah had had a secure home.

Now that she was about to lose it, she vowed never again to fall upon the charity of the parish. Somehow, she was going to make a decent life for herself and the girls.

"Glad to meet you, Mrs. Pruitt."

"The pleasure is all mine, Mr. Locke," cooed Mrs. Pruitt.

Sarah felt her teeth clench, and forced herself to relax her jaws. Nothing good could possibly come of this meeting. Not when the damnable Scot held on to Mrs. Pruitt's hand, smiling at her as though he'd wrecked his ship on their shore for the express purpose of making her acquaintance.

"Your country reminds me of my own lands," he said. "My people take braw pride in the fierce beauty of our landscape."

"Your *lands*?" asked Mrs. Pruitt, her attention increasing even more, if that were possible. "Are you close to the sea?"

"Aye. Verra close," he said, moving almost imperceptibly closer to the woman. His voice was low and intimate and sent a frisson of heat down Sarah's spine. "'Tis in my blood."

"We feel the same, of course." Reluctantly, Mrs. Pruitt removed her hand from his grasp. "Please do join us, Mr. Locke. I'm sure Miss Granger can manage to pour another cup."

Her neighbor's subtle insult, even as she graciously invited Mr. Locke to join them, grated on

Sarah, but she poured, then handed Mr. Locke the cup as he sat down with them.

"What brings you to our modest parish, Mr. Locke?" asked Mrs. Pruitt. "Surely you'd heard of poor Captain Barstow's demise."

He gave a nod. "'Twas the strangest thing. I was sailin' only a mile or so off your coast, and a sudden wind came up just as I got caught in a strong current. I started to adjust the jib, but the boom swung loose and hit me. Knocked me overboard."

"Oh gracious! Were you injured? Was the doctor called?"

"I'm happy to say 'twas no' necessary," Mr. Locke remarked with an engaging smile. "I was fortunate that Miss Granger and the children happened by. I'd have been in dire straits otherwise."

Tittering as though he'd said something clever, Mrs. Pruitt replied, "I'm certain we all owe a debt of gratitude to Miss Granger, then."

"Aye," he said, casting a cursory glance in Sarah's direction, dismissing her. "She was verra kind."

"Well, since all turned out well, will you continue on your journey now, Mr. Locke?" Mrs. Pruitt asked, suggesting that his departure would be greatly lamented.

He shook his head. "The old castle interests me,

so I've decided to stay another day or two. Mayhap you would know of a small house nearby that's available to let."

Sarah nearly choked. Hadn't he just given her two full guineas to stay at Ravenfield? Did he mean to leave?

Would he want his money back?

"I'll have to think . . ." Mrs. Pruitt replied as a small crease appeared in her brow.

"Weel then," he said expansively, his burr thicker than Sarah had heard it before. He turned to her, his eyes catching hers in a startling wink that escaped the dragon lady's attention. "I'll just keep my room in the groom's quarters out by the barn for now, if it's all right with you, Miss Granger?"

Brogan decided he'd managed the sour woman masterfully. He'd saved Sarah's reputation by claiming to be an old friend of Barstow, and deflected her questions, insinuating that he was a powerful Scottish landowner. He'd given himself a Tuath status he knew the woman would respect. Yet he wasn't sure why he'd interfered. The Pruitt woman was Sarah Granger's neighbor, and in another day or two, Brogan would have naught to do with either of them.

But the look in Sarah's eyes when Mrs. Pruitt had spoken of the parish school had decided it. He was not going to allow the woman to run rough-shod over her, not after learning she was about to be evicted from this house. Nor would he let Mrs. Pruitt spread tales about the "strange" man she was harboring at Ravenfield. Remembering the dragheen's warning, he realized such a thing would be disastrous to Sarah's reputation.

The lass needed a husband. A protector.

Brogan wondered if there were any reasonable candidates for the post. Mayhap Mr. Ferris, the man Mrs. Pruitt had spoken of. Sarah clearly had no idea of her own appeal, but he had seen fire in her green eyes, and a flash of passion when he'd shoved her beneath him on the sand. He'd seen her hair drifting loose and free, curling gloriously about her shoulders.

And her skin ... those freckles seemed to beckon to him of their own accord. The men in the parish must be blind not to have noticed her.

She sat stiffly, contrary to the relaxed posture he'd noted the night before, when she'd sat sewing at the table during his meal.

"I have a marvelous idea," said Mrs. Pruitt. "Well, that is to say, I'd had the idea before coming here this afternoon, but now that I've ..."

The woman directed her words toward him, leaving Sarah out of the conversation, as though she were not even present in the room. Brogan's brow furrowed, and he wondered at the woman's cold attitude. 'Twas not as though she were vastly superior to anyone. She might have wealth, but she was Tuath, same as Sarah Granger.

"Well, that's neither here nor there," she continued nonsensically. "I've been thinking it's been far too long since we've had a party at Pruitt Hall. At least six years, since my poor Henry died."

As the woman spoke, Sarah's shoulders seemed to shrink. And though she kept a small smile on her face, it seemed frozen in place. She sat as still as a dragheen, her eyes focused upon naught.

"So I've decided to hold a music soiree . . ." Mrs. Pruitt said. "Let's say at week's end, Friday. Will you come, Mr. Locke? Our modest society would be delighted to meet you."

He hoped to be long gone by Friday, but the expanse of territory he had yet to search was vast. Working alone was going to take a while, likely to the week's end.

Making a snap decision, Brogan turned to Sarah. "Miss Granger, are you and the children engaged next Friday eve?"

She blinked her eyes and looked at him, puzzled. "N-no, Mr. Locke, we are not."

"Good." He gave a curt nod and turned to Mrs. Pruitt. "Then we will be—"

"Oh, but I . . ." The woman licked her lips, then pressed them tightly together. She smiled resignedly. "Of course you must all come."

Brogan soon took his leave and went in search of Maud and the keys, anxious to resume his work. The housekeeper was still missing, but he spied a ring of keys hanging on a hook inside a kitchen shelf. Returning to the shed, he found a key to unlock the door and went inside. There were a few tools, but no rope, so he took a shovel and returned to the castle ruins. He was determined to make the most of every day and get back to Coruain before he found himself any further enmeshed in Ravenfield's troubles.

If he managed to find the stone before Friday, he would make some excuse for his early departure. The Pruitt woman could not very well renege on Sarah's invitation to her soiree, and Brogan did not doubt it would be the perfect opportunity for Sarah to socialize with a few prospective husbands. With some attention to her hair and clothes, and a few lessons in mild flirtation, she should be able to net a spouse for herself.

Sarah gazed in puzzlement in Mr. Locke's wake, sighing with relief. She'd felt dangerously off balance when he was in the room, as though she could not take a deep enough breath.

Now, if only Mrs. Pruitt would leave, Sarah could go and find the girls. Their welfare was what Sarah needed to think of, and not parties where she would be an unwelcome addition.

Now that Margaret and Jane had had time to fret over the news about Mr. Ridley and the loss of Ravenfield, she wanted to reassure them and talk about plans for the future. Clearly, they hadn't been ready to listen earlier, but she hoped to make them understand that she really did intend to make a life for them in town.

Unfortunately, Mrs. Pruitt did not appear ready to leave. Sarah had been compelled to pour another cup of tea for the woman, who was too preoccupied with Mr. Locke and his disarmingly agreeable manner.

While he'd taunted Sarah and put her on edge, he'd been affable and charming with the dragon lady. Sarah had no doubt he actually was a wealthy landowner, just as he'd intimated to Mrs. Pruitt. His clothes were of the very best quality, and there was no scarcity of money. He still didn't know how to tie a cravat, leading Sarah to the conclusion that he was accustomed to having a manservant.

Considering he'd likely have drowned without her assistance, he might have shown a bit more tact and courtesy when dealing with her. Even if he was some grand scion of Scotia.

Nonetheless, he'd diverted Mrs. Pruitt from her evil conclusions about his presence at Ravenfield, and impressed the woman with his importance and superiority at the same time. It made no sense for him to include Sarah and the children in his acceptance of Mrs. Pruitt's invitation.

She wondered if Mr. Locke really intended to stay long enough to attend the music soiree.

Brogan climbed up to a promontory near Ravenfield's caves and introduced himself to Seana, a dragheen whose shape was that of a female warrior. She held a shield and spear, and did not move when Brogan spoke to her.

"You know naught of the *brìgha*-stone?" he asked when the formalities had been observed.

"No," Seana replied. "Lord Dubhán did not entrust me with such knowledge."

"But you still keep watch over the Ravenfield family?"

She lowered her brow. "'Tis Colm's wont to meddle. I have no interest in humans, whether Druzai or Tuath."

"What if I tell you that Eilinora has escaped? And that she might come to Ravenfield for the blood stone?"

"'Tis no concern of mine, Druzai lord. I live for the peace of the dale, of the wind and sky, the clouds overhead. Your mayhem means naught to me."

Brogan had never encountered a creature so disinterested in its fellow beings, but left the dragheen to her quietude. He returned to the castle and resumed his search.

The fortress had once been huge. If Lord Dubhán had been given possession of the *brìgha-stone*, Brogan was sure it had been for the purpose of keeping it safely hidden until it was needed. Brogan reasoned that Dubhán would have protected the stone with powerful cloaking spells, preventing its loss or destruction, and keeping any sorcerer from locating it with magic. Still, the ancient Druzai lord must have anticipated the stone being needed sometime in the future. Surely he would have left some clue as to its location.

Taking hold of the shovel, Brogan walked to the stairs that led to the lower levels. Some of them were open to the air, but overgrown with moss and grass. He climbed over rubble and broken walls, seeking more runes, trying to find more of the nested circles, considering the possibility that there might be an overall pattern to the etchings. He considered making a diagram of the ruins and mapping them, marking the places where he'd found runes and *crìoch-fàile*, noting the words that had been etched and the designs drawn. Mayhap the entire castle and all the symbols were part of a massive puzzle.

He gave an inward groan, wishing that Merrick had come with him, for his brother was far more proficient at riddles and puzzles, while Brogan's forte was brute force. He vaulted over a broken-down wall in the southernmost wing and came upon an ancient room that appeared to be a favored playing place for the Barstow girls, with a small table and two chairs set alongside one of the walls, and four small, cracked teacups on it. The younger of the two girls sat alone in a corner, clasping a one-armed doll to her side in a tight hug. The child's knees were drawn up under her skirts, and her head rested upon them, a perfect picture of despair, oblivious to the brown cat rubbing its head against her legs.

He set his shovel aside. "What are you doin' here, lass?"

She looked up at him, her eyes red-rimmed and swollen.

"Miss Granger says we must leave Ravenfield." She sniffed, then laid her head back on her knees. One of her shoes was unbuttoned, and Brogan crouched beside her to fasten it.

"Why must you leave?" He only asked because their departure might very well affect his search.

"B-because Papa is dead and Mr. Ridley is coming to live in our house."

If there was any logic to her words, Brogan did not follow it. But he understood well the child's grief over the loss of her father. 'Twould be a long time before the ache of sorrow in his own chest receded. Mayhap he would find some measure of peace once he dealt with Eilinora.

He would give anything for a sword and a mace and an enemy he could defeat with sheer physical strength. Or a rogue sorcerer against whom he could match power and wits. Instead, he was charged with an impossible task in this mediocre Tuath land where men abandoned their kin and young girls like this one were left to fend for themselves.

He glanced at the cracked and uneven steps that led below, anxious to continue his search. But he found himself turning back to question Jane instead. "Who is Mr. Ridley?"

"Papa's cousin. Ravenfield belongs to him now."

"This cousin will no' allow you to stay?"

She sniffed loudly. "Miss Granger d-does not think so."

Brogan stood, wondering if it was common for Tuath men to turn out their own kin, and what would happen to Sarah and the girls if he did. As it was, this child could not have experienced much joy in her short life.

Surely she'd known no magic.

Reaching into his pocket, he slipped one of his coins into his hand and reached for the child's head. With one easy trick, he produced the coin, seeming to pull it from her ear. Jane's eyes grew huge and round, and the pain in them receded momentarily.

"Have you ever found anything in the caves?" he asked. "Besides mouse bones?"

"Nothing's down there."

"You're certain, then? No runes on the walls, no buried treasure to be found?"

"Miss Granger says there is nothing of interest, and made us promise to stay clear of the caves."

Which was wise, Brogan reflected. The dark spaces and dangerous holes below were not for little girls.

"Mayhap you should hie yourself back to the house and see if Miss Granger has a treat for you." Brogan knew naught of little children, but he knew what would have comforted him had he been a lad in this household. "A bit of bread and . . . *jam* would not be amiss."

"I don't want to go away from Ravenfield," she said, ignoring Brogan's prod.

"Mayhap you willna have to."

Jane shook her head pitifully, and Brogan felt an odd twinge in his chest. She was small and fragile, and had no one but Sarah Granger to look after her interests. Sarah, who was just as vulnerable as the children.

Brogan decided that once he had the blood stone in hand and was ready to return to the Astar Columns, he could risk a bit of magic. The females of this household did not deserve to be displaced by a stranger who cared naught for them. When he was on his way back to Coruain with the stone, he would not care if any Odhar managed to trace him through his magic. By then, 'twould be too late for them to interfere with him, and Ravenfield would belong to those who needed it most.

"Methinks Mr. Ridley will not wish to keep Ravenfield to himself."

Jane gathered her cat into her arms and petted its head absently. She looked up at Brogan with hope in her eyes. "You think he will let us stay?"

"I think you shouldna assume the worst, Miss Jane."

Brogan wiped the tears from the little girl's face with his handkerchief. "I doona suppose Miss Granger will mind if I go exploring?"

Jane looked doubtful. "She will be cross."

He smiled. "I'm willing to risk it, lass."

"Where's Margaret?" Sarah asked Maud. Last she'd seen her, the child was upstairs in the nursery. She was not there now, and Sarah thought she must have left the house while Sarah was entertaining Mrs. Pruitt. "Have you seen her?"

"I thought she was with Jane."

The two women gazed out the window as Jane came across the yard with Brownie scampering after her. She carried her doll and looked as forlorn as Sarah had ever seen her. One of her braids was undone, and her face was dirty. "I wonder if she knows where her sister is."

Sarah went outside and met the child, going down on one knee to face her. "Have you seen Margaret?" she asked, keeping the worry from her voice. Though there were many places where Margaret liked to play, there were also caves and dangerous cliffs on the property. Sarah had made strict boundaries for the children, and hoped Margaret had abided by the rules.

Jane shook her head. "I don't know. She's angry with me."

"Why, love?"

Jane shrugged and hugged her doll, Henrietta, to her narrow chest. "We had a row and she pushed me down. Then I went to the house in the castle with Henrietta and Brownie and we stayed there while Mr. Locke went into the caves."

"Margaret didn't go down to the caves, did she?"

Jane shook her head. "Only Mr. Locke."

"All right, love," said Sarah. "Go into the house and stay with Maud. I'm going to look for your sister."

In all due haste, she hurried through the yard and headed toward the path that led up to the fells, meeting Mr. Locke as he came out of the ruins. He'd tossed his jacket across one shoulder and held it in place with his finger. He wore no collar, and the top buttons of his shirt were open, showing a soft indentation at the base of his neck. His shirtsleeves were rolled up, exposing the thick sinews of his forearms.

Sarah's entire body flushed at the memory of the strength of those arms when he'd caught her beneath him. She ignored her inappropriate and untimely reaction, aware that such men had more interest in the Mrs. Pruitts of the land than the penniless Sarah Grangers. "Mr. Locke, have you seen Margaret?"

He glanced back toward the ruins. "No. Only Jane."

"Yes, she told me she saw you. But—"

"Her sister is missing?"

Sarah had already gathered her skirts to go up the path when she nodded. "It'll be dark soon. I need to find her." As she started walking, she heard him mutter quietly behind her.

"No need to concern yourself, Mr. Locke. If you go back to the house, Maud will have your supper for you."

"I'll go with you." He tossed his coat, sending it to rest upon a shrub along the path, then took Sarah's elbow, surprising her. No man had ever gone out of his way to assist her.

She extricated her arm, discomfited by his firm grasp. No doubt he'd only offered to accompany her due to a gentlemanly obligation to assist a woman in need. Sarah cautioned herself not to read anything more into his simple offer of assistance.

Indeed, she preferred to make the hike up the fell without his haughty company. "There's no need for you to trouble yourself."

"The cliffs—"

"They're not to go near them."

"Then where? Are there any other houses nearby?"

"No. Only a small country cottage a mile or so from our house. It belongs to Mrs. Hartwell, a widow who lives in Craggleton, but it's empty now." They moved quickly up the path toward Squire Crowell's property. It was a steep, rocky course, with dense forest on either side, and Sarah did not like to think of Margaret up here all alone after dark. She'd been upset enough to lose track of time.

"The cottage is abandoned?"

"Yes. But it's locked. Margaret wouldn't be able to go inside."

"Then where would she go?"

"Up this way, toward the squire's house. There's a tree she likes to climb."

He raised a brow. "You're speaking of Margaret? The tidy one?"

"It's a big tree. Before her father went away, he nailed steps to its trunk so that she could climb it." Sarah was sure this must be where Margaret had gone. The child felt closest to her father there, and with the day's upset, she would seek such comfort.

"I see," said Mr. Locke, and Sarah felt his gaze on her. "You don't think she's just gone to pass the time."

Sarah swallowed back a fresh surge of distress. "I should tell you since our . . . situation . . . is likely to affect you, too." And the money he'd already paid.

"About Mr. Ridley?"

Sarah nodded. "Jane told you?"

"Aye. The cousin."

"I understand he'll be coming in the next day or two, to take possession of the house. And the property. He might not want you poking about the ruins anymore."

His brows creased, and he gave a slight shake of his head. "I doona understand English law. How does it allow a stranger to evict the rightful owner of a house?"

"I don't understand it, either." Sarah wondered if the law was so very different in Scotland. "The house is entailed . . . the solicitor told me it means that Margaret and Jane cannot inherit."

"It doesna make sense. How long have their family been Ravenfield people?" He took Sarah's hand to guide her over a stretch in the path that was crisscrossed by thick roots, and the pulsing warmth of his body shot through her.

He was only being gentlemanly, obviously aware of her worry over Margaret, but such courtesy was utterly new to Sarah.

She removed her hand from his grasp. There was no point in getting too accustomed to his touch. "There have been many generations of Barstows at Ravenfield. Centuries of them."

"You should have worn sturdier shoes, Miss Granger." Her concern about Margaret radiated from her body. Brogan did not think she would rest easy until she saw the little lass safely at home, so he did not try to reassure her. He distracted her instead.

"My sturdy shoes have not yet dried after their excursion into the sea, Mr. Locke."

"Ah. The rescue. Have I thanked you for that?"

"I don't believe so, although—as my mother used to say—it's never too late."

"And your gown? I suppose it was ruined by the brine. I will see that it's replaced."

"It was only my everyday dress, Mr. Locke. I laundered it today, and it will continue to serve me well."

The path climbed steadily upward, an easy trek, but he took her arm once again. He enjoyed the touch of her cool, soft skin. And he'd been right . . . his touch *did* cause goose bumps.

She did not pull away this time. "You know you were the inspiration for Mrs. Pruitt's soiree."

Aye, and he could only hope he would not be present for it. "I thought I handled her masterfully."

Walking close beside him, Sarah shook her head. "You definitely roused her interest."

"That was my intention. She was easily impressed, was she no'?"

Sarah gave him a puzzled look, then laughed, the sound of her mirth sluicing through him to ease the deep ache that had settled between his ribs since losing his father. "She was much too easy for a man of your skills."

"*My* skills?"

She blushed deeply then, and he was tempted to mention it to her again, to see the color deepen. But then she might accuse him of using his skills on her. "What skills would those be, Miss Granger?"

She licked her lips, and Brogan reminded himself that he only wanted to engage in a bit of innocent flirtation to prepare her for the Pruitt party. He did not care to encourage any particular interest in him, but merely to show her how to engage in some friendly repartee.

"Well . . . you obviously know how to charm

women, Mr. Locke. Maud thinks the world of you, and Mrs. Pruitt is holding a soiree to introduce you to all her friends."

"But what about you, Miss Granger. Have I charmed you?" he asked, surprisingly distracted by the movement of her mouth.

"'Tis a ridiculous question," she said, hurrying up the hill ahead of him. "There hasn't been a gentleman in my entire life who has wanted to charm me."

Chapter 5

Sarah loved the forest. In the late afternoon sunlight, the leaves often gave the appearance of a mist in the hills. In some directions, the play of light made the leaves look like lace. She liked to stop and listen to the ancient limbs creak as they shifted in the earth, and feel the cool breeze on her skin. But this time, she hardly noticed anything but the path beneath her feet.

Mr. Locke was flirting with her.

He'd been friendly with Maud and the children, flirtatious and attentive with Mrs. Pruitt. Yet he'd been nothing but difficult with Sarah, grudgingly answering her questions and making her feel cornered in her own home. Until now.

She pressed one hand to her cheek and felt the heat that seemed to spring up much too often when she was in the man's presence. She did not understand him, nor could she fathom that he was trying to charm her as he'd done with Mrs. Pruitt.

Not even the most ordinary men in the parish had found her appealing . . . neither would a rich, handsome visitor from Scotland who clearly thought a great deal of his own worth. Fortunately, she was not so susceptible to his charms. He could play at seduction all he liked, but Sarah was not his for the taking.

Nothing had changed. She still had the children to think of, and when Mr. Locke left Ravenfield, she would have to deal with Mr. Ridley. Alone, as always.

She hiked to the peak of the hill, went through the old gate in the fence, and hurried on toward Margaret's tree. Very soon, Sarah was able to see two small feet dangling from one of the branches.

"Margaret!" Relieved to see her unharmed, Sarah picked up her pace and started to run toward the tree, ignoring the heavy footsteps behind her.

She reached Margaret, who had already started down the steps made for her by her father. The child's face was drawn and pale, and wet. She looked as though she'd been weeping for hours.

Sarah lifted her from the step and drew her into her arms, giving her a tight hug. "You're shaking, Margaret. I promise you all will be well, love. I'll take care of you."

"Miss Granger, he's here!"

Sarah pulled away slightly to glance back at Mr. Locke. "Yes, Mr. Locke was good enough to accompany me—"

"No!" Margaret wailed. "*Mr. Ridley!* He's come!"

Sarah's heart began to pound. She was not ready for this. "Mr. Ridley? How do you know?"

"I saw him." Margaret's breath came out in short sobbing bursts. "He's horrible!"

"Are you sure it was not Andy Ferris?" Sarah asked. "He sometimes wanders these woods."

Margaret's chin quivered. "No. Andy has no fine clothes nor top hat. And he drools."

Sarah noticed Mr. Locke's frown and gave a brief explanation. "Poor Andy is simpleminded. He begs in town and sleeps wherever he finds himself. Sometimes in our barn."

"Simpleminded?" asked Mr. Locke.

Sarah nodded. "Surely you've known someone like Andy—a poor soul without all his faculties."

His eyes lost their focus as he pondered Sarah's description of Andy. Sarah felt an eerie prickle at the base of her spine that dissipated the moment he spoke. "I doona believe I have. 'Tis strange . . ." He turned his attention to Margaret. "Where did you see the intruder?"

Margaret looked up at him with teary eyes. "I was up in the tree and I heard him whistling. So I hid in the branches and waited for him to pass."

"When?" Sarah asked, lowering Margaret to the ground.

"A long time ago," Margaret said, straightening her clothes. "Hours and hours. I was afraid to come down."

"Whoever he was, he did not come to the house, Margaret."

Shuddering visibly, she shook her head. "He stood upon Norton's Fell and looked at our lady warrior on the cliff. Then he turned to look at Ravenfield. I stayed perfectly still until he went up the path through the fells to Squire Crowell's house."

Mr. Locke moved away in order to get a clear view of the sturdy stone warrior who stood on the promontory. When he returned, he placed his hand on Margaret's shoulder and went down on one knee beside her. "What did he look like?" His tone was serious, his voice gruff.

"He was nearly as tall as you, but he wore a gray coat and a top hat."

"Did you see his face?"

Sarah did not know why that should matter, but the questions seemed to calm Margaret as she focused her attention on them, rather than her worries.

"His hair was light like mine and Jane's. Like Squire Crowell's. But his eyes were black as coal."

Mr. Locke paused only a moment, then turned away slightly. "We ought to return to the house. Would you care for a pony ride, Miss Margaret?"

When she nodded, he pulled her onto his back and stood, easily managing her slight frame. "In my country, lasses named Margaret are called Meglet. Might I call you that?"

"I . . . I suppose so," Margaret replied.

"Weel then, Meglet, I think you should try no' to worry so much about Mr. Ridley. 'Tis my guess that things will work out much better than any of you could possibly foresee."

Sarah bristled at his words, for he could not possibly have any idea how they would survive after Mr. Ridley took possession of Ravenfield. It was cruel to raise Margaret's hopes.

Brogan doubted that the dreaded Mr. Ridley would climb to the top of this fell to survey his new property and then walk in the opposite direction of the house. The stranger Margaret had seen could very well have been sent by Eilinora.

Or he was merely a visitor to the local squire, a harmless man who'd taken himself on a hike in the hills. In any case, the appearance of the strange man gave a new urgency to Brogan's search. He had not planned on being so distracted by the Ravenfield females.

Or Ravenfield itself.

The land was lovely. From Margaret's tree, he'd been able to see the craggy cliffs of Ravenfield and the sea beyond. Heather and wildflowers grew profusely on the hills, and small, colorful, winged creatures flitted across the fields. Sarah called them butterflies, and Brogan was struck by an awareness that Coruain was not as perfect as he'd once thought. He wondered how the ancient elders had neglected to bring butterflies when they'd created Coruain. And jam. 'Twas unforgivable.

"Who is Squire Crowell?" he asked.

"He's the most comely man in the parish," Margaret announced. "And Miss Granger has—"

"He's a member of our local gentry," said Sarah, cutting off the child's chatter. "And our magistrate."

Brogan ignored Sarah's praises of the man and turned to speak to the child on his back. "And Miss Granger has *what*, Meglet?"

"She has loved—"

"'Tis rude to tell tales, young lady," Sarah admonished before Margaret could finish. But her face turned pink with embarrassment at the little that was said. "I barely know the squire."

Brogan felt an immediate dislike for the man, but only because of his foolishness in ignoring Sarah Granger. "You never saw this blond fellow on the hill before?"

"No."

"I shouldn't think that's terribly unusual," Sarah remarked. "The squire is an important man who must have many acquaintances who visit him. Friends from the city and country alike."

Brogan's dislike grew with Sarah's defense of him. "Do these friends and acquaintances visit him often?"

"I'm sure I wouldn't know," Sarah said, her tone piqued. "My path does not often cross Squire Crowell's."

"You were quite anxious to summon him yesterday, Miss Granger, when you found me on the beach." Brogan knew he sounded equally annoyed. He could not understand why Sarah's esteemed squire had not once sought her company in the time Brogan had been at Ravenfield. Was the man blind as well as a simpleton, like Andy Ferris?

Brogan wondered if the man had noticed her.

Sarah did naught to make herself attractive, wearing clothes that concealed her feminine assets and made her complexion dull. Her glorious hair was forever pulled so tight, 'twas surprising her face hadn't frozen into a perpetual smile.

He realized she had no awareness of her appeal. She was lovely. She needed only to loosen her hair and wear more attractive clothes and her squire would notice her.

"Well, of course I thought of summoning the squire," she said. "I've probably violated any number of laws by neglecting to call in the authorities. I've never heard of a man washing up from the sea."

"And now your squire has a guest, so it would be inconvenient to trouble him," he said.

"Exactly right," she remarked, obviously relieved to have the matter settled. Yet his unorthodox arrival had been the perfect excuse for her to call on the squire, the man she loved.

'Twas curious. Could it be that she was shy? Or lacking confidence?

"Is this the path to his house?" Brogan asked, turning his attention to the more weighty matter at hand—a stranger in the vicinity.

Sarah and Margaret nodded together. "Over the next rise and through the trees," said Sarah. "Corrington is a huge estate. 'Tis much larger than Ravenfield."

But close enough that an Odhar warrior might establish his own base there as Brogan had done at Ravenfield. Mayhap he should pay a visit to Corrington House and see Crowell's visitor for himself. He decided to wait until after dark, then he would make a quick trip to Crowell's estate and try to determine whether the visitor was a magical being, or nothing more than a Tuath gentleman, come to visit a country acquaintance.

In the meantime, Brogan intended to discover what made Sarah Granger so skittish with men.

They descended the steep path carefully in consideration of Sarah's flimsy shoes, and Brogan grabbed her arm when she tripped, keeping her from falling. Her hair came loose, and when it brushed his hand, she quickly drew away and twisted the glorious mass into a tight loop at her nape.

He wondered if Crowell could possibly be Sarah's true *céile* mate. If so, 'twould be a simple enough matter to make him realize it. The Pruitt woman's event would likely be the best opportunity for Sarah to show herself to good advantage. If she wore flattering clothes and softened the arrangement of her hair, the only thing lacking would be confidence in herself.

As to that, mayhap all it would take would be a bit of flattering male attention and she would learn to trust her feminine charms.

"My papa used to carry us this way," said Margaret. "We had to take turns."

"Aye. 'Tis a fair occupation for a father," Brogan said, enjoying the simple pleasure of touching Sarah and carrying Meglet.

Brogan had yet to meet his own *céile* mate, the woman with whom he would share *sòlas* forever. He had come to doubt that he would ever sire the children Kieran had wanted to see before he died.

None of Brogan's past mistresses aroused more than a passing interest. They hadn't needed him particularly, nor had Brogan had much need for any of them, beyond the obvious.

"Did your papa take you on pony rides, too?" Margaret asked.

"Aye. And like you, I recently lost him." He didn't know why he'd said it. The information could make no possible difference to his quest here, or the fact that he would soon be gone.

But when Sarah put her hand on his arm and looked into his eyes with a compassionate gaze of her own, a warm current of contentment flowed through him, an unfamiliar sense of peace.

"I'm so sorry for your loss. I didn't know."

"Was he killed in the Napoleon war, too?" Margaret asked.

"No, *moileen*," Brogan said, using a Druzai endearment as he enjoyed these few moments of tranquility in Sarah's world. He would not have minded if she leaned closer so he could inhale that scent that aroused him every time she was near. But she moved away when she saw Jane running up the hill toward them.

It was for the best. When he left, he wanted to leave no lingering impression on them. Nor did he want any particular memories of Sarah Granger to follow him to Coruain.

"Look, Margaret!" Sarah said. "It's your sister

coming after you, and Maud right behind her."

Brogan let Margaret down and she ran ahead to meet Jane and the housekeeper.

His father had recently died. Perhaps that was why Mr. Locke seemed a bit lost, so otherworldly. It was likely why his attention sometimes seemed to drift. Sarah knew how he felt. After her father's death, she had not gotten her bearings until she'd come to Ravenfield. She'd felt adrift for four long years.

He did not hurry to catch up to Maud and the girls, instead falling into a comfortable pace beside her. "My father was hardly an exemplary parent," Sarah said. "But I missed him terribly when he died."

His expression was desolate when he looked at her. "We used to argue," he said.

"And you are sorry for it."

"Aye."

"Do you not think most fathers and sons argue at times?"

"'Twas different with us, Miss Granger. We argued matters of policy. Of defense. Of marital alliances."

"You make it sound as though your father was king of Scotland." She looked up at him, puzzled. "But there is no Scottish king, is there?"

"No. He was . . ." He hesitated, and Sarah

thought he considered his next words quite carefully. "He was a very powerful lord of our lands. The lives of many were affected by his decisions."

"Even so . . . Your father must have appreciated a lively discourse with the man he could most trust," she said. "His son."

"But we disagreed."

"'Twould be a foolish lord who surrounded himself only with those who agreed with him," she said. "I would venture to guess your father was not a fool."

He shook his head. A lock of his hair dropped onto his forehead, giving her a glimpse of the boy he'd once been. Sarah had the urge to push it back, but such an act would be much too intimate.

"No. He was brilliant in his way."

"You loved him."

His jaw clenched tightly. "Aye. I did."

Sarah's throat tightened, and she felt tears welling in her eyes. She blinked them away and put aside the memories of her own parents' deaths.

He stopped and turned to her. "I loved him, but no more than you did yours."

Sarah took a shuddering breath. "My father was no noble lord, Mr. Locke. After my mother died, he was responsible only for the two of us. And he failed at that."

"It changes naught."

She shook her head. "You're right. It doesn't. He was a drunkard, but I remembered our happier times, when my mother was alive and all was well. After she died, he barely kept a roof over our heads, and food on our table, but he cared for me as best he could."

He'd taught her to play the pianoforte, to draw and to speak French. They were all worthless occupations, except to a wife or a governess, and Sarah knew which she would soon be.

Mr. Locke touched her cheek then, and rubbed away a tear she hadn't realized she'd shed. "We are a fine pair, are we not, Sarah Granger?"

She brushed away the other tears as well as his hand, and started walking again. She did not like to think of her father's last days and the illness that had ravaged him. Nor did she wish to dwell upon the time she'd spent in the parish school or the three years she'd had to rely upon the grudging charity of the wealthy families in Craggleton.

Those days seemed all too threatening now, with Mr. Ridley on his way to Ravenfield. She didn't know if she could succeed in the town that had made her an outcast. Yet there had to be some fair-minded families in Craggleton who wanted to educate their daughters, but could not afford the venerable widows who took in students. Her plan depended upon it.

Mr. Locke fell into step beside her and they

walked in silence to the garden, where he retrieved his coat from the shrubs.

Sarah felt embarrassed by her tears, shed for the father who had already been gone ten years. She was no weak-minded female who dwelled on past sorrows, especially now, when she had to find the strength and determination to make a go of it in Craggleton. She was determined to see that Margaret and Jane fared better in their orphaned state than she ever did.

"You don't think it was Mr. Ridley visiting Squire Crowell, do you?" Sarah asked hopefully while the children washed their hands and faces. She needed a few more days to make plans, to find lodgings, to advertise her services.

"Ridley will come directly to Ravenfield," Mr. Locke said. "What reason would he have to visit the neighboring estates first?"

It was what Sarah thought, though it did not ease her worries. Mr. Ridley would soon arrive, and Mr. Merton had suggested that she and the children should vacate the house before he came.

It distressed her to know that Captain Barstow's cousin, far removed as he might be, intended to cast his cousin's children from their home with no prospects. Could any man be so cold?

She knew he could. Shuddering at the memory of her own experiences before coming to Ravenfield, Sarah renewed her vow to take care of the girls if they were compelled to leave. All advice to the contrary, Sarah wondered if Mr. Ridley might let them stay. She said nothing of this possibility to the girls . . . It was remote at best, and they had to be prepared to leave the home they'd known all their lives.

When they returned to the house, Sarah noticed a few items that were out of place. Books lay on the desk in the library, and a drawer in the writing table was open. She did not think Maud would leave these items out of place, but her chores must have been interrupted by Jane's appearance in the house with tales of Margaret's disappearance. Giving it no further thought, she closed the drawer and replaced the books, and joined the others.

Maud served supper in the kitchen and they all sat down informally at the table with Mr. Locke. It began as a tense and quiet affair in spite of Sarah's attempts to speak cheerfully of the life they would make for themselves in Craggleton.

"What if that man really was Mr. Ridley?" Margaret asked. "Will he turn us out of the house when he comes here?"

"What kind of lodgings will we find?" Jane asked.

"Will we have to take the rooms behind the butcher's shop?" Margaret asked, going pale. She put down her fork. "Before Papa went away, I saw him give money to a ragged little boy who lived there."

"Of course not, Margaret," said Sarah. "Our rooms will be lovely, with windows and . . . a small kitchen. We'll be able to cook our pies . . ."

"And sell cockles, too?" Jane asked.

Sarah nodded. "And I will give music lessons."

"Will we have a pianoforte in our new home?"

Sarah took a deep breath. They would be lucky to have enough beds for the three of them, but she could not tell that to the girls. They would have to face cold reality soon enough. "No, love. I'll have to go to the homes of those who wish to learn."

Mr. Locke stood abruptly and took the pitcher from the table. He said nothing, but went out the door to the well.

"I think Mr. Locke is angry," said Margaret.

Jane nodded. "His brows came together the way Papa's did when he was displeased with us."

Sarah had also noted the dark expression on their visitor's face. "Perhaps he's thinking of his boat and the trouble he's going to have getting home."

Maud snorted. "With the money that one has, he'll have no difficulty hiring his own private carriage to take him home."

He'd told Margaret that things would likely

work out better than they could imagine. Yet Sarah could not see how. She wondered if Mr. Locke also thought it possible that Mr. Ridley would want the girls to remain at Ravenfield.

Brogan had to get out of there. He went to the well in the courtyard, but sat down on the low, rocky wall that enclosed the garden, letting the pitcher dangle from his fingers.

"They insinuate themselves, do they no'?" Colm remarked. He ruffled his feathers, but did not move from his perch in the fountain.

Brogan did not reply, but he knew the dragheen was correct. He was beginning to care what happened to these Tuath females.

Kieran's death had hit him hard, but Brogan's position on Coruain ensured there would be no hardship resulting from his father's demise. Brogan would continue to see to the protection of the Druzai isles, training and commanding the elite sorcerer-warriors of Coruain while Merrick became high chieftain. Merrick would wed the Druzai sorceress that had been foretold at his birth, and Brogan could play doting uncle to his children.

But here ... Captain Barstow's death had caused the impoverishment of his family. Ravenfield did not appear to have been prosperous for a long time, but at least the children and Sarah had a home here. They managed to earn enough money to buy the essentials they needed.

Brogan had not been able to continue listening to Sarah's plans and the lasses' glum questions about their future. It was all too appalling.

"She needs a husband," the dragheen remarked.

Brogan felt his jaws clench, even though he'd already considered this. He just didn't care to hear it from another.

"She needs someone to provide for her. To give her a secure position in life," said Colm. "I've considered planting a thought—"

"In whom?" Brogan demanded, thinking of Crowell, who had not seen past Sarah's drab clothes to the vibrant young woman who wore them. "Is there a likely husband for her in all the parish? Why, then, has no man claimed her?"

"She has no dowry," Colm replied calmly, "no property to bring to a marriage."

"And that's all there is to it?" Brogan demanded. He reached into his pockets and drew out a few of the coins that were so prized here. He would leave all this money with Sarah when he left. Mayhap this would bring a likely spouse to her door.

"Not quite, m'lord. The lass has a certain history in these parts. She is known as a pauper, the daughter of a drunkard. But if she were more comely, mayhap—"

"She's as comely as any Druzai—"

"To an eye that sees beyond the tattered clothes and work-worn hands," said Colm. "If only her father hadna taken to the drink after her mother's death . . ."

"Doona be giving *ideas* to anyone, dragheen," Brogan said harshly. The last thing Sarah Granger needed was to gain a husband who believed he'd been duped into marriage. He'd heard far too many instances of dragheen suggestions going awry. Sarah was more than capable of attracting a man without dragheen assistance. She needed to attract a spouse on her own merit for any love match to succeed.

But Brogan would make a few suggestions of his own, as a man who knew what feminine accoutrements would make her most appealing. Then he could return to Coruain, confident that she would fare well.

The tears she'd unconsciously shed had touched him more deeply than he cared to admit, but he wanted to feel no more. The lass was a survivor, and quite capable of taking care of herself and the two bairns.

"Ah, but think how simple 'twould be if Ravenfield's heir decided to wed our Sarah," Colm said. "I could make but a wee suggestion—"

"Ridley?" Brogan stood abruptly and paced restively. He'd been thinking her squire was her most likely *céile* mate, but marriage with Ridley would mean she and the lasses could remain at Ravenfield.

In any case, dragheen interference was not acceptable.

"You know what would happen, Colm," Brogan said. "Your hints would seem sound for a week or two, mayhap even a month. But once your spell dissipated, her husband would feel he'd somehow been duped. Mayhap even tricked by her."

"Miss Granger was ill used after her father died, before coming to Ravenfield. I would see her secure in marriage, m'lord. Ne'er again should she have to worry about losing her home."

Brogan made a sound deep in this throat. "Ill used? In what way?"

"Beaten on the whim of a bad-tempered mistress. Embarrassed by bored husbands who tried to take advantage. Abused by young men who—"

"Are you saying she was raped?" Brogan asked, his anger rising.

"No' to my knowledge, m'lord. The lass has found comfort in hiding herself here at Ravenfield."

Brogan swore brutally. 'Twas no wonder she did not wish to attract attention to herself. This Tuath world was even worse than Brogan had thought before coming here. Now he knew how barbaric they were.

"I've sent a message on the wind," said the dragheen, "for information about Mr. Ridley. I've learned he is a bachelor, m'lord."

"Bachelor or no, do you no' think Ridley would soon become dissatisfied with a wife he did not choose for himself."

"These are Tuath, m'lord," said Colm. "They are accustomed to accepting their lot, whatever it may be. They are accustomed to accepting marriages arranged for them. They know no *sòlas*. They do not become *céile* mates." Yet a match suggested by a dragheen would never succeed. Ridley could very well grow dissatisfied if his attraction to Sarah did not originate from his own heart and mind.

Brogan fixed his gaze on the dragheen. "Doona interfere. I will deal with her predicament myself."

Even if she would not experience the bond commonly shared between Druzai spouses, there would surely be an acceptable husband for her.

And it would take none of his extraordinary powers to achieve it. She was more than capable of attracting her own mate. He had only to show her how.

Colm's stone feathers crackled. "I'm sure ye know best, m'lord."

Brogan filled the pitcher at the well and started back to the house, though he still felt edgy. He was satisfied the dragheen would make no suggestions on Sarah's behalf, but there was no love spell on earth that actually worked beyond providing a short-lived infatuation.

She would have to win a husband with her own charms.

"Here's a thought," said Maud. "We'll make some extra room at my sister's in Ulverston. Then you and the girls—"

"We couldn't ask that, Maud." Sarah knew that Maud's sister lived in a tiny cottage. There would be barely enough room for the two women. "You've been looking after us for so long—you deserve a rest."

Mr. Locke returned to the table, and Sarah suspected the discussion of their predicament had made him uncomfortable. He was a guest, and they needed to avoid speaking of their private troubles while he was present.

He had his own. Likely his trip away from Scotland was intended as a respite from his own grief. Sarah had somewhat softened toward him upon hearing of his loss, and knew she must guard her heart. He was a man with obligations in Scotland, and she had her own duty here. Wishing for . . . No, she'd learned long ago that wishes were only for children.

"Mrs. Pruitt visited this afternoon," she said, putting her dismal thoughts from her mind.

"Oh! While I was in Craggleton?" Maud asked. "Was she just as evil-tempered as ever?"

"She's decided to hold a musical soiree," Sarah said suddenly. She hadn't intended to mention the soiree, much less attend it, but the girls needed cheering. She swallowed and continued. "We're all invited."

The girls looked up from their plates with bright eyes. Sarah knew the only reason she and the children had been invited was the presence of their guest. As much as she'd wanted to, Mrs. Pruitt had not been able to slight Sarah and the girls, not without offending Mr. Locke.

"Will I have a new dress to wear?" Margaret asked, their troubles forgotten for the moment.

"Will we be allowed to dance?" Jane wanted to know.

Sarah nodded. "I'm sure we'll be able to make new gowns for you . . . and of course you'll be able to dance," she added, hoping it would be so. She'd never been to a soiree herself, and would be attending this one only because of Mr. Locke.

With Sarah's news, the tension in the room eased and the girls began to talk excitedly about the function at Mrs. Pruitt's grand house. Captain Barstow had taken them to a soiree a few years before, but they'd been too young to remember it well.

With the money Mr. Locke had paid for his board and lodgings, Sarah would be able to buy new fabric to make party frocks for the girls. In spite of their reduced circumstances, they would be cleanly and neatly dressed. The way she and the girls appeared at Mrs. Pruitt's party would affect her reputation and whether anyone would hire her services as a teacher.

"When is this magnificent event to take place?" Maud asked, smiling widely.

"Friday," Sarah replied, keeping her eyes on her plate. "Mrs. Pruitt is hoping Mr. Locke will stay long enough to attend."

Brogan shook his head, keeping his features expressionless. In truth, he should not be here now. The more contact he had with this Tuath family, the more complicated things became.

Yet he found himself wanting to show Meglet that the world was not the harsh and unforgiving place she imagined. He'd like to provide teacups for Jane's parties and a doll with two arms. And the list was growing. When he had the blood stone in his possession, there was all manner of magic he intended to perform, from easing the aches in kindly Maud's stiff knees and back, to settling the Ravenfield inheritance in Sarah's favor.

"'Tis likely I'll be gone before Friday." If he located the stone after supper, they would not find him in his room in the morning. If it turned up in the morn, he'd leave before noon.

"But we'll need an escort," Margaret whimpered. "Who will take us to Pruitt Hall?"

"Margaret, hush," Sarah admonished, quick to mask the disappointment in her own eyes. "Mr. Locke is under no obligation to us. Besides, we are quite accustomed to getting ourselves to and from our destinations, are we not?"

He felt like a heartless lout, but he was in no position to make any promises. He did not even intend to stay long enough to say farewell once he had the stone in his possession, not when it was so desperately needed on Coruain.

He had no idea what was happening at home. Eilinora might have already returned for another attack, and here Brogan sat, calmly eating Maud's delicious roasted fowl in the kitchen of a quiet English estate. 'Twas irresponsible.

Sarah turned to him. "Did you find anything of interest in the caves today, Mr. Locke?"

He shook his head, refusing to feel any regret for keeping his distance. Druzai and Tuath were not meant to mix. 'Twas what he'd always believed, and he saw no reason for changing his opinion.

"I saw naught but markings on the walls," he replied, glad of the change in subject.

"The runes?" Maud remarked. "No one has ever been able to tell what they signify. Neither them nor those peculiar circles."

"Except Miss Granger," said Jane. "She knows."

Brogan nearly dropped his fork. He looked across the table at Sarah. "You understand the meaning of the etchings, Miss Granger?"

She shrugged her narrow shoulders, and Brogan caught sight of a line of fine, white lawn beneath the neckline of her gown. He blew out a long, deep breath, refusing to allow himself to be distracted by that bit of her beguiling feminine undergarment. He would not wonder whether 'twas the same worn chemise he'd handled earlier.

"They're only children's tales. I don't really know what the symbols mean."

Brogan shifted his gaze and looked into her eyes. "The stories are your own, Miss Granger?" he asked. He wasn't sure what he was hoping for . . . perhaps that she would say her tales and the clues given by the runes had been passed down from generation to generation.

"Of course," she replied. "No one knows the meaning of the runes. Even Captain Barstow did not know."

'Twas only a small disappointment. He'd never really expected Sarah to come out with a tale of runes or *crìoch-fàile* that were clues to the location of the ancient blood stone.

The quest that had seemed so straightforward and simple only two days ago now seemed next to impossible. Brogan was going to have to search every one of those caves, as well as the castle, inch by inch. There had to be a hidden compartment, a door, or some small niche where the blood stone might have been concealed.

He had to hurry. If a Druzai seer had located the blood stones, 'twas likely one of the Odhar had done so, too. Eilinora would know the stones could be used against her. She or one of her minions was sure to turn up here sooner or later, and Brogan wanted to be long gone by then.

He only wished he'd spent more of his idle hours playing with puzzles.

Mr. Locke's eyes darkened, and he seemed deep in thought. His lashes were long and thick, spiked as though he'd been caught in a summer rain. Sarah wished she could answer all his questions about the runes in the caves and high upon the tower walls, but she knew nothing about them. None of the amateurs or scholars who had visited the ruins had been able to offer anything but theories about the strange markings.

They reminded Sarah of the etchings on her Luck—a small tin box given her by her mother just before her death. The marks on the tin were worn nearly smooth, but Sarah had been able to feel them in the dark hours of the night when she'd missed her mother so desperately. She'd held the box in her hands, hoping to feel closer to her, but the cold tin had been a poor substitute for her mother's gentle hands on her hair and skin.

Looking for a diversion from her maudlin thoughts, she turned to the housekeeper. "Supper was wonderful, Maud. Thank you."

"Yes, well, you can thank Mr. Locke . . . his coin was what put this fine bird on our table."

Looking up blankly, Mr. Locke seemed not to hear Maud's words of appreciation. "Have you a pen and paper?"

A bit of his hair came loose from his queue, and he seemed quite distracted.

"We surely do," Maud answered him. "I'll just get it from the library."

But when Maud started to rise stiffly from her chair, he bade her to remain seated, not to trouble herself on his account. "Just tell me where to look and I'll see to it myself."

He went toward the door, but came back to the table and dropped two guineas on it. "This should be enough to buy a few new party gowns for you ladies."

Chapter 6

Brogan took four sheets of paper and put them together on the desk in the library, making one large square of white. Then he drew a complete diagram of the castle and caves in four quadrants, marking the runes in the locations where he'd found them. On the morrow he would make exact copies of the *crìoch-fàile* patterns and see if he could fit them together and make sense of them.

If there was a puzzle or riddle in the words, he still had to find the clues that put them together. He read and reread the runes he'd already found, but was distracted by the voices in the drawing room.

Then he heard music.

Brogan had never heard such sounds on Coruain, where the soft strings of their lutes and *teilinn* soothed and lulled the uneasy to sleep. He got up from his chair and opened the door to the drawing room.

Sarah and the lasses were sitting together on a long bench before the huge instrument. Sarah's hands flew over the white and black strips, making the most complex combination of sounds he'd ever heard, while the children's feet swung in time with the music.

Sarah caught sight of him and faltered.

"Doona stop, lass. 'Tis verra fine."

She resumed playing the piece, slowing down the pace and telling Meglet to join in. Sarah moved her hands to the left and played the deeper notes, while Meg played the lighter, more delicate part, keeping time with Sarah. Meglet made a few mistakes, but Sarah did not chide her. They continued until the piece came to a satisfying conclusion. It did not drift to a subtle end as Druzai music often did, so ethereal the listener sometimes thought he'd imagined hearing it.

There was silence for a moment, and then the girls asked Sarah to play another piece on the pianoforte. Brogan leaned back against the doorjamb and crossed his arms to listen as she started to play, considering that any Tuath man who heard Sarah Granger's music would be a fool if he did not immediately want to wed her.

Sarah and the girls went upstairs to prepare for bed after the music lesson. Sarah had played two more short pieces, and yet a third at Mr. Locke's request.

She had never played for an audience before. Her father had taught her well, but she doubted her own abilities when she caught sight of the expression on Mr. Locke's face as he listened to her play. He looked as though she were playing Mozart in a manner he'd never heard before.

Yet she quickly realized he did not disapprove. Whatever she'd done that was different had not displeased him, and Sarah felt an unfamiliar pleasure at his good opinion, in spite of his abrupt departure when she'd told the girls it was time for bed.

They bid Maud good night and went up to the nursery. "Miss Granger, can you not convince Mr. Locke to stay and escort us to Mrs. Pruitt's party?" Margaret asked.

"Of course not," said Sarah. "A lady never asks a gentleman such a thing. Never."

"I don't see why we can't go alone," Jane grumbled. "We know our way to the dragon lady's house."

"I would like a pink gown for the soiree," said Margaret. "One with ribbons and bows."

"All right," said Sarah, smiling as Margaret lightened the mood. "What about you, Jane?"

The little girl shrugged and drew on her nightgown. "Pink, too."

"No, you cannot have pink if I am to have pink," Margaret scolded. "Yellow. You look quite good in yellow."

While the girls washed and cleaned their teeth, Sarah gathered up their stockings to be laundered for tomorrow, and lined up their shoes beneath the window ledge. "Please may we have a story tonight, Miss Granger?" asked Margaret.

"Oh yes, please! About a fairy princess at a ball?" Jane added.

"Come and get into your beds," Sarah instructed. She set the lamp on the table between their beds, then drew back their blankets. The two sisters climbed into the same bed, and Sarah sat on its edge.

"Where is Brownie?" Jane asked.

"She's outside looking for mice," Margaret replied impatiently, turning to Sarah. "Ready."

"Once there was a sad, sad yeoman."

"Why was he sad, Miss Granger?" Jane asked.

"Be quiet, Jane," Margaret admonished, "and listen."

"The yeoman was tall and handsome, and he lived in a beautiful land, with tall cliffs and fells to hike in."

"Just like Ravenfield!"

Margaret jabbed her sister with her elbow to quiet her, but she was right. Sarah often made Ravenfield the setting of her tales. She'd never seen the castle before taking her post as governess here, yet it had been a part of nearly every one of Sarah's earliest dreams. She could not explain it, nor did she try. Somehow, Ravenfield's castle had always been a part of her, and when Captain Barstow had brought her here, she'd known she was home.

"The yeoman, whose name was Robert, was lonely," Sarah continued. "There was no young lady in all the kingdom who would have him for her husband."

"Why?"

"Because a powerful witch had put an evil spell on him when he was born. Because of it, he was unable to speak."

Sarah enjoyed inventing amusing tales for the girls, and answering their inevitable questions about the characters or the plot. Every story was greatly enriched by the girls' contributions, and tonight was no exception. Their embellishments kept Sarah's attention fixed on the tale, and not on Mr. Locke's company in the drawing room.

He'd sat on the sofa between Margaret and Jane, and when Sarah had dared a glance in his direction, he'd seemed entranced by her music. It gave Sarah pleasure to know she had done well, performing for a man who seemed to have the resources to have heard the best musicians in the country.

Yet she'd felt unnerved at the same time. His scrutiny had been intense, and Sarah had almost been able to feel him touching her skin . . . the back of her neck, her upper arms. She knew it was not rational, but the feeling had been strong, nonetheless, and not as unpleasant as such contact had been in the past. He was no cloying lecher who felt he had a right to touch her or speak indecently to her. He did not amuse himself with embarrassing her.

Sarah drew out the tale of the mute yeoman, adding as many interesting elements as she could imagine. "There was a beautiful fairy princess whom the yeoman loved, but she took no notice of him because he could not speak."

Sarah wove the tale, capturing the children's fancy, until she stranded the fairy princess in a giant's lair.

"What was her name, Miss Granger?"

"Adriella. And the poor thing could not escape."

"Was the giant huge and fierce?"

"Of course," Sarah said. "But he had a very surprising wit."

"What do you mean?"

"He enjoyed a good jest. He took her down into the cave on Robert's land, and guarded the entrance so that Adriella could not get out."

"Did Robert come and save her?"

"Not right away. The giant told Adriella that he would give her one question every day for three days. If she could answer all three correctly, he would let her go on the third day."

"Did she know the answers?"

"No. For they were questions about men's crafts. Carpentry, smithing, and weaponry. Adriella nearly despaired."

"*Then* did Robert come and save her?"

Sarah nodded. "He tried. But the fierce old giant caught him, too."

The girls' eyes grew large and round then, worried about their hero and heroine. "The giant knew that Robert could not speak, so he had no doubt the two would become his supper on the third day. With supreme confidence, the giant promised to go away forever if Adriella managed to answer all three questions.

"The giant asked the first one, and when neither Adriella nor Robert could answer, he laughed and settled himself down for a nap. Then Robert took up a sharp rock and carved the answer into the rock wall. When the giant woke up, Adriella gave him the correct answer."

Sarah repeated the same process with the next two questions, and Robert and the princess were soon freed.

Happy with the ending, Margaret started to complete the story the way Sarah had done so many times before. "The princess was so grateful to Robert that she gave him the tin Luck—"

"And told him," added Jane, "that if he kept it safe for all time, the luck of the fairies would stay with him."

"No!" Sarah laughed, pleased to be able to give them an end that they had not been able to predict. "She removed the spell that kept Robert from being able to speak, then flew away to the land of fairies. Robert found himself a wife and was able to tell her with words that he loved her. They lived happily ever after in the land of cliffs and caves!"

"So the circles and dots on our castle walls are the ones Robert made?"

"Of course," said Sarah. "Someone had to have drawn them."

When the house was quiet, Brogan slipped out and went to the castle. He looked for the torch he'd left inside the mouth of the first cave, but it was not in the sconce where he'd left it.

He considered whether one of the children might have taken it, but knew it was unlikely. The sconce was well above their heads, so they could never have reached it. He didn't think either Sarah or Maud had come down here . . .

Brogan had seen no sign of any Odhar, yet who else would have an interest in these caves? Who else might have taken the torch? He stepped inside and lit a match, holding it high. In the faint light, he saw the torch, lying near the opening to the next cave. He dropped his match, then lit the flare, looking for signs of an intruder.

At the sound of stealthy movement in the next chamber, Brogan prepared to attack. If Eilinora or one of her sorcerers was inside, Brogan had trapped them. Their only escape would be through the hole in the lowest cave. They might not yet know about it, for the passage to it was extremely narrow.

Moving silently, he gathered the energy he needed to vanquish the witch, then stepped into the next cavern, tossing the torch to the floor in front of him. He lifted one hand, prepared to shoot a killing bolt at the intruder, but stopped short when he heard a pathetic whimper nearby.

Brogan faced no Odhar, but a small Tuath man. He was unkempt, with filthy clothes and a week's growth of whiskers on his chin. He had only a few blackened teeth in his mouth . . . and Margaret was correct. He drooled.

"Andy Ferris?" Brogan asked, lowering his hand.

Quivering in fear, the man nodded. "Andy Ferris. Andy Ferris."

Sighing, Brogan lifted the torch and beckoned to him. "Come on. You doona belong in here."

"Sleep. Sleepy."

"Aye," Brogan said, disgusted with himself for frightening such a pitiful creature. He hadn't really understood Sarah's talk about the simpleminded one, for there were no such beings on Coruain. "Come. The barn is a better place for you."

Ferris was still frightened and refused to move, pointing to the next cave and speaking gibberish.

"What is it?"

He made jerking movements with his hands and legs, shifting back and forth. "Do you understand me, man? 'Tis time to come out."

"Buh . . . buh . . . buh . . ." He began to weep, pointing into the deeper cave.

"What is it?" Giving Ferris a wide berth, Brogan walked 'round him to enter the next cave. He raised the torch high and looked for signs of anything frightening, but saw naught. "Come and—"

He stopped abruptly. On the floor of the cave was the shape of a cat, its ashes in a perfect silhouette of the creature it had once been. The animal had been killed instantly, scorched by a powerful surge of heat. Only a few tufts of brown fur remained.

Brogan swore under his breath. He wondered whether Ferris had seen Eilinora, or if the mere sight of Jane's dead cat was all that had frightened him. And what had Eilinora found? Had Ferris's arrival forced her away from the cave before she could complete her search?

Brogan had a talent for hunting magic, but when he engaged in the search, his perceptual abilities became dangerously diminished. He might not see or hear someone approaching, making him vulnerable to attack.

He decided to risk it. Without leaving a trace of magic for any other sorcerer to find, he would be able to sense any magic that had recently been used in the vicinity, and if had not been too long ago, he could track down its source.

As he shifted his attention from the physical world, everything took on a shadowy form. Brogan opened his senses and looked for the yellow sparks of magic, the sure sign that Druzai power had been used nearby.

He saw a few fading sparkles over the cat's ashes, and noticed the familiar tangy scent of magic. Yet he saw no signs that Eilinora had used her power to search the walls of the cave. There was no indication that the walls had been disturbed in any way. She hadn't found the stone, at least not down there.

Stepping carefully, he walked out of the cave and searched the vicinity outside for a trail of sparks. He doubted Eilinora would stay near, fairly certain she would not want to be exposed before finding the *brìgha*-stone. She wouldn't want to bring any Druzai attention upon herself before she possessed the additional power she needed to defeat Brogan and Merrick.

Yet Jane's cat must have startled her. As would Ferris's appearance in the cave. She'd acted rashly, defending herself with Druzai power, thereby drawing Brogan's notice. But the sparks were dissipating even now, and Brogan could not see any beyond the garden. 'Twas strange. There should have been a clear trail of her retreat, but Eilinora had somehow managed to mask it.

Puzzled, he let his vision return to normal, then went to the shed for the shovel he'd used before. Though Jane was unlikely to enter the cave and see her cat's remains, Brogan could not leave them for anyone else to find.

He dealt with the ashes, then took a trembling Ferris by the arm and led him to the barn. "Here you are," Brogan said, as though he had any right to settle the man into any part of Ravenfield. "Stay away from the caves."

Ferris wasn't likely to go back there after his fright. He must have walked into the cave just as Eilinora blasted Jane's cat, and Brogan wondered why she hadn't killed the man, too. 'Twas exactly the kind of mischief the Odhar would commit solely to torment the Tuath, just for their own amusement. Mayhap Eilinora had not realized Ferris's reduced mental capacity and hoped he would tell "strange" tales to incite panic among his peers.

He doubted she would want to risk an outright confrontation, at least not until she had possession of the blood stone. For she could not be sure there wasn't a whole army of Druzai warriors just waiting to stop them.

Brogan jammed his fingers through his hair and wished Merrick had not decided that the two of them should recover the stones quietly and alone.

"Colm!" he whispered, heading to the fountain.

"M'lord, something . . . I feel something amiss."

"How do you mean?" Brogan asked.

The dragheen's demeanor showed subtle signs of distress. "I canna say. I saw naught, but I feel . . ." Slowly, he moved his hands to his stomach and hugged his body. "Something is verra wrong."

"Aye," said Brogan. "The Odhar were here. Mayhap Eilinora herself."

Colm groaned. "I saw naught."

"But you felt it."

"Aye. And something more . . . I canna say what, but 'tis disturbing."

"She must not realize you are here, else she'd have immobilized you as she did my father's guardians," said Brogan. The royal dragheen should have been able to warn Kieran of a coming attack, but the Odhar had rendered them useless. "Take care that you do not give yourself away, Colm."

Brogan had a feeling he knew where he would find Eilinora, or at least one of her minions. Doubtful that she would bother the Ravenfield household again this night, he headed up the path toward Margaret's tree. His normal vision was better than most, and the moon was bright, so he moved quickly and quietly through the yard and up the steep path.

Following the directions given earlier, he found Corrington House easily, for there were lights blazing in all the windows on the main floor.

As Brogan approached, he heard Tuath music and convivial voices through the many panes of glass. He climbed onto a lower branch of a nearby tree and glanced through the windows, looking for anyone who fit Margaret's description of the stranger.

Two well-dressed women sat at a pianoforte, but their music did not come out half as well as Sarah's. A third young lady stood alongside two gentlemen nearby, her dark hair a sharp contrast to theirs. Both men were fair-haired and reasonably good-looking, and Brogan could not determine which was the squire.

He eyed the two men and wondered which was the one who had captured Sarah's affections.

They were soft, pampered men, dressed in fine suits of clothes, but neither one wore gray. The first was a bit taller than the second, who wore a heavy, jeweled ring on his hand. Neither appeared full-blooded enough to satisfy a woman's needs . . . a woman like Sarah.

There was no indication to tell him which man was Crowell, and which was the visitor. But Brogan was prepared to dislike the former, whoever he was.

He knew it was not sensible. His world was entirely separate from this one, and as soon as he found the blood stone, he would leave. At that time, he intended to alter the entailment of Ravenfield so that Sarah and the children would be free to stay, but he could not make Squire Crowell fall in love with her.

Nor did he particularly want to do so. There had to be a better man for her.

Deriding himself for losing his concentration, Brogan turned his full attention to the house. There was no outward sign of any Odhar presence, but he wanted to be certain.

Shifting his perceptions once again, he shuttered his awareness of the physical world, impeding his ability to see any physical objects in the area. The sheep in the hills, the trees, the ground beneath his feet, the house and all within . . . everything became filmy, ghostly images as he concentrated on locating even the slightest residue of magic.

Brogan hoped that if the Odhar who'd killed Jane's cat was here, there would be at least a few residual sparks. He hoped they had not seen any need to hide their presence so far from Ravenfield.

Extending his hands in front of him, he opened up his senses, allowing streams of his awareness to flow from his body. He searched for the bright sparks and the peculiar tang in the air that would indicate the recent use of magic. Beams of light streamed from him, invisible to anyone but another Druzai hunter.

He sensed the exterior walls of the building and listened to the voices of those inside, talking and laughing together. Using all his perceptive senses, he perused the gardens for the yellow sparks, but saw none, nor did he did smell any magic in the air. If Crowell's visitor was Odhar, he had not performed any sorcery here.

Or he had somehow concealed his trail.

Pulling out of his hunting form, Brogan shook his head to restore his vision just as a door crashed open. He heard barking dogs as they spilled out of the back of the house, panting as they ran toward him. Fast.

With only a moment before they would be upon him, Brogan had no time to run, no time for prudence. There was no choice but to vanish and hope that none of the men or women in the house was Odhar. He moved quickly, bringing together his sorcerer's will and his fae power. A second later the dogs were upon him.

But Brogan was gone.

Though he had not moved, the dogs could not see or smell him, nor could the servants who'd followed close behind. The animals caught whatever scent Brogan had left behind and sniffed the ground, frantically searching for their prey.

They were unsuccessful. Brogan hoped there were no Odhar hunters nearby to see the sparks of his own magic.

A window flew open and one of the two fair-haired men leaned out. "What is it, Gray?" Brogan looked up at him. Taking note of his weak chin and pasty skin, he decided this one must be Crowell.

"Naught, my lord. The dogs just caught a whiff of something."

"What did they find?"

"Naught, sir. They'll settle down now."

The house had been quiet for well over an hour, but Sarah could not sleep. She lit a lamp, pulled a wrapper over her nightgown, and went down to the library for something to read.

She assumed Mr. Locke had retired for the night, and that opinion was confirmed by his closed door and the lack of light underneath it.

In Sarah's opinion, the library was the most comfortable, coziest room in the house. With heavy, book-laden shelves built into the walls, it also had one large, overstuffed chair, and a lamp beside it to provide plenty of light for reading. On cold days, she and the girls liked to light a fire and sit together in the big chair, reading from one of the tomes that had been in their family for years.

There were books of every kind in Captain Barstow's library, subjects ranging from botany to history, as well as works of poetry and fiction. Sarah was filled with sadness when she realized that all these books would come into Mr. Ridley's possession when he took control of Ravenfield. The girls would have no claim to them.

She took out one of her favorite volumes and considered what she could do to remedy the situation. Mr. Ridley could not possibly know how many books were in the library. Sarah might choose a few—just the ones she thought would be most treasured by Margaret and Jane—and see to it that they went with the girls when they left Ravenfield.

Sarah wiped her palms on her gown, shocked that she would even consider stealing from the new master of Ravenfield. The man had not even arrived, yet she was jumping to conclusions and considering taking his property like a common thief. What if her crime were discovered and she was hauled up before the magistrate and—

"You are up late."

She whirled around to the sound of Mr. Locke's voice, and let out a sharp cry.

"You startled me, sir!" she said, lowering her voice. "I did not hear you!"

"I apologize. I did not mean to frighten you." In spite of his good intentions, he looked savage, like a jungle beast on the prowl, yet somehow out of its element. He was not merely the intense music lover who'd sat on the drawing room sofa a while ago. He was entirely too dangerous for her peace of mind.

"I th-thought you were asleep." She felt half naked, wearing only her thin sleeping gown. Her nipples pebbled against the cloth, and Sarah reached for her shawl to draw it over her breasts, but it was not on her shoulders. It lay on the chair at the other side of the room.

"I was . . . out walking," he said. His hair was thick and dark, and so glossy that the highlights shone nearly blue in the lamplight. His jaw was shaded by the day's growth of beard, and the dark shadow added to the primitive air of danger. He was in shirtsleeves, his collar gone and his sleeves rolled to the elbows.

Sarah knew she should not be alone with him, yet she could not move. She was struck again by his untamed appearance and his masculine strength, even in stylish clothes. Her eyes were drawn to the hollow at the base of his throat, his only vulnerable spot, brushed by the dark hair of his chest.

She'd seen most of him when he'd washed up on their shore, but he seemed even more potent now, with his powerful body confined inside the bounds of his civilized clothes.

Sarah felt almost breathless as his eyes drifted over her barely concealed figure, and she curled her toes underneath the hem of her gown, hoping that he would not find her lacking.

Yet he was a stranger who would soon be leaving. His opinion could not possibly matter.

Unbidden came the image of Sarah curled up with him in one of those big chairs, reading her favorite book of poetry together as a fire crackled nearby and the fall rains pelted the windows. Stunned by the clarity of the image, she felt her face heat. She tried to walk away, to move from his presence, but her feet would not obey her will.

Neither of them spoke.

It was so quiet in the room that Sarah could hear the rustling of the trees and the occasional haunting cry of an owl nearby.

Mr. Locke's blue eyes pierced her with a direct glance. He moved a step closer. "Miss Granger, why have you never wed?"

She crossed her arms over her breasts and looked up at him, disinclined to enumerate the reasons no man had claimed her. It would be too embarrassing to recount the way the boys in town had ridiculed her frayed clothes and leaky shoes. Or how they'd teased her for her freckles, and called her clumsy when they tripped or pushed her. They'd been cruel to her, citing her poverty, her father's overfondness for drink, and his failure at business.

And when she'd gotten older, they pinched her and tried to corner her, putting their hands where they shouldn't, frightening her with their cruel strength.

"'Tis not your concern, Mr. Locke."

"Are you waiting for Squire Crowell, then?" A muscle in his jaw clenched, but there was no mockery in his question.

Sarah clenched her own jaw. "Of course not. He is well above my station." But at least he'd nodded kindly to her whenever their paths had crossed. She'd been free to dream her improbable dreams about him . . . but she could barely picture Squire Crowell's face while Brendan Locke stood so near.

"Then why? Is the thought of marriage to any other man so distasteful to you?" Mr. Locke moved closer, and Sarah could see his pulse beating steadily in his neck. He raised his hand to her cheek, cupping her chin, tracing the slight cleft with his thumb. No man had ever touched her so kindly, yet it was not kindness that Sarah sensed in him.

Her eyes drifted closed and she dropped her hands to her sides. Her breasts tingled uncomfortably, and her womb felt tight and languid, hot and sensitive. His touch had triggered the compelling sensations; she knew it could quell them, too.

Sarah leaned toward him and spoke, her voice almost a whisper. "You would not understand."

"Try me, lass." His voice was a caress, as much as his touch on her face. His hand glided down her neck and over her bare collarbone. Sarah's knees quivered when he slid his fingers just inside the frayed neckline of her gown. He skimmed his other hand around her waist and pulled her toward him.

She swallowed. She did not want to talk about Squire Crowell or her difficult years in Craggleton, not while Mr. Locke was drawing her so close that she could see flecks of black in his dark blue eyes.

Not for the first time, Sarah felt as though he were from a different world, a powerful Celt from days of old, a warrior lord who could take her without resistance. She snapped her eyes open. No man of Mr. Locke's stature would give her the time of day, which only meant he was toying with her, just as he'd done on the beach after she'd pulled him from the water.

Sarah stepped away, appalled at her behavior. She gathered up her shawl and her book, then started for the door.

"There are carriages for hire in Craggleton, Mr. Locke. Once you tire of our ruins, no doubt you will be anxious to be on your way."

Chapter 7

The evening had nearly been a disaster, in every possible way. Brogan had left traces of magic for any Odhar hunter to find, and he'd come very close to kissing Sarah Granger. He could hardly explain what had happened in the library with Sarah.

She was Tuath, a woman with no true magical arts. She had put no spell on him, nor had the dragheen *suggested* this attraction to him, for Brogan—being forewarned—would have felt it.

Yet she'd intrigued him from the moment she'd dragged him out of the sea, and her feats of Tuath magic had beguiled him. The jam she made was superb, but her pies were pure sorcery. Her music, with all its complexity, puzzled and enchanted him. And when he'd come inside to find her standing in the library with her hair curling loose about her shoulders and wearing naught but her shift, he'd wanted her with a ferocity he could not explain.

Though she'd left the room several minutes ago, Brogan was still aroused, pacing, and having to force his attention on the diagram he'd made and the runes he'd translated. He closed his eyes and tried to picture the *crìoch-fàile*, but he could not shut out the image of Sarah, nearly exposed beneath the thin shift. She was as lush and seductive as he'd imagined, from the fire in her eyes to the full, pink lips that he longed to taste.

If not for her abrupt interruption of their encounter, he'd have seduced her. He, a disciplined Druzai warrior, would have laid her on the drawing room sofa and made love to her as though there would be no consequence to his actions.

His desire made no rational sense. 'Twas best for Druzai and Tuath to remain separate. Yet when he was in Sarah's presence, his ability to think logically escaped him. Thoughts of *sòlas* came unbidden, unsettling him even more than his primal urge to possess her.

'Twas absurd. None of his Druzai mistresses had ever awakened such a driving need in him. Surely, this Tuath lass didn't, either. He could shut her out of his mind and turn his attention to more important matters, such as his unfortunate use of power at Crowell's house.

If Eilinora had hunters, they would be able to

see the sparks left behind by his disappearance, which only made Brogan's search more urgent. He'd remained hidden in the tree near the house, waiting to see if anyone of Crowell's party would come out after they'd all retired. But all had remained quiet, which led him to wonder if any of the company at Corrington House was Odhar. Mayhap they felt so confident with Kieran's scepter that they were not concerned with the possibility of a Druzai warrior nearby.

The morning dawned cloudy and cool, threatening rain, but Brogan intended to pursue his search in the walls of the castle itself, whether it rained or not.

As the occupants of the house began to stir, he took the last piece of Sarah's pie and carried it outside before he would have to face the woman herself. He needed to find the stone and get away from Ravenfield before there were any more interludes like the one in the library the night before. Or near encounters with Eilinora, though he almost wished she would appear so that he could deal with her once and for all.

He did not like knowing she or one of her minions had been here during the night, and could return at any time. The thought of it was unnerving.

Brogan headed straight for the castle, but stumbled upon Andy Ferris in the garden. The poor fellow looked even worse in the early morning light. One of his eyes was skewed to the left, and the other focused directly on the pie that Brogan had just raised to his mouth for his first bite.

Brogan could almost taste the sweetened fruit and the vanilla and cinnamon flavors that gave Sarah Granger her alluring scent. The pastry was so fine it almost crumbled in his hands, but he gave it one longing look before lowering the succulent treat and handing it over to Andy. The pathetic little fellow obviously had a much greater need.

Brushing the pie crumbs from his hands, Brogan collected his shovel, then proceeded to the castle, thinking Lord Dubhán might have hidden the stone inside the castle itself, to keep it close to him. Mayhap 'twas in the chamber where the man had slept. Just the thought of finding the stone and leaving this confusing world was enough to spur him on.

He removed his coat and cravat and jammed his shovel into the dirt beside one of the stone staircases. Placing his hands on his hips, he gazed upward.

There had once been three towers. The roofs were long gone, but the steps to the top were relatively intact. The floors were missing, but indentations in the walls and a few stone supports still remained. Brogan saw ancient fireplaces on all three levels, brushed clean and smooth with disuse over time. At the rear of the building was a passage to the foundation that led to the underground caves.

The urge to use sorcery was strong, but Brogan knew better. His search for the *brìgha*-stone would take no minor use of power, nor had his quick vanishment the night before. He hoped his mistake would escape the notice of any Odhar who came to find the stone.

Using magic would likely be a futile effort, anyway, for he'd been warned that the stone would be protected against every spell he knew. Brogan reasoned that he would be able to find it through one of two means. Either the runes would give him clues to a puzzle that would lead to the hiding place, or he would have to find it physically— look at every inch of every wall and floor to discover its hiding place.

The underground runes and *crìoch-fàile* had not made any sense, so he decided to climb up to the tower rooms and see if the etchings on the high walls were more intact . . . and more obvious.

He started up the curving steps to the largest tower chamber. Stones broke away as he climbed, but he soon arrived at the topmost landing without mishap. The inside walls were jagged and uneven, and the markings closest to the stairs had faded so that Brogan could not make out their meaning.

But there were more on the far side.

As he looked across the distance, his attention was diverted by the sight of Jane Barstow running through the courtyard, past the dragheen, heading south. She was calling for her cat.

Brogan swore. 'Twas another thing he'd have to remedy before he left. Though he could not return the wee beast to life, he could certainly see to it that she had another to replace the one Eilinora had killed.

He rubbed one hand across his face, then looked back at the house, half expecting Sarah Granger to come out after the child. He found himself wondering if Sarah would see fit to wear her best gown again.

"*Mo oirg,*" he muttered when he realized the ridiculous direction of his thoughts. What Sarah Granger wore made absolutely no difference to him.

Resolved to finish his task in the shortest possible time, Brogan returned his attention to the castle walls and looked for a handhold to steady himself.

Every wall had deteriorated over time. From his place on the top stair, he saw naught that looked like a niche where the blood stone might have been stowed. Turning his attention to the etchings on the opposite wall, he took stock of the space, then rolled up his sleeves.

Grabbing hold of a jutting rock overhead, he stretched one leg to step on a narrow floor support. He'd nearly reached it when a black, leathery figure jumped down from the top of the wall and perched on the very spot where Brogan had intended to step.

Brogan lost his balance and fell, sliding down the wall. The jagged rocks tore at his hands and elbows, knocked into his knees, and bruised his feet before he came to an abrupt stop on a rocky ledge that had once supported the second floor. He grabbed hold of a jutting ledge and caught himself before plummeting all the way to the ground, cursing the sìthean that had intentionally sabotaged him.

The miserable little sprites were unpredictable and capricious, and to Brogan's knowledge, they bore no allegiance to anyone or anything. They existed only to trip the unwary, causing accidents and mayhem wherever they willed. And Brogan's fall could have killed him had he not had the strength to slow his descent and hold on when he'd reached the ledge.

He steadied himself and looked up. "When I catch you, you are dead, sìthean!"

It twitched its tail and looked down at him in horror. "Ye can see me?"

"Aye," he called, marking the sìthean's surprise, "and I'm comin' for you!"

Brogan had forgotten the dragheen's warnings about the mischievous sprites. Judging by the creature's surprise that Brogan could see him, he concluded they must not be visible to the Tuath. He shuddered at the kind of havoc the invisible little beasts could wreak in this world.

The damned sìth blinked its huge eyes and woggled its pointed ears at Brogan, then flitted to the top of the wall as quickly as it had jumped down. Scrambling over the top, the wee devil slipped out of sight.

'Twas no matter. He would seek it out later, and then exact his revenge.

Carefully, Brogan stood up on the perch that had saved him, and made his way across the rocky wall to the steps. He sat down and wiped blood from the small scrapes and cuts on his hands, avoiding his inclination to use a simple spell to heal them. Here, he would have to live with them.

"Oh my heavens! Are you all right?"

Brogan muttered a curse, whipping his head 'round to see Miss Granger hurrying to the bottom of the tower's stairs. To her, he must have looked like the clumsiest oaf, rather than a man who'd been foozled by a sìthean. From below, his mishap must have looked ridiculous.

He jabbed his fingers across his scalp, annoyed that her opinion mattered. "Aye, I'm fine. Just a few scrapes," he said, but his assertion did not convince her, for he could see her trembling even from his high perch. Her face had no color whatsoever, and she was pressing one hand so hard against the center of her chest, he was surprised she could breathe.

She clearly did not believe him, for she lifted the skirts of her best gown and started up the stairs, her expression alternating between worry and annoyance. "Mr. Locke . . ."

"I assure you I am quite all right." He headed down the steps, intending to send her away from the dangerous staircase. 'Twould be too easy for her to misstep and fall, especially with a sithean on the loose.

But she climbed up, meeting him halfway. "Perhaps you should not go climbing about up here," she said, as though he were a clumsy child.

The color returned to her face. A few small wisps of her hair had become dislodged, and they softened her censorious attitude. In a very businesslike manner, she took hold of his hands, turning them over to assess his injuries.

In spite of her coolness, she slid her fingers over the scrapes, and Brogan noticed her brow was furrowed with care.

His chest tightened at her touch, and he couldn't

seem to draw sufficient air into his lungs. Heat arrowed down his spine when she looked up at him, and his blood left his brain. Arousal hit him sharply, with an intensity that was nigh impossible to control. He pulled his hands away.

"These will need bandaging," she said, pressing her empty hands to her waist, nervously smoothing her skirts.

Such small injuries needed no skilled healer on Coruain, but when Brogan looked into Sarah's eyes, he couldn't recall the spell he'd have used to heal them had he been at home.

Nor could he quite recall his reasons for believing Druzai and Tuath should remain separate.

Unable to help himself, he reversed their positions, taking her hands in his. He pulled her closer and inhaled the alluring scent that was hers alone. He felt the pulse in her wrist beating harder and faster, and when her breasts touched his chest, her breath caught. Without thinking, Brogan lowered his head and brushed his mouth against hers.

Though he knew 'twas impossible, the earth seemed to shudder beneath his feet.

When she let out a small sound, Brogan pulled her closer. His need to touch her was more potent than any magic he'd ever experienced. Turning her on the step, he pressed her against the rock wall of the staircase, wildly aroused by the sensation of her breasts quivering against his chest.

Sighing, she lowered her eyelids, and Brogan slipped his tongue between her lips to deepen the kiss.

The earth beneath him seemed to wobble again when he tilted his head to savor her taste and the texture of her mouth. He could not get close enough to her, even when he pulled her hips tight against his own and she drew her hands up to his shoulders and slipped her fingers into the hair at his nape.

He pulsed against her, his erection hard against her soft, welcoming cleft, and he felt a driving urge to raise her skirts and bury himself inside her. He sensed her arousal as deeply as his own, and knew she would fit him perfectly. Desire was hard and hot as he slid his hands up her sides, drawing his thumbs to the lower curves of her breasts. He was about to lift her into his arms and carry her down to the Druzai caves when a shower of rocks and dust rained onto them.

Sarah suddenly realized where she was, and what she was doing. She had intended to keep her distance from Brendan Locke, but when she'd seen him falling from the tower, she hadn't been able to remain aloof. Now that she knew he was unharmed, she pulled away from him, though doing so felt as if she'd just stepped off the castle steps and into the void below.

In spite of her withdrawal the Scotsman did not release her. He sent a quick glance to the top of the tower wall as though he could see the cause of the rocky shower. Sarah pressed a hand to her mouth, mortified that she'd succumbed to him once again. Only this time . . . She gulped audibly and tried to slip away from him, but he pinned her with his dark blue gaze, his expression as bewildered as hers must have been. "'Twas just a kiss, lass."

Just a kiss? If he could dismiss it so easily, then he was far too worldly for Sarah. For she felt as though her very blood was afire, and was certain that he could hear her heart pounding in her chest.

She made a strangled sound and pulled her hands away, then hurried down the steps alone. Lifting her skirts, she hastened back toward the house, hoping for a few minutes alone to compose herself.

But Andy Ferris stepped onto the path in front of her.

He had crumbs and bits of sweetened apple on his face, and he grinned adoringly at her. Sarah took a deep breath and calmed herself. She knew he was ill-treated in town and would not add to his misery. "Good morning, Andy."

He wiped his sticky hands on his filthy clothes, and Sarah realized either he'd come in and stolen the last of Brendan Locke's pie, or Mr. Locke had given it to Andy himself.

She glanced up to the castle wall again and saw him standing where she'd left him, his gaze still hot and intense.

"Andy Ferris g-g-go."

It would be a kindness to take him to the house and get him a more substantial breakfast, but Sarah could hardly think clearly. She had to manage a few minutes alone to recover from Brendan Locke's kiss.

Andy went on his way, but Maud approached from the garden carrying two baskets laden with vegetables, and met her at the garden gate. "What's happened, Sarah?" she asked, no doubt taking note of her flushed face and obvious discomfiture.

Sarah could hardly mention what had just happened with Mr. Locke. Respectable young ladies did not allow such liberties with young men . . . especially strange young men who had no ties to the vicinity and would soon leave. She was no better than the rude young men in Craggleton had thought her.

Her lips still tingled from Mr. Locke's kiss, and she bit them. Deliberately slowing her breathing and composing herself, she looked at Maud. "'Tis nothing. I'm just winded from my walk."

Together, they went up the path toward the

house, near the fountain. "When will Mr. Ridley arrive?" Maud asked.

"Mr. Merton knew very little, but he said he thought it would be soon."

Maud clucked her tongue and took a seat on the low stone wall. "'Tis impossible to think the heir will turn the children from their house and home. And you, my dear girl—"

"I've made some plans," Sarah said.

"Oh?"

"I'm going to take the girls and let some rooms in town. I'll offer my services as a teacher and—"

"But Sarah . . . in Craggleton?"

Sarah's hands went damp at the thought of it. "It's been six years since I came to Ravenfield. I can do it."

"You despise that town. You know you never go unless you must."

"I can adjust, Maud. And besides, I'm not the same pitiful child that I was. I can take care of myself."

"And the girls? Won't Mr. Ridley be their guardian? Will he consent to your taking them?"

Sarah shrugged as though the heir's wishes did not matter. She'd raised the girls since they were infants, and was not going to turn them over to some London gent who cared not a whit for them. Besides, Mr. Merton had made no mention of Mr. Ridley being the girls' guardian.

Maud shook her head in dismay, but then her gaze drifted off to the winged figure that stood in the center of the defunct fountain. "Sarah," she said, her voice sounding strangely distracted. "What . . . what kind of man is Mr. Ridley? Did Mr. Merton tell you anything about him?"

"Only that he's fabulously wealthy, and lives in London," Sarah replied. "And that he probably has no need of any more property than he already has. Nor will he have any interest in raising his cousin's children."

Maud appeared dazed for a moment, then she looked up at Sarah. "I think you should wait and see for yourself what kind of a man he is before you take rooms in Craggleton. Perhaps he will want to keep Margaret and Jane at Ravenfield until they come of age. They—"

"I didn't get any such impression from Mr. Merton," Sarah said, her heart heavy with worry. "Mr. Ridley is an unmarried man, Maud. He isn't going to want children underfoot."

Maud clucked her tongue and scrutinized Sarah. "But what if he should marry?"

"I still don't think—" Sarah started, then she realized what Maud was suggesting. "We both know what an unlikely event that will be. I've no dowry, no family, no—"

"Never say you have no family. You have us.

And besides, you descended from the original Ravenfield family, did you not?"

She gave a weak nod. "So my mother used to say." Sarah's mother had also told her that the tin Luck resting at the bottom of her wooden chest had been given to the family by fairies. She'd said that at one time, the runes on the box had been visible, and in their ancient language, they'd read, *Be thy casket lost or broak, Then Ravenfield's luck will dissolve in smoke.*

After her father's death, Sarah had been allowed to keep the tin box because it had no obvious value. Though it was cracked and wouldn't open, it was her only keepsake from her mother, and so she'd kept it, all through the years when she'd moved from house to house, working for her keep.

"Well, you'll be attending the dragon lady's soiree. There is sure to be more than one likely suitor there."

"For me? Without a shilling to my name?"

Maud clucked her tongue, as though Sarah's lack of dowry and connections were inconsequential. "Sarah, you intend to make *yourself* a new gown for Mrs. Pruitt's soiree, do you not?"

"I hadn't thought there would be time."

"There will be plenty of time, since I'm going to help you," Maud said firmly. "Why don't you plan to go into Craggleton this afternoon and buy a few bolts of cloth. With Mr. Locke's money, you can afford to outfit yourself as well as the girls."

Sarah tamped down a flood of panic at the thought of going into Craggleton alone, and it crossed her mind that Maud was using the occasion to illustrate Sarah's long-held opinion of the people there.

"But you do so much already—"

"You sew the girls' new dresses. I'll make yours. It will be something magnificent."

"Oh but Maud, I—"

Maud laughed and started toward the house. "You'll have to indulge me in this, my girl. I know what suits you better than you do yourself."

Sarah took one of Maud's baskets and fell into step alongside her as she headed for the house, so preoccupied with what she would do when Mr. Ridley arrived that she nearly forgot Brendan Locke and that kiss.

"I have a few ideas of my own, my girl," said Maud.

Sarah raised an eyebrow.

Maud nodded. "Do as I say, and you'll have a husband before a fortnight's done."

Brogan scrubbed one hand across his face in frustration. His brain had gone soft if his loins were in control. He went back up to the tower, keeping a wary eye out for the sìthean and the gathering clouds. The runes were worn and faded, just as they'd been in the caves. Nothing pointed to the location of the stone.

He stepped carefully across the supports in the walls, tracing the etchings with his fingers and wondering how life must have been for Lord Dubhán, stranded here among the Tuath. Mayhap he'd had a Tuath wife.

Brogan glanced down to the garden where Sarah stood talking with Maud in the presence of the dragheen. They would not know that the guardian could hear their conversations, that he could influence their thoughts.

He hoped that Colm heeded his warning to refrain from influencing any Tuath man to take Sarah to wife.

Brogan decided to make sure she knew how to use her own feminine qualities to attract a mate. Her lack of fortune would mean naught once she caught a man's interest. Besides being beautiful and caring, she possessed many talents. And if she wore better clothes, loosened her hair, and softened her hands, even Squire Crowell would be hard-pressed not to notice her.

And once he kissed her . . .

Brogan swore under his breath when he cut his finger against a sharp edge of stone. There was no point in thinking about what would happen once the witless men of the parish took notice of her.

* * *

Sarah had not yet recovered from Mr. Locke's kiss when she heard the sound of horses galloping toward the house in the rain. She pressed her fingers to her lips and tried to put that brazen interlude aside just as Margaret scampered up the wooden steps to the second floor. "Miss Granger!" Margaret wrapped her arms 'round Sarah's legs and held on, quivering. "'Tis Mr. Ridley! He's coming!"

Sarah's knees started to shake at the news. She'd worked on drawings for the girls' new gowns to divert herself from her encounter with Mr. Locke on the castle stairs. So preoccupied had she been, she'd done nothing to prepare for the heir's arrival.

Dislodging Margaret from her legs, she took the girl's hand. "Well, then . . ." She took a deep breath and bolstered her own courage. "Let's go down and meet him."

"I'm frightened! What if—"

"Let's not borrow trouble, love. Surely Mr. Ridley won't turn us out in the rain."

They reached the main floor and found Maud welcoming two gentlemen into the entryway. Their cloaks and hats were wet, and they were stamping the water from their feet. It was not until they removed their hats that Sarah saw that one of them was John Crowell. The man beside him was a stranger.

"Ah, Miss, er . . . Granger, isn't it?" said the squire, and Sarah blushed at the thrill of being recognized. He gave a short bow and turned to his companion. "This is Mr. Malcolm Rutherford, one of my guests up at Corrington House."

Sarah let out a shaky breath as she curtsied, grateful that it was not Mr. Ridley, but wondering what had brought the men to Ravenfield. "I'm pleased to meet you, Mr. Rutherford. Please come in and warm yourselves."

The men went into the drawing room, and Margaret pulled on Sarah's skirt. Sarah bent down to listen to the child's whisper. "That's the man I saw on the fell yesterday. He looks mean."

"I'll bring tea," said Maud.

As Margaret left the room with Maud, Sarah was left alone with the two gentlemen. She was glad she'd worn her best dress again, and that she'd been inside when the rain had begun. Her hair was neatly bound as it should be, and her shoes presentable.

"We were on our way to Fullingham when my horse went lame," said the squire as he hung his cloak on a hook by the door. Both men were very well-dressed, though Mr. Rutherford's attire was rather too formal for the country.

His waistcoat was a beautiful, multicolored silk, and he wore a jeweled stickpin in his cravat, one that matched the heavily jeweled ring on his right hand. The top of his walking stick was solid gold, molded into the shape of a ferocious tooth-baring beast. Sarah did not care for it.

"We were caught in the downpour and hoped you wouldn't mind giving us shelter until the squall passes."

"Not at all, Squire. Please make yourselves comfortable."

"You might send someone up to Corrington House for a carriage," Rutherford said to her.

Sarah shook her head regretfully. "I'm sorry, but we have no one to send. And there's no one to put the horses into the barn."

"The servant woman—"

"Not to worry, Miss Granger," Squire Crowell interrupted. "The horses are sheltering under the eaves. Once the rain passes, we'll return to the house and collect another."

Mr. Rutherford went to the window and pushed the curtain aside. "Another castle here? It looks quite old."

"Yes," Sarah replied civilly, even though she was irked by the man's effrontery. How dare he suggest that Maud walk through the rain to fetch him a carriage? At least Squire Crowell had had the decency to reject such a suggestion. "Raven-field has stood for many centuries."

"Fascinating," their guest remarked, though his tone indicated he was not fascinated at all. Nor was Sarah interested in the haughty Mr. Rutherford, not when John Crowell stood so near. The squire had visited Ravenfield in the past, but his attentions had always been engaged by Captain Barstow. Sarah had never stood so close to him or felt his gaze as keenly as she did now.

His clothing was expensive and well-made, and suited to a country squire. His shoulders might be only slightly wider than her own, but at least he knew how to tie a cravat. And he was a respectable denizen of Craggleton society who knew how to treat a woman. His boyish good looks were more than appealing. His cheeks were smooth, and if there were whiskers present, they were so light, they were invisible.

His features were altogether the most charming she'd ever seen, bright and open, rather than dark and forbidding. He was a civilized Englishman who would make a fine husband for a worthy young lady.

"Miss Granger is governess here," said the squire to his friend. "She has been in charge here at Ravenfield ever since Captain Barstow was killed in Spain last year."

He smoothed his hair with his fingers and straightened his coat, giving a handsome smile as he did so.

His familiarity thrilled Sarah to her toes, and she knew her regard was not misplaced. There was much to admire in such a steadfast gentleman, one whose solid presence would remain at Corrington House. Not even Mr. Ridley could object to raising his wards in such an environment. Looking at his pleasing form, Sarah couldn't have provided a greater contrast to the uncivilized adventurer who was clambering over the castle ruins if she'd tried.

"I understand there will soon be a new owner here," the squire remarked.

Sarah nodded. "'Tis true. We've just learned that Captain Barstow's cousin—a Mr. Charles Ridley—will inherit the estate."

"Such as it is," drawled Rutherford. Sarah wondered at his attitude. If he truly was the man Margaret had seen on the fell, then he'd already seen Ravenfield in its entirety. Yet he'd given the impression of not realizing there was a castle here.

Perhaps Margaret was mistaken.

She turned to Squire Crowell and ignored his friend's offensive tone. Ravenfield might be a notch below the grand houses he was accustomed to, but it was a fine and venerable estate, nonetheless.

"I should think the new heir will want to clear away some of that rubble," Mr. Rutherford added.

"No doubt," said Squire Crowell. "There's good pastureland wasted here. Your Mr. Ridley will likely enclose it and start growing grain. The way the army is paying these days, only a fool leaves his fields for the sheep."

Sarah felt her face heat with dismay at the realization that the squire agreed with Mr. Rutherford. He could not be so callous as to think Ravenfield would be better served by removing any part of the ancient building. Where was his sense of history, of their noble heritage?

She dearly hoped Mr. Ridley would not clear any part of her beloved castle. If only he shared Mr. Locke's respect for the structure, its continued existence would be secured.

Yet it was not for Sarah to say. She would soon have no reason—or time—to visit Ravenfield again. It gave her a pang of sorrow to think she would never see the castle or grounds again. She and the girls would not have the freedom to walk the beach as they willed, or climb in the fells whenever they liked.

The changes were going to be difficult for all of them.

Unless she married.

Maud returned to the parlor, carrying a large tray with their tea, and Sarah knew this would be one of her few opportunities to make an impression on the squire. Her gown was acceptable, her hair in place; she was clean and articulate. Now she needed to show him that she was a competent hostess.

Sarah poured, careful to perform the ritual with as much grace and elegance as possible to demonstrate her wifely skills. But when she suddenly took note of her red and chafed hands, it was all she could do not to sit on them.

Even as she hoped the squire hadn't seen her work-worn hands, she told herself it did not matter. Everyone knew that times were hard at Ravenfield. It was common knowledge that Captain Barstow's pay had stopped upon his death, and that Mr. Merton had not yet managed to sell his commission. If the lack of army pay had escaped anyone's notice, their selling cockles and pies in town would have told the tale.

In any event, Sarah did not doubt that the squire would take note of her character rather than her rough hands and tattered surroundings. Surely he was astute enough to understand that character was what made a good spouse, not the garments a woman wore or the contents of her purse.

"Come along, Rutherford, and sit," said Squire Crowell.

Mr. Rutherford dropped the curtain and draped himself without decorum in a chair near the table. He cast Sarah a look that she could not fathom, one that made her feel like a lowly villein of old when the lord of the demesne deigned to visit.

Had Squire Crowell come alone, she'd have sat down and joined him. But Mr. Rutherford's indolent superiority made it clear that he would not welcome the company of a lowly governess. She finished pouring and smiled graciously. "I'll just leave you gentlemen to your—"

"No, no, Miss, uh . . . Granger. You must join us," said the squire.

Sarah took a seat in spite of Mr. Rutherford's sour expression. Maud would never forgive her if she did not make the most of this opportunity to impress the squire with her affability.

"How are you enjoying Cumbria, Mr. Rutherford?" she asked, in spite of her uneasiness.

The man sipped his tea before answering. "'Tis tolerable."

He did not openly ridicule her, but Sarah felt degraded by Mr. Rutherford's disdain. There was no kindness in him, and yet he was a friend of John Crowell. Sarah realized it would be the responsibility of the squire's wife to play the gracious hostess to friends such as these. If she ever became his wife, she would hope to influence him to improve his acquaintances.

"Have you long been acquainted with one another, then?" Sarah queried, attempting to initiate a polite interchange.

"No, as a matter of fact, we only met recently," said the squire.

That news reassured Sarah. Surely Squire Crowell had few such disagreeable friends.

"We have a mutual friend in York." Mr. Rutherford turned his dark gaze on the squire. "An old, old friend."

John Crowell's brow dipped slightly, then he turned to Sarah. "I went away to school in York . . . I think I . . ." He gave a slight shake of his head. "Mr. Rutherford also went to Farrowdale. He and I know many of the same families."

"I see," said Sarah, though his demeanor seemed vague and distracted. She realized with chagrin that he was anxious to be on his way.

He lifted his cup to his mouth, and Sarah noted his long, slender fingers. His hands were softer than hers, his nails neatly manicured, and she could not help but think of Brendan Locke's big, square hands and the strength she'd felt when he'd held her.

Heat surged through her at the thought of their kiss, their embrace. No man had ever held her in such an intimate manner, pressing the length of his body against hers, holding her as though she were the most precious treasure in the world.

Surely Squire Crowell's hands were strong, too. Just because he did not amuse himself with climbing all over the rocky ruins of Ravenfield did not mean he was weak. He was a gentleman with responsibilities that kept him from haring off in sailboats to strange shores, only to be knocked overboard and nearly drowned.

He was a far more likely husband.

"It sounds as though the rain is letting up," he said, glancing toward the window. "We should forgo the trip to Fullingham and get back to the ladies."

Rutherford muttered something that Sarah could not quite hear. He left his tea and headed for the door as though he could not wait to take his leave. The squire followed close behind, her chances to impress him fleeting. She tried to think of something to induce him to stay, but he took his cloak from the hook in the entry hall.

"We'd better go while there's a break in the clouds," he said as he tossed his cloak over his shoulders. They left the house, and Sarah closed the door behind them, wondering miserably who the ladies were that awaited them.

She went toward the back of the house seeking Maud's motherly comfort, and found Mr. Locke coming toward her. "You can do much better in a husband, Sarah Granger," he said. "And I'm going to find one for you."

Chapter 8

Brogan could not credit that Sarah would waste her aspirations on the dandified milksop who couldn't bear a bit of rain on his precious top hat and cloak. There was too much fire in her to be satisfied with that scrawny, overfastidious dandy.

The taste of her kiss was still on his lips, and he could still feel the impression of her soft curves pressed against his body. Crowell was the last man she should consider, with his pale skin and soft hands. She would be better off with a man who was poor as dirt, but knew how to make love to his *céile* mate.

"And what would you know of it, Mr. Locke?" She spoke with annoyance, and started to go 'round him. He stopped her and prevented her from leaving.

"I know how your mouth feels against mine."

Her jaw clenched tightly, and he moved in front

of her to stand toe to toe. "I know how your body feels against mine."

She closed her eyes and tightened her lips into a straight line. "And you should forget such things, Mr. Locke. Now, if you'll let me pass—"

"You could attract any man in the district, Sarah."

"*Miss Granger,* if you please, sir."

He reached up and pulled two wire pins from her hair. She protested as the curling mass drifted to her shoulders and down her back, but Brogan did not relent. He slid an arm 'round her waist and pulled her close, preventing her from hindering his actions. "You are soft and feminine, Sarah. And your hair is beautiful."

She trembled in his arms. Or mayhap 'twas his own arms quaking.

"You jest, sir. 'Tis wild and unruly, as you can very well see. No man would ever want—"

He placed two fingers against her lips. "*I* am a man and I like to see it curling softly about your face . . ." He swallowed heavily and stepped away. "If I were to stay and court you."

She turned 'round and headed for the stairs. "But you are *not* staying."

"Nay, I am no'," he said.

"So your opinion is of little consequence," she snapped. "Perhaps Scottish women—"

"Wear their hair down for their men. Aye." He

slid his fingers through her soft curls. "You are lively and spirited, lass. You need a husband to match your own mettle."

"I need a husband who understands how a woman wishes to be treated."

"And you believe Squire Crowell is that man," Brogan demanded. Angry that she could not see that fop for what he was, he pulled Sarah into his arms again. "You canna think that such a *lùigean*, such a mollycoddle of a nim-nam like Crowell could ever satisfy you."

The blacks of her eyes dilated and she started to yank away from him, indignant at his words. Brogan prevented her, crushing his mouth to hers, hungry for another taste of her, yet furious that she could cause such a primitive reaction in him.

She stood perfectly still at first, but her lips quickly softened against his, and when he thrust his tongue through her lips, she did not resist. He invaded her mouth as he drew her close, savoring the tightening of her nipples against his chest and the sweet softness of her body cradling his erection. Gladly would he show her the kind of fire that could be shared between a man and a woman.

She wound her hands 'round his neck and touched her tongue to his, tentatively moving her body against his, seeking the promise of pleasure as intensely as Brogan did. She made a small sound in the back of her throat and Brogan broke the kiss, pressing his lips to her jaw, then her neck, savoring her essence as he moved his mouth toward the edge of her bodice.

He heard a desperate whimper, then her eyes flew open with a suddenness that left him breathless and bewildered. Breathing hard, she wrenched her arms away from his neck and pushed against his chest, turning at the same time, propelling herself out of the room and up the staircase.

Brogan stood still, his heart pounding, his arousal pressing painfully against his trews. He closed his eyes and struggled to recover his own breath, telling himself that he'd only demonstrated the kind of passion Sarah would miss if she won Crowell for her mate. 'Twas not personal. Not at all.

Maud came in through the front door with Margaret, brushing droplets of rain from her skirts and shoulders. "Oh! Mr. Locke! Where are Squire Crowell and his friend?"

"They've gone," Brogan growled.

Fortunately, Maud did not take note of his frustrated tone, for he could give her no explanation of his present mood.

"Oh, well, I'd hoped . . ." She stopped, casting a speculative expression in his direction. "Mr. Locke, are you sure you won't stay for Mrs. Pruitt's gathering?"

He shook his head, still feeling nonplussed and incomplete. "Absolutely sure. I canna stay."

"Well, then. 'Tis no matter," she muttered. "Our Miss Granger plans to walk into Craggleton this afternoon to buy cloth for the new frocks. If you go along with her, she can show you the livery."

Brogan clenched his teeth, determined to try another tack with Sarah. "I would enjoy that walk verra much, Maud."

Sarah had to get away from the house. Away from Brendan Locke.

And he had instilled a seed of doubt about John Crowell. "How dare he?" she whispered fiercely against the fingers she'd pressed to her mouth.

He had just spoiled the most important day of her life, her one chance to impress Squire Crowell with her grace and poise. Brendan Locke had no intention of claiming her for himself, yet he'd taken liberties like a legitimate suitor. Why couldn't he leave her alone?

Standing in her bedchamber, she looked at herself in the glass at the gown she'd worn again today. It fit her well and showed her figure to good advantage. There were still those damnable freckles, but at least her hair had been neatly arranged and pinned at her nape.

The squire had seen her at her best.

Yet Mr. Locke could only criticize her . . .

and befuddle her with his kisses. She had surrendered to his demonstration of passion, but fortunately had come to her senses once again. She had no intention of becoming his "holiday conquest," for when he returned to Scotland, he would go alone. He did not even intend to stay long enough to escort them to Pruitt Hall on Friday.

She pulled her hair back into order and pinned it tightly to her head, silently castigating the Scotsman. He knew nothing about her situation or her needs. She certainly did not need a husband who felt compelled to make her skin quiver with his touch, or her mouth tingle with his kiss. She wanted a staid and stable spouse who would provide a decent home for her and the girls.

She took her bonnet from its box and put it on, stopping short when she caught her reflection in the mirror once again. Somehow, she'd left a few soft curls around her face where Brendan Locke had put them.

"Oh fiddle," she muttered, grabbing her shawl. She felt as though she could crawl out of her skin, and the only remedy she could think of was a long walk. The weather had cleared, so it was the perfect afternoon to walk to Craggleton for new fabrics for the girls' dresses, just as Maud had suggested.

She went downstairs where Maud was gathering up the teacups from the drawing room. "That was an unexpected visit!" she said.

Sarah nodded. "I think it went well, though."

"Oh my dear saints, yes! You looked beautiful in your good dress, and I'm sure Squire Crowell took note of your fine manners."

"Maud, do you . . ." Sarah paused, unsure quite what she wanted to ask.

"What is it, Sarah?"

She frowned. "Do you think that the squire is . . . is . . . Oh, never mind. I'll be back soon."

"All right, dear," said Maud. "And Sarah, don't come back without buying some fine cloth for yourself."

She took an umbrella from the stand by the door and went out toward the front gate. The sky was still cloudy, but the rain seemed to have passed. Considering how little time remained to make gowns for the girls—and herself—she needed to get into town today, no matter what the weather.

She watched the ground as she walked, avoiding the mud and puddles, so she did not see Mr. Locke until he had fallen into step beside her.

She stopped abruptly. "What are you doing?" she demanded, unwilling to walk one step farther with him.

"I am allowing you to take me to the liveryman in Craggleton."

"As your legs are so much longer than mine, I

am sure you can reach the livery much faster than I," she said. "I will just give you the direction and you can—"

"You mistake me, Sarah."

"You know that I have not given you leave to use my Christian name, sir. Do you say it just to annoy me?" It was just a word. The sound of it on his lips should not make her heart pound or her breath catch. She should not allow her eyes to drift to that mouth, to those lips. His kisses were not only forbidden, they were unwanted.

"Crowell would never consider using your familiar name, would he . . . *Sarah*?" He crowded too close, his leg brushing her skirts as they walked.

Sarah moved closer to the edge of the path, wishing that the contact of his arm against her shoulder did not generate such an earth-shattering sensation in her womb. She gathered her shawl tightly around her shoulders to avoid touching him. He was not the man for her, and he had no right to criticize the one she'd revered and respected since her girlhood.

"Of course he would not. Squire Crowell is a well-bred Englishman who would not dream of taking liberties with a respectable woman he hardly knew."

"Because he has no spine."

"You are the most impertinent—"

"Aren't there any other well-heeled gentlemen in Craggleton? Men with . . ."

"With what, Mr. Locke?" she demanded, suspecting he'd nearly said something entirely inappropriate.

"With the *brass* to treat his woman like—"

"A trollop?"

"No." He stepped in front of her. "Like he doesna wish to take another breath without touching her, without holding her in his arms while the ground shifts beneath his feet."

Sarah's heart lurched and she found herself dangerously close to touching him, to falling with her entire body into his improbable romantic fantasy.

She snapped back to the reality of her life. Of his being a stranger who intended to leave in another day or so, of her responsibility to Margaret and Jane.

"The squire's suit was very finely made, wasn't it?" she remarked with a nonchalance she did not feel.

Brendan Locke stepped aside and let her continue.

"And his boots—so well-polished that even the rain and mud couldn't spoil them."

Mr. Locke looked down at his own scuffed top boots. "Signifying what, exactly?"

She smiled with feigned sweetness. "Oh, I did not mean to imply that your boots were anything but . . . Well, you've been mucking about at the castle, haven't you?"

Surprisingly, Mr. Locke continued in silence until they reached Craggleton, giving her some peace as well as the opportunity to reflect on her few precious moments with Squire Crowell.

Brogan wanted to shake her.

Then he wanted to kiss her, to lay her down in a secluded bower and show her what a woman was meant to do with the man she took for her *céile* mate, her husband.

He shouldn't have touched her, and he certainly should never have kissed her, not when the memory of their intimate embrace caused such an instant, painful arousal.

She was more responsive than any mistress he'd ever known. Innocent and inexperienced, she possessed a wealth of natural sensuality, and he feared her kiss, her touch, her scent, would haunt him for the rest of his life. He'd never had the urge to pledge *céile*, and now he knew he never would. Not unless he found a woman of his own kind who roused him as Sarah Granger did.

Craggleton was a lively town with plenty of foot traffic as well as riders on the muddy streets. Sarah kept her attention focused on the space before her, never turning her head to look into the shops or greet passersby.

Nor did they greet her.

She stopped and gave a nod in the direction ahead. "Follow this street until you reach Mr. Merton's office." She indicated the solicitor's sign. "Then turn right. You'll see the livery after a few minutes' walk."

Brogan remembered hearing Merton's name mentioned at Ravenfield and decided to have a talk with the man. He needed to learn about Tuath entitlements and inheritance.

"I trust you will be able to find your way back to Raven—"

Brogan crossed his arms over his chest at her easy dismissal of him, and looked down at her. Her impudent gaze faded slightly.

She gave a small cough and looked away. "T-to Ravenfield?"

"I'll see you right here, shortly," he said.

"'Tis not necessary for you to—"

"Do you ride?" he asked.

"I never had the . . . I never learned, and I have no need of the skill, anyway," she replied, turning away. She started down a narrow lane and went into a small shop. Only then did Brogan make his way to the livery.

He chose a suitable horse and gave the liveryman instructions on saddling the beast and bringing it to the solicitor's office, where he went next.

Merton's clerk ushered him into the small, cluttered office at the back of the building and introduced him to the man behind the desk. The solicitor was a short, round man with a bald pate and a fringe of silver hair around the baldness. He had prodigious whiskers on his cheeks that extended into a bushy mustache. He arose slightly, extended his hand, and asked Brogan what he could do for him.

Brogan took a seat, not entirely sure what a solicitor did, though he assumed his function encompassed more than just handling inheritance matters. Since he dealt with property, Brogan hoped the solicitor could help him.

"I wish to let a house," Brogan said. "I'm a visitor here, and I understand there is a widow who owns a small cottage near Ravenfield."

"Mrs. Hartwell's house. Yes."

Merton told him that the widow would lease the place for no less than a one-month term. Brogan made the agreement and signed a lease, satisfied that in doing so, he was protecting Sarah's good name. When she went to the Pruitt affair, there would be no questions about a strange man staying at Ravenfield.

"The cottage is somewhat closer to town than Ravenfield," said Merton.

"Where, exactly?"

"Take the east path after you've gone about two miles. It's just around the bend."

Brogan nodded. Earlier, he'd noticed the road splitting off about a mile from Ravenfield.

"What is your business here, may I ask?" said Merton.

Brogan hesitated, surprised by the question. He decided to keep it simple and give the same lie he'd told Mrs. Pruitt. "No business, really. I once knew Captain Barstow. Since I was in the vicinity, the ladies at Ravenfield graciously allowed me to explore the old castle grounds."

"Such ruins interest you?"

Brogan gave a nod. "Aye."

"You might wish to consider visiting the old castle at Fullingham. It's in much better condition," said the solicitor. "Besides, Ravenfield has a new owner who should arrive at the estate within the next day or two." He looked out the window at the sky. "Weather permitting."

Brogan furrowed his brow. "What will become of the women at Ravenfield?"

"I'm sure I don't know," Merton replied. "It's only Sarah Granger, after all. She—"

"Is a woman alone, is she no'?"

"Her father was a drunkard, sir," the solicitor said, as though that explained it all. "She is accustomed to making her own way."

Brogan restrained his anger and stood, his business concluded. No woman would be left in such straits on Coruain. Every opinion he'd had about these Tuath was correct. "And the children?"

"A guardian was named . . ." Merton furrowed his brow. "Once the captain's commission is sold, there will be some money for them. With careful supervision, it might keep them for several years."

Disgusted by a society that took such slipshod care of its women and children, Brogan left the office. His horse awaited him, so he gathered its reins and walked to the draper's shop where Sarah had gone.

Preoccupied by the strange notion that Sarah and the children would fare much better on Coruain in spite of their Tuath blood, Brogan dismounted and went into the shop where bolt after bolt of fabric lined the shelves on every wall.

Two women stood waiting on Sarah, their expressions unfriendly and impatient. There was one long, glass case where Sarah stood, pointing out ribbons and buttons to the older of the two women, who wore a pincushion tied 'round her wrist and had a long measuring strip draped 'round her collar.

There were two neatly folded mounds of cloth, one of shiny, pale yellow and the other a delicate pink.

"Are you sure you have the coin to pay for all this, Sarah?"

Brogan stopped short at the comely young woman's sharp, discourteous tone.

"Of course I do," Sarah replied, and Brogan saw her straighten her back and raise her chin at the woman's words. "But I'm not finished."

"The cloth is cut," the older woman said brusquely. "If I have to put it back—"

Brogan stepped up beside Sarah, troubled by the other woman's surly attitude. "Are these the fabrics for the children?" he asked.

The shop woman looked up at him and raised one brow. She was nice looking, if he counted only facial features. But Brogan had felt her ugly animosity. He could not imagine anything Sarah might have done to deserve such a raw opinion in Craggleton. It raised his ire to think she was being judged because of her sire's failings.

"Yes, the pink is for Margaret," she said quietly.

"And the bonny yellow for Jane?"

Sarah nodded.

She had naught for herself. That made Brogan angriest of all. He looked 'round at all the bolts of cloth until his eyes lighted on a shiny, coppery cloth on one of the top shelves. With no doubt it had to be among the most expensive fabrics in the entire shop, but it was the one that best suited Sarah's coloring. He went to the shelf and reached up for it, then found a bolt of rich, brown silk on a lower shelf.

"Add these."

"But sir, white is most fashionable—"

"White would not suit Miss Granger's coloring."

"Oh, but sir—"

"She'll have these, one for the gown, and one for trimming. Miss Granger, choose buttons and any other bric-a-brac you need."

Sarah felt perilously close to tears when Brendan Locke pulled down the very fabric she'd eyed earlier, deciding it would be too expensive. She could hardly meet Frederica Hattinger's cold stare when he put the beautiful, burnished cloth on the counter and handed her the money to pay for it.

The seamstress, Nettie Burrows, had once turned Sarah away from this very shop when she'd come looking for scraps of fabric to make a cloak for herself. It had been a particularly bitter winter, and Sarah's old cloak had been threadbare.

Miss Hattinger was a year older than Sarah and not yet married. But Sarah could not believe she lacked for suitors. In the years Sarah had lived in town, boys had flocked to Frederica's door, carrying her parcels and currying her favor at every opportunity. Her father owned the draper's shop as well as several other businesses in town, and it could only be a matter of time before she made an advantageous marriage. A girl as pretty as Frederica, and with such good connections, could not

have escaped Squire Crowell's notice. But Sarah
hoped the man would consider her unattractive character before falling for her more obvious
charms.

"My word, Sarah," Frederica said in exaggerated astonishment. "I had no idea you had a *protector*—"

"I'm an old friend of Captain Barstow—Brendan Locke," he interjected. He gave a polite bow,
though Sarah noted a tightening of his jaw and
a stiffness of bearing. "I'm staying at Mrs. Hartwell's cottage while I'm visiting his family."

Sarah's heart filled with gratitude at his words,
his explanation thwarting the malicious gleam
in Frederica's eye. She wondered how he'd managed to let Mrs. Hartwell's house, but it hardly
mattered now. Frederica was a practiced gossip. Word of Mr. Locke's presence, his obvious
wealth, and his friendly acquaintance with Captain Barstow's family—including Sarah—would
reach every corner of town by nightfall.

For a moment, Sarah did not feel quite so alone
against the world. She did not like to admit it, but
with Mr. Locke beside her, bolstering her, she'd
had the confidence to face Frederica and the
seamstress without cringing inside. Without feeling worthless, the way she had every day she'd
lived in Craggleton, surviving only because of the
grudging charity of its occupants.

"I'll wait for you outside, Miss Granger," Mr. Locke said. "Take your time."

When he had gone, Frederica leaned forward and gave Sarah a conspiratorial look. "Such a fine-looking specimen he is, Sarah. A Scotsman, by the sound of him. Will he be staying long?"

"Mr. Locke's plans are his own, I'm sure," she said coldly. She did not need to mention that his plans were none of Frederica's concern.

"He must be very rich," the young lady remarked, eyeing the money in Sarah's hand.

"He seems to have what he needs," Sarah said, her tone terse, anxious for the seamstress to hurry and finish cutting her fabric, measuring the ribbons, counting buttons.

"These are our finest fabrics . . . Who would ever have thought pitiful Sarah Granger . . ." Frederica had the good grace to give Sarah a sheepish glance at such an outrageous remark. She shrugged with puzzlement. "Why ever would you need such fine materials up at Ravenfield?"

Sarah clenched her teeth and wished that Brendan Locke were still standing nearby. Perhaps he'd have had the perfect retort, but Sarah did not, and she had no intention of mentioning that she'd been invited to Pruitt Hall. She turned away as though interested in some other goods, letting Frederica's question and insulting manner go unanswered, the way she'd done all her life.

"If you'll just come into the back," said Miss Burrows. "I'll take your measurements—"

"That won't be necessary," Sarah responded, unable to forget the woman's past cruelty. She would not give her business to Nettie Burrows now. "I'll do the sewing myself."

"Oh," Frederica interjected, "but you obviously have more than enou—"

"'Tis surely a sin to waste money on a task I can very well do myself," Sarah said. "I am a fair seamstress and I know what will best suit the children."

Miss Burrows pursed her lips and stepped away as Frederica wrapped Sarah's purchases in paper and tied it with a string.

"Well, here you are—"

Sarah took the parcel from Frederica's hands and hurried away, eager to leave the shop.

She found Mr. Locke around the corner, standing beside a massive gray horse. When he beckoned to her, she realized she was gaping at him as though he'd made the animal appear out of thin air.

Even as properly dressed as he was, he looked like a barbarian warrior with his mighty destrier. Sarah could almost see him dressed in leather and armor, a sword at his waist and a lance in his hand, with small braids at his temples and paint on his face.

"Have you found all you need?" he asked.

She swallowed and nodded once again, dispelling the odd sensation of seeing something that was not really there.

"Good. Hand me your package and let me help you up."

"Oh no, sir," she said, backing away from the huge horse. "I've never ridden in my life."

"'Tis time you started, then."

Sarah glanced left and right. There was no one about, no one to witness her cowardice when she moved away. "On the contrary, Mr. Locke, I have no need—"

But Mr. Locke did not let her escape. He took her arm and relieved her of her umbrella and her bundle of fabric. These he stowed in a pack on the side of the saddle. "'Tis no great accomplishment to ride. The smallest of children can do it."

"But I really—"

He placed his hands on her waist, and she could no longer think of anything but the wall of strength that stood so close before her. His outdoor scent surrounded her, and when she looked up, she saw the lips that had kissed her senseless.

She couldn't breathe.

"When I lift you, just throw your leg to the opposite side—"

Sarah exhaled abruptly and pushed him away. "*Astride?* Absolutely not!"

It would be scandalous. Any hope she had of gaining students in Craggleton would end the minute one of the townspeople saw her. Even now, Miss Burrows might very well be peeking out of some hidden window to watch them.

"Sarah, it's going to start raining soon. We're going to ride back to Ravenfield."

"Together? Oh no. That would be even worse."

Mr. Locke shook his head as though she were the most unreasonable creature on earth.

"Men and women might ride together . . . astride . . . in Scotland," she said, "but it is not done here."

She took one step, but Mr. Locke picked her up and lifted her onto the saddle. With ease.

Sarah grabbed hold of the pommel to keep from falling.

"There's naught to it, lass," he said, and Sarah thought there might be a mirthful sparkle in the man's eye.

Contrary to Mr. Locke's opinion, there was much to it. The horse was so tall, she was likely to break an ankle were she to try jumping down. "Please do not mount this horse with me," she said as he took hold of the reins. "It will be ruinous to my reputation."

He did not reply, but turned the horse into the street and led it to the end of town. Sarah held onto the pommel and braced one foot in a stirrup as she struggled to sit up straight and achieve some dignity, and accustomed herself to the swaying of the horse.

To her dismay, she soon found her anger mollified as she watched Mr. Locke's easy manner and purposeful stride. He tipped his head and made polite greetings to the people he passed, who responded in kind.

His legs were long, and they covered the pretty terrain much more easily than Sarah could do. However, with one quick glance at the sky, she could see that they were not going to make it back before the rain started again.

They were well out of town when he stopped the horse and came around to the side. Sarah thought something must be wrong, but he took her by surprise, suddenly vaulting onto the horse's back behind her. Before she could object, he clucked his tongue and they set off at a trot.

Sarah grabbed hold of his forearms as they bracketed her on either side of her waist. "Mr. Locke!"

"There is no one out here to see you. So try to enjoy the ride, Sarah."

It took several moments to accustom herself to their speed, but once her initial fright subsided, Sarah managed to ease her grip on his arms.

He leaned close so that his mouth grazed her

cheek, and she could feel his breath. "I think you've left a few scars on me, lass."

The warmth of his voice sent a shiver of awareness through Sarah's body, and she unconsciously tipped her head to allow him closer access. She hardly felt him press her shoulders back so that she leaned against him, her body languid, yet expectant.

Surely she did not long for another kiss. She knew next to nothing about Mr. Locke besides the fact that he intended to leave soon. Imminent travel was his only reason for buying this horse. With his boat lost at sea, he could easily return to Scotland at his own pace on horseback.

Sarah could not imagine Mr. Locke resting content inside a stuffy, stomach-churning carriage. He was the kind of man who would ride like the wind, his cloak billowing out behind him, his horse burning up the ground as he passed. He would go hatless, as seemed to be his wont, and every woman in his path would take notice of the powerful rider who passed so quickly over the land.

"You turned a number of heads at your passing through town," he said, voicing the reverse of her own private thoughts.

"If so, it was only to see my escort," she replied, remembering Frederica Hattinger's reaction to him. If he stayed long enough to attend the Pruitt soiree, he could have his choice of any gentle-woman in the parish.

"They were male heads, Sarah." He pulled on the ribbons that held her bonnet in place, untying them, removing the hat from her head. "You have bonny auburn hair. You must show it."

She knew very well her hair was not only un-ruly, but a nondescript color that was neither blond, nor black, nor red. But when she felt Mr. Locke's lips so close, it hardly seemed to matter. He tucked her head under his chin and pulled her against his hard chest, and Sarah wondered if he could be persuaded to stay in Cumbria.

Chapter 9

Holding Sarah felt much too good.

But Brogan was not about to deny himself the small pleasure of feeling her body against his own. His horse was a spirited mare, but it was easily controlled, so he gave the horse its head and relaxed his hold on the reins. With his hands relatively free, he brought them to Sarah's waist and held her close.

He inhaled deeply of her scent, an echo of the wonders that came out of her kitchen. She always smelled good enough to eat, her fragrance giving him a surprising sense of comfort and contentment. In spite of his reasons for leaving Coruain and his urgency to return with the stone, he was drawn to this prickly yet tenderhearted woman. He wanted to show her how to attract a man who would appreciate her. There had to be a man who would pledge *céile* to her.

He had thought more of *céile* since coming to

Ravenfield than he had in years. Neither he nor his brother had met his life mate, though Merrick's had been foretold at his birth. His brother would pledge to a powerful Druzai sorceress before his thirtieth year.

But no marriage had been predicted for Brogan.

It did not surprise him. He'd spent his life in the company of men, commanding Coruain's warriors, continuing the Druzai tradition of protecting their realm from dangerous forces that threatened them. Brogan had enjoyed the occasional liaison with a comely Druzai sorceress, but he'd never considered the possibility of establishing a lasting bond with any of them.

'Twas not that he hadn't liked or respected his mistresses. But there had been naught beyond the obvious physical gratification they'd shared. There had been no challenge, no real sòlas.

It had been years since anyone but his own father had gainsaid him. Sarah Granger could not be more different from the obsequious Druzai women who had shared his bed. She would be the last woman to pay homage to a Druzai prince.

"Why do you laugh?" Sarah asked, and he realized he'd let a chuckle escape.

"You, Sarah," he replied.

"You find me comical?"

"No . . . I find myself comical. Look, it's starting to rain."

He kicked his heels and held her securely before him as the horse began to gallop.

"Mr. Locke, you're going the wrong way!"

"We should come upon Mrs. Hartwell's cottage in a moment."

"Well yes, but—"

"We can wait out the storm there."

She said something he could not hear over the sound of the rain and the galloping of the horse, but they were soon 'round the curve in the bridle path and at the house. He pulled up to the barn at the back of the house and dismounted, quickly shoving open the door and leading the horse inside.

"You really *have* let the house?"

"Of course. Your reputation is precious to you, Sarah," he said, reaching up for her. "I doona wish to cause you any trouble."

He lifted her down, taking his time. His pulse kicked up a notch with the caress of her body as he brought her to the ground.

"We should not be here alone," she said.

"Who will know?" He felt like a raw lad, sneaking away with a forbidden lover. He tossed her bonnet onto the pommel of the saddle. "You're trembling."

She went to the barn's door and looked out at the rain. Though her back was to him, Brogan could almost see her hands clasped tightly in front of her.

He shouldn't have brought her here, but there had been no better option for getting them out of the rain since he could not allow himself to stop the weather. Besides, this was the perfect opportunity to show her how attractive she could be. She had the beauty, now all she needed was the confidence to pursue the man of her choosing.

Brogan approached her, and standing close behind, he placed his hands upon her shoulders. He turned her to face him. "Are you afraid of me, lass?"

She shook her head, then spoke quietly. "But surely you understand that if I am to make a home in Craggleton and earn a living there, I must be beyond reproach."

He lowered his head. "One kiss do no' a harlot make." Her mouth trembled and he hungered for it.

This time, when he touched his lips to Sarah's, she did not resist. It seemed he'd been holding his breath since their last kiss, waiting for this moment. Yet he'd been breathing all day, hadn't he?

Without thinking, he pulled her hair loose from its pins while he deepened the kiss. He felt her tremulous sigh, and the slipping of her arms 'round him. With no further urging, he speared her mouth with his tongue and felt her hesitant response.

Her innocent reaction inflamed him.

He sucked her tongue into his mouth and lowered his hands to her hips. Pulling her flush against him, he hoped to ease his throbbing erection, but his need only increased.

He broke the kiss and took her by the hand, leading her to the house. They ran together through the rain and stopped only long enough for Brogan to find the key and unlock the door. They fell into a darkened room, and he kicked the door closed, pressing Sarah against the closest wall, savoring the soft pull of her body. She cupped his face in her hands, drawing him down to meet her kiss, and Brogan shuddered with desire.

There had to be a bed somewhere.

Yet a bed was the last thing he should seek with Sarah. His unquenchable lust was a madness, brought on by some kind of Tuath magic, and he needed to rise above it. He wanted to show her how desirable she was. Not seduce her.

Ignoring his own better judgment, he encircled her waist with his arms and took her mouth once again, dipping his tongue inside, tasting her sweet fire. He felt her slip her fingers into his hair, sliding up from his nape, pulling him closer.

The rain came down sideways, viciously pelting the windows and shaking the glass in their panes. Brogan hardly noticed. Quaking with pleasure at her touch, he wanted more. He wanted her naked, lying beneath him.

After he removed her cloak, the buttons of her bodice were easily released. He slid the gown from her shoulders and shoved his own coat down his arms, letting it fall to the floor. Her underclothes posed a greater challenge, but he managed to free her breasts. Their pale, pink tips were visible in the dim light, and Brogan touched them gently, groaning low in his throat when they hardened in his hands.

She arched into him, letting her head fall back, intensifying the contact between her soft, womanly cleft and his hard arousal. Brogan moved against her and felt her tremble with the same kind of pleasure he felt. He pressed his lips to the tender skin just below her ear, then kissed her shoulder, moving his mouth lower and lower, until he reached her nipple.

He swirled his tongue 'round it, then sucked it into his mouth.

"Brendan," she sighed, and Brogan wished 'twas his own name she'd called.

He licked and sucked one nipple, then turned his attention to the other, while Sarah shivered in his arms. Her pleasure was all that mattered, and Brogan dropped to one knee before her. She grabbed a fistful of his hair as he slid her skirts up her legs. She pulled tightly and gave a small cry of distress.

"Trust me, Sarah."

She whimpered once again, but made no further protest, sighing deeply when he parted her legs with his hand, then touched her womanly center. He laved her nipples with his tongue, each in turn while he stroked her, feeling close to his own climax when he slid one finger inside her.

"Oh!" she whispered.

"You feel it, *moileen*, the pleasure I can give you."

"Brendan, you must not."

"Aye, I must. Let go, sweet. Feel the *sòlas* between a man and a woman."

The room was nearly dark, but with her skirts raised to her waist, he could see her, fully exposed to his gaze. In hopes of quieting the fire that raged within him, he pressed one hand against his erection, then bent to her and blew a kiss against the nub that gave her pleasure, then licked it as he slid his finger inside her moist channel.

Brogan's heart pounded in his ears. He felt Sarah's breath coming in spurts, and knew that they moved close to the edge together. Her hands were on his head, holding him in place, and when she gave out a low cry and pressed her legs tightly together, he knew she'd reached her climax.

She shuddered in his arms while he tamped down his own driving need for culmination. His thoughts might be muddled, but he had a clear recollection that a Tuath maiden's virginity was a valued commodity. He would not take it from her, not when it would be treasured by the man who took her to wife.

Now that she'd experienced a fraction of the pleasures to be shared with a man, she would surely know how to flaunt her charms. She knew he found her desirable, and she could not lack the confidence of a beautiful, sensual woman . . . a woman no Tuath man could resist.

"Your blushes are charming, lass," said Brendan . . . *Mr. Locke*, Sarah reminded herself, yet she could hardly think of him in such a formal manner, not after the intimate act he'd just performed.

She blushed even more deeply, but she had no desire to push him away after her skirts dropped to their proper place and he rose to his full height. He nuzzled her neck and called her beautiful.

Sarah could almost believe it. Brendan gathered her hair into his hands and pressed his face to it, whispering words that were foreign to her ear, but felt soft and endearing. He slid his hands over her shoulders, then down to her breasts to cup them once before pulling her chemise over her shoulders.

Was it possible that he did not intend to leave? He was so adamant that she stop thinking of Squire Crowell as a possible husband, saying that he would find her a better man. Did he mean himself?

"I have little experience . . ." But she was no fool. He had given her pleasure without taking his own. Even now, he pressed light kisses to the skin that was still exposed, sending wonderful tingles from her nipples to her most private parts.

Parts that he had kissed, licked, and nuzzled.

She swallowed heavily, tentatively moving her hand to the placket of his breeches. The powerful ridge of his erection strained against the fabric, and Sarah was encouraged by his obvious arousal. "You must feel . . ."

He must feel as she had before those intense sensations had peaked, hurling her into a world of pure physical pleasure, where she had no awareness of anything but his perfect touch.

As she drew her fingers along the length of his arousal, Brendan exhaled sharply. "I would give you the same pleasure," she whispered.

"Sarah." His voice was a harsh rasp that sent shudders of awareness to that sensitized area between her legs. He leaned his forehead against hers, allowing her to unfasten the straining buttons of his breeches. She felt him then, his naked manhood, surging powerfully against her hand. It was long and broad, and hard as a rod of iron, yet smooth and soft as the satin she'd just bought.

Sarah slid her fingers over the tip, and felt a bead of moisture there.

She rubbed it over his length and felt his sharp intake of breath. She withdrew abruptly, afraid she'd done something wrong. But he caught her hand and put it back, groaning at her touch.

Sarah felt emboldened. "Tell me what will please you. Show me."

His large hand engulfed hers and he demonstrated, shuddering as she stroked him, moving his hips reflexively. "*Mo oirg*," he muttered on a hoarse breath, and though Sarah did not understand his words, she comprehended the tumultuous sensations running through him. She knew of only one other thing that might intensify what he was feeling.

She dropped to her knees and pressed her face against him.

"Sarah—"

He made a strangled sound when she took him into her mouth and used her tongue the way he'd done to her. She closed her eyes and savored the taste and texture of him, and the knowledge that she was pushing him toward the same burst of pleasure he'd given her.

It shocked her to realize she was heading toward that same peak again, too, even without his touch. Merely the awareness of his impending culmination was enough to push her over that precipice.

He braced his hands against the wall above her as she found a rhythm, moving down his heavy length and up again, sucking and swirling her tongue 'round him. Her climax came as he pulled away from her and took himself in hand, holding his shaft with his kerchief.

"*Ainchis ua oirg*," he whispered.

Shuddering with her own pleasure, Sarah looked up at him and met his incredulous eyes, and knew she'd pleased him. He drew her up to her feet and kissed her soundly. She felt sated and confused, content and puzzled. But she was not embarrassed as she should be. They stood together on more intimate terms than Sarah had known with any other, but she did not feel mortified. Or sinful.

All she felt was the need to be enfolded in his arms. He held her against him and stroked her hair and her back. Sarah had never felt quite so cherished.

"You make a man forget himself, Sarah Granger," he said.

"'Tis kind of you to say so, even though it isn't true."

"Aye, it is. Can you no' understand the power of your allure?"

She would have laughed at such a notion, but his caring touch and sweet words brought tears to her eyes. She quickly blinked them away.

"The rain has stopped," he said.

Before righting his own clothes, he helped Sarah with her bodice, then fastened her buttons. He picked up his jacket and slipped it on while Sarah searched for the pins for her hair.

"Turn 'round," he said. When she did, he gathered her hair into a loose knot and kissed her neck before trying to pin down her tresses. "Have I told you your hair is verra fine, lass?"

His words against her neck gave her a shiver of delight, and she turned in his arms. "Brendan, what is *sòlas*?"

He looked at her strangely. "You must have misheard me, Sarah. I likely said *solace*."

Even during their intense encounter in the shadowy room of the cottage, Brogan would not have spoken of *sòlas*. He couldn't have. 'Twas a bond shared only between Druzai mates. This liaison with Sarah, as intense as it had been, could not be permanent. Fortunately, some instinct had kept him from carrying her to a bed and taking full possession of her.

Yet he could not resist pulling her close as they rode back to Ravenfield, and nuzzling her ear. He must make her understand how desirable she was. "I'm glad you're not above a bit of scandal in private, lass. A man enjoys knowing he can make a woman mindless with pleasure."

"I should never . . ." She did not finish the thought when he pulled the lobe of her ear gently through his teeth. He could not continue this way. In Sarah's arms, he'd completely forgotten his reason for coming here. It was imperative that he regain his focus.

Sarah suddenly stiffened against him.

"What is it?"

She did not reply at first. "I don't know . . . just an odd sensation. Like a premonition."

"A premonition," Brogan repeated, wondering if Sarah's strange sensation actually was a premonition. He'd never heard that the Tuath were capable of auguring, but in the past few days, he'd found many gaps in his knowledge of these people.

She nodded against his chest. "Foolish, I suppose."

Not half as foolish as his persistent reaction to her. His body still pulsed with desire, even after their wildly sensual encounter. He could barely keep from turning 'round and going back to find a bed in that small house, and fully mating with her.

It was some sort of madness.

His intention had been to show her that she was attractive and desirable. Surely that was the only reason he'd allowed that desperate seduction in the cottage to occur. He had not intended to let it go so far, and he berated himself for losing control, for playing the selfish *lùigean* who sacrificed his better judgment for the attentions of a comely lass.

It would not happen again. Nor would he allow her suggestion of *sòlas* to haunt his thoughts.

He would return to Ravenfield and his search for the stone, and Sarah could go to the Pruitt event with the confidence of a beautiful woman, one who knew she'd been wanted. A woman who understood her power to drive a man mad.

Brogan tightened his hands on the reins, ready to put some distance between them. 'Twas well past time to locate the blood stone and take his leave of Ravenfield before he became any further enmeshed in these Tuath affairs. He'd never anticipated caring what happened to Ravenfield's residents. . .

Or wanting Sarah with every drop of his blood.

They soon arrived at Ravenfield. Brogan helped Sarah dismount and watched her head for the house, straightening her bonnet and brushing the moisture from her cloak. She seemed slightly unsteady on her feet, as Brogan did himself.

He jabbed his fingers through his hair, then turned to the horse's flank. Lowering his head, he laid both his hands on the mare's sides. He took a deep breath before collecting Sarah's umbrella and her purchased cloth, and taking them inside.

* * *

Sarah began work on the new dresses immediately. She had to occupy her mind with something other than the interlude in the cottage and Brendan Locke's cool attitude toward her since returning to the house.

She should never have let matters go so far. It was Squire Crowell whose attentions she'd yearned for, not those of a strange Scotsman who had clearly not changed his plan to leave in another day or two. He had not even promised to stay for Mrs. Pruitt's soiree.

What could she have been thinking?

"Your face is red as a beet, Sarah," said Maud, who worked nearby, cutting out the sleeves for Jane's frock. "You must be too close to the fire."

She felt her cheeks grow even ruddier at the thought of Maud or anyone else learning of her tryst with their handsome visitor.

He'd come in only to drop off her parcel and collect his own satchel, then gone out again. The girls had followed him out to the caves, but they'd soon come back for permission to go exploring with him. "I don't think so," Sarah said. "'Tis damp and slippery down there, and dangerous enough for a grown man."

"Oh, but—"

"Jane, some of those caves open out to the cliffs over the sea. If either of you were to fall . . ."

"I won't fall! I want to look for Brownie!"

Sarah looked across at Maud, who shook her head. "Brownie has found a nice, dry place to wait out the rain," the housekeeper said.

"Jane, Mr. Locke is unaccustomed to little girls," said Sarah. "He's liable to forget all about you and leave you stranded."

"Do you think it's just the runes that interest him?" Maud asked.

"What else could there be?" Sarah remarked, sorely aware that her presence had not been interesting enough to keep him inside the house. While she had helped Maud with supper preparations, he had remained glaringly absent.

"Remember the fellow that came up from Oxford a couple of years ago?" Maud asked. "He couldn't be pried away, either. Not until Captain Barstow told him it was time he moved along to Fullingham."

"Will you tell Mr. Locke to move along, Miss Granger?" asked Margaret.

Sarah's heart filled her throat. "I'm sure Mr. Locke will leave of his own accord, Margaret. He already told us he would not be escorting us to the soiree."

"'Tis a shame," said Maud with a rueful chuckle. "If only he could see you in the fine new gown we're making, he would just beg to stay."

He would not wish to stay. He might have

availed himself of what she'd offered in the Hartwell cottage, but Sarah knew better than to fool herself. Those moments in the cottage had changed naught.

The trot of a horse's hooves drew the girls' attention, and they went to the drawing room window, pushing aside the curtains to see who approached.

Margaret turned to face Sarah and Maud, her face starkly white. "It's him! This time, it's him for certain!"

"Come to me, girls," Sarah said. Hadn't enough happened in one day? "Maud, answer the door, please."

Chapter 10

Mr. Ridley was nearly as tall as Brendan Locke, and his hair almost as dark. His black eyes scanned the room as he entered, removing his gloves, then his top hat and cloak, and handing them to Maud.

His build was compact, and he wore a thick mustache after the fashion of the gray-haired men Sarah had seen in town. But he was not much older than Brendan. She supposed he was fair of feature, but she was no one to judge, at least not today, when Brendan Locke's and John Crowell's comely faces haunted her every thought.

"This is Barstow's brood, then?" he asked, his voice deep and thundering.

Sarah felt the girls flinch at his words, and they clutched at her skirts. She nodded. "Do we have the honor of addressing Mr. Ridley?"

"Yes, yes, girl. I'm Ridley. Who are you? The governess, I suppose?"

Flustered by the man's brusque tone and questions, Sarah nodded. "Yes, sir. I am Miss Sarah Granger and these are Captain Barstow's daughters, Margaret and Jane." She placed a hand on each girl's shoulder and squeezed as she said their names. "You met Maud, our housekeeper, in the foyer."

Mr. Ridley hardly acknowledged them, but went to stand before the fire to warm himself. "Beastly night. Would have stayed at an inn, but I was so close . . ."

"Yes, sir," Sarah said. A stunned silence ensued, none of them entirely prepared for the man's appearance, even though they'd expected him at any time.

Maud broke the silence. "We've just finished supper, if you're hungry."

He rubbed his hands together and gave her a curt nod.

Sarah gathered the materials she and Maud had been working on, and put the girls to work collecting the new thread and ribbons and placing them in their sewing basket. "We did not know when to expect you, sir."

He shrugged. "I'll want a full tour on the morrow, but for tonight, it'll be a quick meal and then bed. I assume a room has been made ready for me."

"Yes, sir. Maud prepared the master's rooms

when we learned of your impending arrival."

He nodded and turned back to the fire. Sarah wanted to know what he intended to do about the girls. And her. But dreading his answer, she was willing to put off the question.

"Will you b-be staying long, sir?" she had the temerity to ask.

"I have established no particular plans, other than to stay long enough to make an immediate assessment of the property." He looked over his shoulder at the girls. "'Tis late for my wards, is it not?"

Sarah swallowed audibly at the realization that the children were under his guardianship. "Yes, sir. We'll retire to the nursery now."

"Send them on, Miss Granger. I'd like you to summon a groom to take care of my horse."

"We have no groom, sir."

He gave a great, irritated sigh. "Well, you're a country girl. You must know what's needed. See to it."

Brogan climbed out of the cave and over the stone wall of the ruins. He looked up at the towers and wondered if his cousin Ana could have been wrong. Mayhap the stone had been hidden here at an earlier point in time and removed by one of Dubhán's successors.

If so, his time here had been wasted.

Mo oirg, not wasted. He could never think of the moments with Sarah as wasted. Even now, he could not stop thinking of her sweet responses to his touch, or of her magical lips and tongue.

He hardened at the thought of her sensual reaction to his kiss, his touch. No other woman had inflamed him so . . . and Sarah had done it without even completing the sexual act.

Thoughts of being inside her had made it impossible to concentrate on his search. Yet he knew his duty, and knew he had to return to Coruain, soon. With the *brìgha*-stone. He folded the diagrams he'd made and placed them in a pocket, then climbed up to the promontory to see if Seana could tell him who had come down to the cave the night before. From her height and position, she would have had a good view.

As he headed in her direction, he did not see her silhouetted against the sky. He decided her form must be obscured by the trees, so he continued until he reached her pedestal.

She was gone.

'Twas impossible. Dragheen were never known to move more than a few feet from their positions, and if danger threatened, they were unable to move fast enough to save themselves. Brogan searched the vicinity near Seana's promontory, but found no sign of her. He clambered up to her thick stone platform and turned his gaze toward Ravenfield's caves.

Through the branches of the trees that lined the path, he was able to see the castle below. Seana would have had even a better view. He pulled himself all the way onto the pedestal and looked down.

Seana lay in pieces at the bottom of the dell, sections of her gray stone body scattered at the base of the promontory a hundred feet below.

Brogan pushed back, horrified by the sight of the dragheen's vicious death. Seana would not have fallen. Someone had done this to her, had killed her just as they'd killed Jane's cat. It had to have been Eilinora, or one of her followers, for there'd been no lightning, no other reason for a dragheen to fall to her death when she'd stood in the same place for centuries.

Brogan had no need to shutter his vision and hunt for sparks of Odhar magic. Without a doubt, he would find them there. Seana must have seen the Odhar at Ravenfield the night before. They'd become aware of her and decided to eliminate her. They would not have known that she had no interest in their—or anyone else's—activities.

Feeling a renewed urgency to find the blood stone before Eilinora could do any more damage, he went back down the path, intent on resuming his search. He took a side path to go into the garden and approach Colm, the winged dragheen. He'd told Brogan that something was amiss the night before. If he'd had a bond with Seana, he must have felt what was happening to her.

"Greetings, m'lord," said the guardian.

"Colm . . ."

"M'lord." His wings shifted slightly and his brow shadowed his eyes. "I know aught is . . . Ye must tell me."

"'Tis Seana. I found her dead."

The sound Colm made was harsh to Brogan's ears, reminding him of the sound of teeth grinding teeth. Had it been louder, 'twould have been intolerable.

"It grieves me to bring you such tidings, dragheen," Brogan said. "I canna think 'twas anything but Eilinora or one of her followers that caused Seana's death."

The dragheen gathered his wings close to his body. "Ye must defeat her, m'lord. Avenge Seana now, as well as your father," he said, his voice choked and gravelly.

Brogan gave a quick nod, feeling the dragheen's grief, though he himself felt little for the aloof dragheen. "Colm, it would be helpful if you could try to remember back to Dubhán's time. I have yet to find the blood stone, and there is some urgency to my search."

"What would ye have me remember, m'lord?"

"Was there ever any talk of riddles? Of puzzles, or secret places?"

"M'lord, someone comes." The dragheen became still as stone once again as Sarah came 'round the house, carrying a lamp and leading a black gelding. She seemed tiny beside the great beast, and Brogan could understand why she was afraid of horses.

She glanced up at him, but turned her eyes down and kept walking toward the barn where Brogan's horse was housed, alongside the Ravenfield pony. He caught up to her.

"He's come, hasn't he?" he asked, recalling the premonition she'd had earlier.

But when she bit her lower lip in a gesture so completely feminine and enticing, Brogan almost forgot his question. He pushed open the barn door for her and took the horse's reins from her hand. "He sent *you* out here with his horse?"

"We have no groom to take care of such tasks, Mr. Locke. And Mr. Ridley is master here," she said resignedly, setting the lamp on the ground. She'd reverted to their formal address, obviously respecting the distance he'd put between them since their interlude at the cottage.

Yet Brogan longed to hear her familiar use of his fictitious name.

The lamp cast a soft light, throwing their shadows in distorted forms against the wall. Brogan caught sight of Sarah's shoes, now caked with mud, and felt his ire rise precipitously. What kind of man had not the decency to see to his own horse when he knew there was no one but a young woman to do it?

Angrily, Brogan unfastened the saddle and pulled it off the gelding, wondering how Ridley had ever thought Sarah would be able to manage it. The man was an idiot.

"He'd better hire a groom to take care of these chores," Brogan said.

"I am sure he will." Sarah kept her eyes downcast and started for the door. "I-I think it would be best if Mr. Ridley did not find you here tonight."

He caught up to her and raised her face, forcing her to meet his gaze. "Sarah."

Her eyes were glazed with tears that spilled when she looked up at him. Her face seemed to crumple, but she turned away quickly and reached for the door.

Brogan stopped her and pulled her into his arms. "What did he say? Will he send you away?"

She shook pathetically, weeping in silence as he held her. "I was h-hoping he would w-want to keep the g-girls here."

He placed his hand at the nape of her neck and gently rubbed, saying naught, wondering what it would mean to Margaret and Jane to be sent away from Ravenfield. Would they have to rely on the grudging charity of Craggleton's residents as Sarah had done?

"He sent them to b-bed barely ten minutes after he arrived," she said quietly, sniffing into his chest. "He did not want them near. You can imagine what—"

"Sarah, I have money enough to spare," he said. "You and the children are welcome to it."

He hardly knew what he was saying, only that he was being pulled into this Tuath mire when he needed to be solving the *crìoch-fàile* puzzle. "Go back to the house. I'll return in the morning," he said, though he had no intention of leaving her and the rest of the household alone tonight. Someone with more power than Colm needed to keep watch.

Sarah took a deep, shuddering breath. "Maybe it would be best if you didn't. I doubt Mr. Ridley will take kindly to a stranger puttering among his ruins."

"Did he say that?"

"No, but he gave a certain impression . . ."

Brogan caressed her head and savored the press of her body against his. Small as she was, she fit him like no other. He pressed a kiss to the top of her head, wishing he could do more, certain he should not, at least not until he had the stone and was well on his way home.

"You should go back."

Sarah nodded against him, then stepped away. "Maud is getting his supper—oh, I nearly forgot." She handed him a wrapped package. "It was all I could take without attracting Mr. Ridley's attention."

She left the barn, and Brogan opened the paper. Inside was half a loaf of bread, generously slathered with jam.

Sarah was not able to escape Mr. Ridley to go up to the girls. He'd apparently tired of Maud's company, and appeared to be awaiting her when she returned from the barn.

"Tell me about your duties here, Miss Granger," he said, though did not ask her to take a seat as he ate his supper in the dining room.

She remained standing. "Before Captain Barstow died, I was responsible for the girls. For their care and schooling, I mean."

"Yes, yes. A governess's duties, I'm sure. And now that Barstow is dead?"

Sarah shuddered at the man's cold tone. "The captain's income ended. So we have been compelled to earn our keep as well as we can."

Mr. Ridley took a sip of Captain Barstow's port and studied her. "Your keep, Miss Granger? How does one do such a thing? By selling my wool? Has my land produced any saleable crops during the past season?"

"N-no, sir," Sarah said, realizing she needed to tread carefully. They'd certainly used his fruit for their pies, and he gave every indication of being a man who would begrudge them that. "We collect cockles on the beach and sell them."

"Cockles." He looked at her with disbelief.

"They're very popular in Craggleton," she remarked. "And our needs are small here."

"What of Barstow's commission? Has it been sold? Should be worth a good six or seven hundred pounds." He went back to his food. "Suppose I'll have to ask the solicitor . . ."

"It has not yet been sold, sir. We were told it might take some time."

Mr. Ridley chewed his food, leaving Sarah standing quietly for several minutes before dismissing her.

Anxiously, she climbed the stairs and went into the nursery, where Margaret and Jane were huddled together in Margaret's bed with their nightclothes on. "See?" Margaret whispered tearfully. "I told you he would be horrible."

Sarah sat on the edge of the bed and wished she could crawl in with them. And that Brendan Locke could come up and gather them all into his strong arms and take care of them.

In a way, he'd already done that, with his generous overpayment for his room and board. Now he would not even make use of what he'd paid for.

He'd been kind to mention to Frederica Hattinger that he'd taken Mrs. Hartwell's cottage, sparing her reputation, but Sarah had begun to doubt her ability to make a living in Craggleton. She wondered whether the people in town would ever accept her as a teacher. Her experience that afternoon with Frederica Hattinger had made her realize that memories were long. There were some who would never let her forget she was Paul Granger's daughter, and that the parish had had to support her one way or another for four long years.

"Margaret says he'll turn us out of our beds, Miss Granger," Jane cried.

"Hush, love," Sarah admonished. "Keep your voice down. And no, he's not going to turn you out of your beds."

"You, too, Miss Granger."

"Well ... There may be other ... arrangements for us," Sarah replied, attempting to keep her voice bright. "Do you remember my plans to move us to Craggleton?"

The girls turned their watery eyes up to Sarah, who felt overwhelmed by responsibility. It was one thing to remain here at Ravenfield, sharing the care of the girls with Maud, making their way as best they could. She could not bear to think what it would mean if she failed in Craggleton.

"Will you stay with us tonight, Miss Granger?" Jane asked somberly.

"Of course," she said as she tucked the girls into the bed. Jane's cat was conspicuously absent, but Sarah did not mention the missing animal. Matters were bleak enough.

"Will you tell us a story, too?" Margaret added.

"A happy one," Jane said through her tears.

Brogan spent the early morning hours going over every inch of the first cave before daylight, but he knew he had to speak to Ridley soon. He'd hoped for a sight of Sarah, coming out early to feed the pony and Ridley's horse, but it was Maud who showed up.

"I've no worries about what will happen to me," the woman said. "I'll soon be going down to Ulverston to live with my sister. A couple of old widows together." She clucked her tongue. "But those little girls . . . They're much too young to be turned out of their home. And Sarah . . . she's already endured more than she should in her short life."

Brogan was quite sure he could change all that. Before he departed the Tuath world, he would return ownership of Ravenfield to the girls, and make certain that Sarah had the funds she needed to survive. But he didn't want her to be alone.

For a few of his shillings, she would have a new gown that would show her coloring to particular advantage. And once her delectable figure was displayed, he did not doubt she would have more men than Crowell groveling for her attentions.

The thought of Crowell fawning over Sarah did not give Brogan the satisfaction he expected. On the contrary, he took no pleasure in the knowledge that the man wouldn't be able to resist her.

He walked back to the house with Maud, aware that he needed Ridley's consent to wander the grounds, and he still had to map the rest of the *crìoch-fàile* clues. The housekeeper led him into the library and introduced him to the new master before disappearing into the kitchen.

"Scottish, are you?" Ridley asked. He sat behind the big wooden desk, with papers and journals spread out before him.

Brogan let the question go unanswered as he glanced 'round the room. He had not been in the library since he'd stumbled upon Sarah one night, disheveled and beautiful in her sleeping gown. She'd been wary then, a prickly female whose situation he had not understood.

Even now, he barely understood it, or the man who sat across from him, so intent upon dusty journals when his magnificent lands lay no farther than his door. 'Twas a clear, bright morning, and if Ravenfield had belonged to Brogan, he'd have taken his wife to one of the lushly wooded fells and made love to her there.

Brogan sat down abruptly, taken aback by the clarity of the thought. If only he could think so clearly of the *brìgha*-stone and the puzzles he needed to solve, he might find it and be on his way back to Coruain. "While I'm visiting your district, I'd like your permission to look over your ruins."

Ridley picked up a bell from the desk and rang it. "Damned incompetent servants," he muttered when there was no immediate response.

Brogan had met Druzai elders who appeared less formidable than Charles Ridley and wondered how Ridley would react to a man of greater status or wealth. Likely as equals, though the man surely did not feel the same with anyone whose fortunes seemed less.

Sarah came into the room and dipped in a slight curtsy. She kept her attention on Ridley. "You beckoned, sir?"

"Get me coffee," he said without even looking at her.

"I'm sorry, sir, we have no coff—" She jumped

when he slammed a journal onto the surface of the desk.

"By damn, is nothing in order here?"

Brogan stood.

"W-we have tea, sir," Sarah said quietly. "And the kettle is hot."

Brogan loosened his fists and bit back his angry reproof. Sarah would be able to forget Ridley's meanness once Brogan negated the man's inheritance. But her discomfiture rankled.

He decided the mere negation of Ridley's inheritance would be too kind. He was going to strip him of his property and leave him at Sarah's mercy. She would surely be kinder to him than he deserved.

But Brogan could work no changes yet, not when he was wasting time with visits to Corrington House and trips to Craggleton. His priorities had been clear from the start, but he'd allowed himself to be distracted. He waited for Sarah to go for Ridley's tea, then posed his question again.

"Ravenfield interests me, Ridley," he said, annoyed that he even had to ask. "Do you have any objections to my wandering through the ruins?"

"Waste of time, but do as you please," Ridley said. "They'll be gone soon enough, so avail yourself of them while they last."

"You plan to remove the ruins?"

"Waste of space. When my man of business

arrives, we'll determine what needs to be done here."

"You'll need to do some hiring before then if you want your horse tended."

"Eh?"

"Miss Granger is no groom, sir. She has not the strength to lift your saddle."

The man made an inconsequential sound and returned his attention to his books.

"And what about Captain Barstow's children?" Brogan persisted, even though 'twas clearly none of his concern. "Have you a plan for them?"

"Loncrief School will accept them next term," Ridley replied, fully engrossed in the columns of numbers in the Ravenfield ledgers. He hardly glanced up when he spoke. "I am a bachelor, Mr. Locke. And as my mother is recently deceased, she obviously cannot see to their needs. They must go to school."

"And Miss Granger?"

Ridley replied in an impatient tone. "I am not her keeper, sir. If she is competent, she will find other employment. 'Tis not my concern."

Brogan unclenched his teeth just enough to ask, "When does the term begin?"

"A few weeks. Long enough for Miss Granger to outfit them accordingly."

Brendan shuddered at the thought of Sarah's reaction when she learned of Ridley's intentions.

The sooner he found the blood stone, the sooner he could alleviate her worries. He should take his leave immediately and return to the castle and resume his search, but decided to broach one other subject first.

"They'll be able to attend Mrs. Pruitt's soiree, then." He mentioned it on Sarah's behalf, willing to fight for their right to go, in case Ridley objected.

He looked up at Brogan then, with narrowed eyes. "Soiree?"

"I believe it's being held to introduce me to the neighborhood. Miss Granger and the children were included in the invitation. Friday."

"I suppose I'll have to attend," Ridley muttered.

"I expect so," Brogan muttered in return, then made his way out of the house and back to the ruins.

"Our lady warrior is gone, Maud," Sarah said, feeling foolishly close to tears.

"Gone? How can that be?"

"Crashed to the ground. She lies in pieces at the bottom of the precipice."

"Struck by lightning?"

Sarah shrugged sadly. "I suppose. 'Tis like an omen of all that will be, now that . . ." She bit her lip to keep it from trembling. "Oh, Maud."

"The girls will be upset, too. Maybe you should tell them before they discover it on their own."

Sarah nodded and accepted Maud's comforting hug.

"Why don't you go and get some sewing done. Those dresses won't finish themselves, you know."

Maud was right, but the only thing Sarah wanted to do was follow Brendan Locke into the ruins and spend the rest of the morning with him.

She'd seen him from her window early that morning, climbing over the stone walls, looking at all the scratches and etchings, and remembered every moment of their interlude in the cottage.

Yet he'd given her no indication that he wanted their involvement to continue. He'd been kind last night, holding her as she'd wept. But he had said nothing of changing his departure plans. He'd bought a horse and a saddle with traveling packs. Obviously, their interval at Mrs. Hartwell's cottage had changed nothing. He still intended to leave before the Pruitt party.

Sarah swallowed her disappointment, and tried not to feel ashamed of her actions. Yet she wondered if those who'd denigrated her for being Paul Granger's daughter had been right. He'd been a drunkard and Sarah was a . . .

She pressed her hand to her mouth and sup-

pressed a quiet sob. She was *not* a strumpet. She'd
behaved as a woman in love.

Dear God, that was even worse.

Hadn't John Crowell been the object of her
affections for years? Sarah tried to recall all the
times she'd encountered the squire, and the way
he'd treated her. He'd never made any advances,
nor had he treated her with any particular regard.
She had never felt the same jolting attraction for
Squire Crowell that she'd immediately felt with
Brendan Locke . . .

It was all so confusing. The squire's visit yesterday morning should be at the forefront of her
mind. She was certain she'd made a decent impression, in spite of Mr. Rutherford's disdain. Yet
she could not imagine John Crowell ever kissing
her with the kind of fervor that Brendan Locke
had done. The squire's touch would not send
spears of fire shooting through her veins. He
could never rouse in her the same kind of passion
Brendan Locke did with just a glance.

But he had given her no more than a polite nod
since those few quiet moments in the barn the
night before. Disheartened, she managed to make
progress on the girls' dresses, and Margaret's was
ready for a fitting by the early afternoon. She left
the house in search of the girls, who'd been admonished to stay near. She found them together,
following Mr. Locke's progress as he climbed

over and around the castle's ruined walls, drawing representations of the runes and the ancient circle patterns that were carved on the walls.

"We're helping Mr. Locke," Jane said.

"Oh? Doing what?" Sarah asked.

"He's looking for a secret hiding place."

Chapter 11

Brogan glanced across the high castle wall at the fluttering wings of a hundred butterflies in the overgrown field. Each one seemed a different color, but all were radiant, all were magical. He'd thought Coruain was perfect, created by the ancient elders after the Druid wars to provide a home for the Druzai and keep them separated from the Tuath. Yet they'd neglected to bring any number of wonders to the Druzai world.

Sarah's pies, for example. And jam. And though there was music on Coruain, 'twas only the soft, lyrical sounds of the stringed instruments. There would be no pianoforte, for without contact with the Tuath world, the elders had not learned of such an instrument. They'd either forgotten, or never known, about the rainbows that appeared magically in the Tuath sky, or the glowworms that shimmered beside the paths just after dark.

Brogan rubbed one hand across his face.

Naught was going right. He'd been certain of finding the *brìgha*-stone within a day or two, and he'd had no doubt he'd be able to remain aloof from these Tuath women at Ravenfield.

He'd been wrong.

And now he'd practically committed himself to staying at Ravenfield long enough to escort Sarah and the girls to Mrs. Pruitt's soiree. He could not leave her at Ridley's mercy before she had her chance to appear at the party, showing herself as the most comely lass in the district.

Yet if he found the blood stone, he would need to return immediately to Coruain. He decided he could delay his departure long enough to make a few drastic changes to Sarah's situation.

He would give her a dowry, but not too large, for he didn't want her to have to deal with suitors who were only after her fortune. He would make a few slight changes to the rooms at Ravenfield, making them more presentable to her gentleman guests, and remove all signs of redness and chafing from her hands.

Yet the thought of those tender hands caressing him made it nearly impossible for him to think. He muttered a low curse and forced his attention back to work. In whatever manner events played out, he still had to find the blood stone.

He climbed to the top of the southernmost wall

of the largest tower and discovered more *crìoch-fàile*. There were several pieces to the puzzle, and with each one were more runes, not all in good condition. Brogan drew the symbols on his paper, as well as the *crìoch-fàile* designs, hoping he would be able to put the words and symbols together and understand the clues Dubhán had left him.

Carefully, he made his way to each of the opposite walls until he reached a stone shelf that jutted out slightly. He examined it, then pulled on it, even though he doubted it would separate easily from the wall. If it was solid enough to last centuries here, his sharp tug wouldn't dislodge it. Underneath were runes, and they had been brushed clean of the debris that surrounded them.

It meant someone else had discovered them, yet Brogan had seen no one. He braced himself and shifted his attention to look for magic sparks. He stood perfectly still on the ledge as his vision changed and everything became hazy 'round him.

He cast his glance over the walls and the grounds, looking for the yellow sparks that would signify use of Druzai power, but there were none. Even so, it wasn't reassuring, not when he knew they'd learned to cover their sparks.

Brogan translated the words he found under

the shelf. *Muscle and stone are hers to say.* His heart sped at the words. 'Twas the first seriously promising sign he'd found.

He moved farther down the wall and found another set of runes, but these were mostly covered by residue, indicating that he was the first to notice these.

With blood and bone that shimmer in light, he read, then swore softly. "Riddles," he muttered, recalling that the blood stone was said to glow red when held in a Druzai hand.

He had to find another foothold before he could move any farther. He looked 'round for any loitering sìthean pests, and carefully held on to a niche in the wall while he shifted to the next secure floor support.

There was a wide crack that obscured the next line of runes, but it looked like *daughter* again, or *woman*. The symbols underneath were clear. *Precious gift of the fae.*

He leaned back and looked again. Without a doubt, the markings referred to the *brìgha*-stone. But what was the clue? Was there some hidden meaning that he could not discern?

He had to try to piece together the *crìoch-fàile* and mayhap the meaning of the runes would be clear, though he was almost certain the most important clue was the last line . . . *gift of the fae.*

Had the stone once been hidden beneath the

shelf, or was it somewhere within these stone walls? Mayhap it had been an actual gift to a Tuath. If that were true, it could be anywhere.

No, Ana had seen it here at Ravenfield. In this time and place. It had to be in the castle.

One thing was certain: He was close. Soon he would have it in his hands and be able to leave Ravenfield. He made drawings of the *crìoch-fàile*, then carefully copied the runes onto his chart. Last, he had to make sure the Odhar who was dogging his steps would not be able to make out the clue of these runes. Taking a hammer from his belt, he struck the runes, destroying their integrity and obscuring the key words.

Brogan heard voices below, Sarah and the children calling for Brownie as they scoured every hidden corner in the yard for the missing cat. Jane was distressed, and the sight of her tears gave Brogan an unusual ache in the center of his chest. If only he could give her another cat . . .

'Twould have to wait until he was ready to leave, for he did not know how to conceal traces of his own magic.

Sarah glanced up and caught sight of him. She gave him a shy smile, and he felt her glow to the depths of his soul. More magic? He wondered whether there would be bright yellow sparks 'round her if he looked.

Her touch was pure enchantment. Their stolen moments had been all that he'd imagined *sòlas* to be. Yet she was Tuath. It was not possible.

He saw Meglet throw her arms 'round Sarah's legs, and Sarah embraced the child in return. Both girls were fragile, Meglet more so than Jane, in spite of the missing cat. He wondered how the children would fare once they were removed from Sarah's kind care.

How would Sarah fare?

He did not like to think of her as a young girl, cast to the kindness of the people in Craggleton. She'd been alone and mistreated, but she had not become bitter or cruel like the women he'd encountered at the draper's.

He vowed she would never again suffer the derision of those Tuath harpies. Once he secured Ravenfield for them and provided Sarah a dowry, all would be well.

Brendan Locke's money weighed heavily in Sarah's pocket. She felt compelled to return what they had not yet used. He'd overpaid for his room and board, and now he could not even reap the benefit of his payment.

She could not keep it.

Glancing up at his precarious perch, Sarah bit her lip anxiously and watched him sidle across the wall to the steps. Loose rock fell to the ground as he moved, but he reached the top step and descended without mishap.

"I don't want to go back to the house, Miss Granger. Ever!" said Margaret, hugging her tightly, while Jane wept quietly as she continued her search for Brownie. By now, Sarah was worried, too. The cat had never stayed gone so long.

"We must adjust, Margaret," Sarah said. "Avoiding Mr. Ridley will change nothing."

"He hates us!"

"How could he hate you, Meglet?" Brendan asked, jumping down agilely from the third step. "He doesna even know you."

He gathered Jane into his arms and lifted her onto his shoulder, making her tears subside for the moment.

"Brownie has run away!" Jane cried.

"Ah, 'tis the way of cats," said Brendan, unconcerned. "She'll turn up. Or there'll be another just as pretty."

"No!" cried Jane, holding on to his head for balance. Giving a watery smile, she seemed unable to decide whether to enjoy the ride or weep for Brownie.

"You must have found something," Sarah said, realizing she'd never before seen his smile.

"Aye, lass." He pinned her with his gaze, and Sarah could not help but think he was remembering what they'd shared in Mrs. Hartwell's cottage.

She could still feel the rasp of his beard on her sensitive skin, and hear the sound of his strangled groan when she'd . . .

She could hardly believe what they'd done. She'd behaved like the most brazen of women, without a care for her virtue. Yet those moments in Brendan's arms had been pure heaven, and it was only Mr. Ridley's arrival that had diverted her from thinking continuously about them in spite of her realization that they did not hold the same significance for Brendan Locke.

"The runes in the tower are exactly what I sought," he said, his voice rumbling through her, making her knees tremble. If he'd found what he was looking for, he would soon leave. Her heart sank.

"I thought you were looking for a hiding place," Margaret said, lifting her head from Sarah's skirts to look at Brendan.

"Ah, but you are a quick one, Miss Meglet. I've found runes that tell me the item I seek is here."

"You can read the runes, Mr. Locke?" Sarah asked hopefully. "I thought . . ." She felt confused. He'd asked her about the runes and what they meant, yet *he* could read them. And he had not yet found whatever he was looking for. Or had he?

"There is a puzzle to be solved, my bonny Miss Granger," he said, reading her thoughts.

"Miss Granger tells us the most wonderful stories about the runes and the castle and giants and—"

"I'm sure she does," Brendan said as he lowered Jane to the ground. "So, my fine lasses, did you find any secret places in the walls?"

Margaret shook her head ruefully. "The rocks are crumbling."

"I've been looking for Brownie," Jane said and went off to search some more.

"What do the runes mean, Mr. Locke?" Sarah asked.

He looked at her quietly for a moment, as though weighing his answer. "They tell of a special stone that was owned by Dubhán, the first lord of Ravenfield," he finally replied.

"I've never heard such a tale," she said. Though her mother's family was said to have descended from the ancient Ravenfield family, she had died when Sarah was very young, before telling much of her heritage.

"You will have to trust me, then," he said, and Sarah recalled those same words the day before, when he'd made her go mindless with pleasure.

But Sarah could not count on such fleeting happiness. For all she knew, Brendan would be gone before Mrs. Pruitt's soiree on Friday.

* * *

Brogan could not say any more. If Ridley had any idea there might be an artifact of value in the ruins, he seemed the sort to restrict access to anyone but his own personal excavator. He half expected the man to come out and see what they were doing out there, anyway.

Brogan was close. After reading those runes, he could almost feel the stone, see it glowing red in his hand.

All he had to do was focus his search now on finding the place where it was hidden.

There was no sign of it having been hidden in Lord Dubhán's private quarters or anywhere within the castle walls. That left the caves.

Brogan felt a renewed urgency to locate the stone and return to Coruain. He hoped Merrick had already completed his own quest so they would be able to engage Eilinora and her mysterious mentor immediately. The power of both stones, combined with the strength of the Mac Lochlainns and all the elders, could not fail to defeat the sorceress, even though she held Kieran's scepter.

Then he thought about leaving Sarah, and his urgency dissipated. She walked beside Meglet, appearing lost in thought, and Brogan realized she did not know what Ridley had planned for them.

Would that he could spare her from worry, but

she would not believe him if he told her what he was going to do. She would only think him daft. In the meantime, she would make herself ill fretting and worrying, and so would the children.

"Meglet, go and find your sister," he said, wanting a moment alone with Sarah.

The little girl looked up at Sarah with questioning eyes. Sarah gave her a nod, and the child trudged away to find Jane.

"You have a nice way with the girls," she said.

His ease with the lasses surprised him, for he'd not spent any time with children in his own world. Yet they'd won his regard, Meglet with her fretful mien and Jane, who was her complete opposite.

They walked to the other side of the ruins, and Brogan had to steel himself against pulling her into his arms and kissing her senseless. He was confounded by the strength of his need for her touch. He could not explain his reaction to this woman, a Tuath who should have held no sway over him whatsoever.

But he wanted her as much as he wanted his next breath.

Her hair was different today, bound at the nape of her neck in a soft cascade that fell down her back. Pretty auburn waves framed her face. She wore her plain gray gown, but she'd adorned it with a ribbon 'round the high waist, and pinned a sprig of tiny flowers at the center, just below her breasts.

He'd known she could be as comely as any woman on earth. And Brogan knew he should feel better about it.

She spoke to him, but he did not hear her words. He only saw her delectable mouth moving, smelled her fresh, spicy scent.

"Mr. Locke? Brendan?"

"Oh, aye, lass. I was just . . ." He didn't know what in Hades he was doing. He shoved his hair back from his forehead and gave her his attention. "What is it?"

"Did . . . did Mr. Ridley say anything to you about his plans?"

"Aye. He did."

He looked back and saw that she'd stopped walking.

"You must tell me. No matter how bad it sounds, I'd rather know than not."

"Weel, he's given his permission for you and the lasses to go to Mrs. Pruitt's soiree," he said, though he knew this was not the subject that was foremost on her mind.

"Brendan, tell me." She came and put a hand on his arm, and he wanted naught but to draw her into his embrace and tell her that all would be well.

"There's a place called Loncrief—"

"Oh dear heavens!" She whirled away with one fist pressed to her mouth

"'Tis a school."

"An awful place! Cold and drafty in winter . . . not enough food . . . no one to care for the children . . ."

He pulled her 'round to face him. "Sarah, I have . . . influence . . . in, er, certain quarters. I will see to it—"

"He is their guardian, Brendan." Her green eyes were as stormy as the sea that had tossed him onto her shores. "He can do what he likes with them."

"And I am telling you that I can influence him to change his mind."

She crossed her arms over her chest and began to pace. "I do not see how."

"You must trust me. Do you, lass?"

She stopped. Standing still, she looked up into his eyes. "I want to."

Sarah's heart and soul were in turmoil. She hoped Brendan would be able to do something about Mr. Ridley's plans, but she had her doubts. The new master was the most stubborn, disagreeable man she had ever met.

She'd been the brunt of bullies for a good number of years. Yet their taunts seemed nothing compared to Mr. Ridley's callous attitude toward Margaret and Jane, children who were his own blood relations, distant though they might be.

She started back to the house in order to let Brendan continue his search for his precious artifact, but remembered the money in her pocket. Turning back to him, she picked up his hand and placed the coins and notes into it. "We cannot keep your money. Now that Mr. Ridley is here, and you've got Mrs. Hartwell's—"

He reversed the position of their hands. "Sarah, you must keep it. I have much more—"

"But we—"

"I insist."

The thought of Margaret and Jane at Loncrief School made her accept it. Life at that place would be every bit as wretched as her own awful state after her father's death. Somehow, she was going to make certain that the girls never saw the inside of that school.

She would need money to do it.

Preoccupied with plans when she returned to the house, she was surprised to see Andy sitting on the ground outside the kitchen door. The children were frightened of him and flocked to her sides when they saw him.

He unnerved Sarah, too, but she did not let on, focusing her attention on his one good eye. "Are you hungry, Andy?"

He gave her a vacant smile and nodded. "Andy eee . . . Andy eee!"

"Wait here," she said. She sent the girls inside, following close behind. She cut a thick slice of bread and a generous piece of cheese, then returned to the kitchen door.

Stepping outside, she handed him the food. "You'd better not come around anymore, Andy," she said. "I'm afraid our new master won't take kindly to . . ." She did not finish when she realized the poor fellow wouldn't understand her explanations. She hardly understood people like Ridley herself.

Sarah left him to his meal and went back inside, meeting Maud, who'd come downstairs with the dress she'd been making. "Come, Sarah, and let me see how this fits you."

"Andy's outside," Sarah whispered, looking toward the library. "Where is Mr. Ridley?"

"No need to worry. He's gone to Craggleton. Mr. Locke told him he couldn't be relying on you to take care of his horse. Told him go and hire himself a groom in Craggleton. Don't look so astonished, my girl," Maud added, smiling. "'Tis no surprise that your Scotsman wants to look out for you. Anyone can see he's smitten."

Sarah swallowed, wishing it were true. But he'd found at least part of what he'd been looking for—a clue to the location of his special stone. Soon he would have that, too.

"He plans to leave here, Maud. If he stays until Friday, I'll be surprised."

"We'll see about that, Sarah, my dear." She held up the coppery gown she'd pieced together. "We'll just see about that."

Chapter 12

Before going back to the clues and the ridiculous puzzles, Brogan carried out a physical search of the caves. The walls were roughly hewn, and he suspected they had not occurred naturally. It seemed likely that Lord Dubhán had produced them for his own purposes, one of which might have been to hide certain treasures.

Taking a broom and ladder from the shed, Brogan climbed to the uppermost reaches of the cave walls and examined every rock, sweeping away loose stones, looking for a concealed space. Mayhap he would find a hollowed-out area concealed by a tight-fitting rock.

"*Gift of the fae*," he muttered, trying to understand what Dubhán could have meant. No one knew where the blood stones had originated, but he was certain they had not been bestowed with any fanfare. The ancient elders had wanted to keep them secret.

They were so secret that Brogan had not even believed they existed until Ana had actually *seen* them. He'd always thought the tales told of them were myths.

He ran his hands across the stone walls, pushing and pulling, brushing, painstakingly going over every surface, forcing himself to stay focused on his search when his thoughts wanted to drift to Sarah. He did not want to think about Crowell and every other swain in the parish crowding 'round her, seeking her favor. He despised the thought of any other man touching her, bringing her pleasure.

Muttering a vicious Druzai curse under his breath, he thought of Ridley and his rude treatment of her. Every masculine instinct he possessed urged him to go into the house and see to it that he gave her a modicum of respect while he was still master of Ravenfield.

She deserved no less. Yet Ridley was a man who took for granted his own power over others. Brogan was going to enjoy taking him down a few notches when he left.

Any satisfaction he enjoyed at the thought of Ridley's comeuppance was dampened by the reality of leaving Sarah. He would never have believed that a simple Tuath woman could insinuate herself into his every thought, his every desire.

Finding the *brìgha*-stone was still his priority.

Yet touching Sarah, tasting her, making love to her had become an impulse that was difficult to control. He wanted her.

"Mr. Locke . . . Brendan."

He could almost believe he'd conjured Sarah when he looked down and saw her standing near the base of the ladder. She looked ethereal in the firelight, holding a plate and a mug in her hands. His manhood stirred at the sight of her.

He climbed down and shoved his hands into his pockets to keep from reaching for her.

"'Tis late," she said, her voice echoing in the cavernous space. Her manner was hesitant and unsure, as well it might be. She was no seasoned mistress who understood the bounds of casual pleasures and physical intimacies. "Well past dark."

Glancing toward the mouth of the cave, he realized he had no idea how many hours had passed in his search down there.

"Where is Ridley?"

"Abed. Everyone is asleep. I . . . I thought you'd be hungry."

"Hungry? Aye." He set the plate aside, slipped his fingers into the curls near her ear, and pulled her close. Aye, he was hungry.

She made a small, feminine sound and tipped her head back. He descended upon her mouth, kissing her like a starving man. A storm raged through him, a tempest rousing his blood, clouding his mind and burning him all at once. He sucked her tongue into his mouth, tasting her, relishing her ardent, brash response to him.

She slid her arms up his chest and 'round his neck, pressing her body against him. He felt her nipples harden against his chest, and a spear of pure desire arrowed through him. He kissed her like a starving man, unfastening the buttons of her bodice. He slipped her gown from her shoulders and took but a moment to free her breasts, cupping them in his hands.

"You are so lovely, Sarah," he said, bending to take one nipple into his mouth. He circled it with his tongue while he teased the other with his fingertips.

She pushed her hips against him, her body seeking the same pleasure he'd given her at the cottage. Brogan obliged her, reaching for her hem, pulling it up and out of his way. He touched her then, his thumb finding the sensitive nub between her thighs.

And nearly came to his own climax.

He wanted to be inside her. Yet the cold, dark cave was no fair bower. He could not make love to Sarah on this filthy, clammy ground. Nor would he take her to the barn or anywhere else at Ravenfield.

"Sarah . . ."

She bucked against his hand and shuddered, and would have slipped to the ground had Brogan not caught her and lifted her into his arms. He held her close to his chest and pressed his forehead to hers as her spasms slowed. As painful as it would be, he had to stop now.

Holding her securely, he carried her out of the cave. 'Twas fully dark outside, though the moon cast a soft light since it had barely begun to wane. He was clearly able to see her questioning eyes.

No doubt there was puzzlement in his own.

"You must go inside, lass," he said, though his words went against every urge in his body. He lowered her to the ground, but she clung to him for a moment before turning and hastening to the house.

Sarah did not know how she could face Brendan this morning. Her wanton behavior had shocked her, and it must have had the same effect on him, for she'd brazenly pursued him.

And he'd effectively dismissed her before she could give herself to him, body and soul.

He was not indifferent to her. She realized he'd ended their tryst because he was leaving. Soon. And without her. He was trying to be honorable.

After a night of tossing and turning in her bed, Sarah knew what she had to do. Brendan Locke was not her savior. He would no more take a poor, insignificant country girl for his wife than he would want two orphaned children. It was too much to ask of an influential man like him, like Squire Crowell.

Brendan's father had died, and for all Sarah knew, he had become lord and master of his father's estates. He would have to return home to his responsibilities. To an advantageous marriage.

She brushed away a sudden spate of tears and tried thinking of something else.

She did not understand his fascination with the castle ruins. Nor did she know how he could find one special stone out there. The entire site was made of stone, and there was rubble on the ground. Could he possibly intend to sift through all the rocks to find that one particular stone he sought?

He'd said the runes provided clues. Sarah supposed that was why he seemed to be concentrating his search in the caves. She'd seen the drawings he'd made, etchings of the circles and runes that had been carved on the castle walls. It all seemed so strange, yet none of it made any difference now.

Surely Brendan knew that whatever he found on the property would belong to Mr. Ridley, and Ravenfield's new master did not seem to be a man who would relinquish any of his possessions easily. Especially if he heard of some unique stone that had brought a Scottish adventurer here to look for it.

None of it had any bearing on what Sarah had to do. She recognized that it was past time to face her own responsibilities and deal with them alone, just as she had always done. She was going to move into Craggleton with the children before Mr. Ridley had a chance to send them to Loncrief. Surely he would not object to her intention of keeping them and providing them with a home and an education.

He would likely appreciate the relief to his purse.

She asked Maud to keep an eye on the children and walked into town, without even looking toward the ruins for a glimpse of Brendan Locke.

There was a milliner's shop off the main street where she knew there were rooms to let. It was a respectable location, not too far from the homes of the prosperous townsmen she hoped would hire her as a teacher for their children. When she stepped into the crowded shop, the bell on the door jangled loudly in her ears as all conversation stopped.

She saw a number of matrons inside, women who had known of Sarah's impoverished state, but had done nothing to help her. Her tongue froze in her mouth and she nearly turned around to leave, but something compelled her to approach the counter where the milliner stood, choosing fabrics for one of the ladies.

"Mr. Yardley, might I have a word with you?" She used the same imperious tone used by the wealthy ladies who stood listening to her. None of them needed to know that her knees were quaking beneath her skirts, especially when the milliner gazed down at her through his quizzing glass.

"Speak, young woman."

Sarah pressed her lips together and raised her chin as haughtily as Frederica Hattinger would have done. She reminded herself she was no longer a poor waif, but a grown woman of some means, and no small ability. She spoke firmly. "In private, if you please."

It worked. The man set his feathers and ribbons on the counter and gestured to a workroom at the back of the shop. Sarah led the way, making the rash assumption that he would follow.

She walked into the room and turned to find the tall, angular man standing with his arms crossed over his bony chest. "I am not hiring any shopgirls."

"I haven't come seeking employment."

"State your business, then."

"There is a sign upstairs for rooms to let. I'd like to—"

He started to turn away.

"Wait! I have the money. I—"

"The Craggleton cockle seller has money?" he sneered, amused by his own silly alliteration.

Sarah took two of Brendan Locke's sovereigns from her reticule and held them out. "How many months will this cover?"

Something woke Brogan from a sound sleep. He reached for his *tarmach*—his staff of power— then remembered where he was and why his neck felt stiff. The cold rock floor of the cave had not been his most comfortable bed.

He rose quietly to his feet and made his way to the entrance of the cave, aware that one of Ravenfield's sheep might have wandered near the ruins. But he did not think so. Eilinora wanted the *brìgha*-stone as badly as Brogan did. She or one of her followers had come to look for it.

The sound of a scuffle and a stifled cry brought him outside, but naught seemed amiss. There were no sheep, or any other intruders; only a cool wind that rustled the branches of the nearby trees. Staying close to the walls of the castle, he searched for an intruder, but could see no one in the dim starlight.

Nor did he hear any more unusual sounds.

Stealthily making his way to the house, Brogan let himself inside and searched for signs of an intruder. He moved quickly through the main floor, then went upstairs to the bedrooms. He checked on Sarah first, then the children. Maud came next, and when he found no sign of anything out of order, he opened the door to Ridley's room, where the man was snoring contentedly.

He resisted the urge to return to Sarah's room, instead, going back to the castle. Not even Colm was awake.

He sat down on the grass near Jane's tea table, just outside the cave entrance. The sense of foreboding was strong, but Brogan was unable to pinpoint the reason for it until the sun rose. It was only then that he saw the blood.

Sarah had no opportunity to speak to Mr. Ridley of her desire to take the girls with her to Craggleton, for he closed himself inside the library for most of the morning and refused to be disturbed.

She spent the time fretting over her eventual meeting with Ravenfield's new master. While she sewed the girls' dresses, she practiced what she would say to him, stewing over what she would do if he refused her. She considered what would be the most effective strategy, whether to ask him for guardianship of the girls outright, or to wait until he mentioned Loncrief and his intention to send them there.

Practicing what she would say, she tried out

different lines of reasoning and the best way to appeal to him.

She tried not to think of Brendan Locke and whether he'd come from the Hartwell cottage to putter in the caves while she and the girls had done their lessons. Whatever his reason for staying at Ravenfield, Sarah knew it was not for her. It was quite clear that, in spite of all that had transpired between them during the past few days, he had not changed his intentions.

Or had he?

Her face heated from embarrassment as well as a startling arousal at the thought of their passionate exchanges. Her palms became damp, her nipples beaded, and she felt a desperate longing for his touch in her most private places.

Yet he had never come seeking her at the house, or taken her for a turn in the garden. Surely he'd have promised to escort them to Mrs. Pruitt's if he intended to stay. Her chest ached when she thought of his leaving, but she knew of no way to induce him to remain at Craggleton.

How could he stay, when he had his own lands in Scotland? Sarah had her own obligations here with the girls, and even if Brendan *did* ask her to go with him, she didn't think Mr. Ridley would allow her to take the girls to Scotland.

Sarah worked on the new dresses, forcing herself to keep at her sewing, even though she'd have preferred to go down to the cave to seek out Brendan. She wanted to know more about the stone he sought in the cave and why he wanted it. She wondered who his family was, and what would be expected of him when he returned to Scotland.

Mostly, she just wanted to be near him, to hear his voice and feel the heat of his body when she stood near.

But he had not encouraged her to join him. He seemed to prefer working alone, and hardly even noticed the passage of time.

Sarah finished work on the children's dresses, then went down to the kitchen to find Maud. The girls had finished their lessons and were upstairs, playing in the nursery.

The kitchen was a quiet comfort to Sarah, with its homely cupboards and shelves, and the warm smells of whatever was in the oven. She found Maud working on the gown made of the beautiful copper cloth Brendan had bought her.

"I was just about to come looking for you," said Maud. "I need you to try this on."

Sarah took the nearly completed gown and started for the door. "Are you coming?"

"Put it on and come back. I must keep an eye on my biscuits."

In the privacy of her room upstairs, Sarah slipped on the dress. Its capped sleeves were short and gathered at the shoulder to add a bit of fullness. The waist was high, allowing the skirt to flow gracefully to the floor. The bodice was cut low, much lower than any gown Sarah had ever worn, leaving her shoulders bare and the upper swells of her breasts exposed.

None of the rich brown trim had been added yet, and Sarah was glad the stitching remained loose. Changes could still be made.

Certain that Mr. Ridley would not venture into the kitchen, she returned and stood on a step stool as Maud directed.

"You'll have to raise the neckline, Maud," Sarah said as the woman knelt to pin up the hem. "'Tis indecent this way."

"I'll do no such thing, my girl. This is the fashion, and you'll be quite the drab if we raise it."

"Oh, but I—"

"You have a lovely figure. And these colors complement your hair and skin. You'll look just right."

Sarah turned, finding herself in a position to glance out the window toward the castle ruins.

"Why do you suppose he wants that stone so badly?" asked Maud.

"He?"

Maud laughed. "You know very well who I mean."

Sarah pressed her hands to her cheeks. "Maud,

sometimes when he's near, I feel as though I could crawl out of my skin. He is . . ."

Maud took a pin from her mouth. "He is quite different from Squire Crowell, is he not?"

Sarah agreed. She could hardly recall what it was about the squire that had ever appealed to her. When she thought about his pale good looks and soft hands, she knew she would never feel the deep pull of attraction that came over her when Brendan Locke was near.

She could no longer think of those pretty hands caressing her and making her heart flutter with desire. Nor could she imagine the sound of her name whispered in passion from his lips. With Squire Crowell, Sarah could never bear the kind of intimacies she'd shared with Brendan.

"The man is maddening," she said, remembering how he'd disregarded her wishes and placed her onto his horse. "He cares naught for convention. He can be rude and thickheaded. But—"

"He fascinates you."

"Yes," she whispered. "I don't understand it."

"Has he . . . made any advances?"

She nodded and pressed her palm to the center of her chest.

"Has Mr. Locke said anything of his intentions?"

"No," Sarah replied, tamping down a wave of misery at the thought of his leaving. "He'll return to Scotland, and I'll remain here with the girls."

"But you said Mr. Ridley intended to send them to Loncrief."

"Maud, I can't let them go there. You know about that place."

Maud's brow crinkled. "What can you do about it, Sarah? If the master decides—"

"I've taken rooms in town. Somehow, I'm going to convince Mr. Ridley to let me keep them with me. I can provide for them, and I'm sure he won't mind saving the money he would otherwise have to spend on them."

With Maud's worried frown, Sarah had the first inklings that she might fail to convince the new master. Maud clucked her tongue. "I don't know . . ."

Brogan saw no source for the blood on the ground near the children's table. He shoveled dirt over it, obscuring the sight. It was an ominous sign, but without knowing what had happened to cause it, he could do naught but caution Sarah and the lasses to stay away from the ruins. It could not be long before he figured out where the stone was hidden.

It was not in the caves, or any of the castle walls, for Brogan had searched every inch and found naught. Neither of the dragheens had been able to tell him anything of use in his search.

Magic would not expose the stone, for it would be much too well-protected to be discovered so easily. He was certain Lord Dubhán would never have hidden it in the trees or under the ground, or any other place that might be temporary or obviously changeable.

There was only one other possibility before he attempted the near-impossible task of trying to work out the *crìoch-fàile*.

He headed toward the house, but one sight of Sarah through the window in the kitchen made him forget his purpose. She'd worn her hair the way he liked it, with loose curls softly edging her face, the mass of it tied at her nape.

Neither she nor Maud saw his approach, for they were engaged in some kind of work on Sarah's new gown. Sarah stood in profile, and Brogan's body tightened at the sight of her elegant form in the new dress.

The color suited her as he'd known it would, and Maud had created a gown that displayed her feminine curves to such advantage that every man at the Pruitt soiree would fall over his feet noticing her.

And lusting for her.

Growling low, under his breath, Brogan reminded himself that that had been the point. He *wanted* Crowell to take notice of Sarah and see her as a likely mate. 'Twas the only way to assure that she would enjoy some marital satisfaction, for the squire was the man she loved before he'd come to Ravenfield and interfered.

He hardly remembered she was Tuath when he gazed at her through the glass. Her neck was long and delicate, her chin delicately cleft. Her shoulders and arms had strength, yet they were soft and feminine, and had held him with a spontaneous, innocent passion unlike anything he'd ever known.

He could not keep from wanting her.

He closed his eyes and relived those all-too-brief passionate moments with her, aware that he should not entertain such arousing thoughts. The taste of her nipples was going to haunt him forever, as would the sensuous sounds she made when he touched her.

He'd broken the Druzai law he revered in the short time he'd been here, yet he could not regret touching Sarah.

She would always have the ability to arouse him, no matter what her clothes, or how she wore her hair. There was much to admire in a woman who had managed so well on her own in this harsh world, and he could not help but compare her to the indolent Druzai women of his acquaintance. The women of his kind had every whim answered with the flick of a finger, the whisper of a thought.

Sarah could not be more different.

Brogan took a deep, shuddering breath and went into the house.

"Why, Mr. Locke, come in," said Maud. She gestured with her open hand toward Sarah. "What do you think of our Miss Granger?"

Sarah stood on a stool, putting her at eye level with him. She did not look in his direction, but clasped her hands tightly in front of her, giving away the nervousness she felt.

For a moment, Brogan thought his throat would not work. He swallowed, and then managed to speak, though there were no words that could convey his appreciation for her beauty, her fortitude, the depth of her compassion for the children in her care. "She is verra lovely, indeed."

"Oh!" cried Maud, taking pins from her mouth and dropping them on the table. "Sarah, stay right there . . . Er, I'll be back shortly." The woman quickly disappeared from the kitchen, leaving Sarah alone with him.

The last place either of them ought to be.

He wanted to touch her, but knew he could not. His quest for the stone had already taken much too long, and he could waste no time once he found it.

He could not kiss her again, nor could he sample the delights hidden beneath the wonderful gown Maud was making for her.

Even if Brogan could take her back to Coruain, he understood her well enough to know she would not leave Meglet and Jane to the mercy of Charles Ridley. She was a woman who understood responsibility.

And she would appreciate what Brogan had to do.

"Sarah." He moved to the opposite side of the table to put some distance between them. He had to concentrate on finding the stone.

He dreaded the prospect of sitting down with his drawing of all the *crìoch-fàile* and trying to solve what might or might not even be a puzzle. "You know the library well," he said. Mayhap there was some recorded folklore regarding the earliest lords of Ravenfield and their treasures. "Have you ever seen a book—a very old book— about Ravenfield? Mayhap some old records or a history?"

She bit her lower lip, as was her wont when she was pensive, and he berated himself for making things more complicated for her. She held herself aloof, obviously sensing his desire to keep a distance between them.

"If you tell me about the stone, I might know where to find it."

"Ah, lass . . . 'Tis an old, dull stone, dark red in color."

"Large or small?"

"'Twould easily fit in the palm of Jane's hand."

"And is it v-valuable?"

"No, Sarah." If he were to explain its significance, she would never believe him. "I wouldna take anything of value from Ravenfield. The stone is an artifact of interest to my family. My father . . ." He shoved his fingers through his hair, at a loss for words.

Her expression softened. "It was of importance to your father? Is that why you came here?"

"Aye." He did not enjoy lying to her, but no other explanation would do.

"I have never seen such a stone," she said, picking a nonexistent bit of lint from her skirt. "But you might ask M-Mr. Ridley to look at the books in the library. That's where you'll find him."

He would rather stay and loosen the stiffness from her shoulders. 'Twould be so easy to kiss her . . . as she stood on the stool, he would not even need to lean down to meet her mouth. He could slide his hands 'round her waist and pull her close, and press his erection against her, make her come to climax with barely a touch.

He let out a harsh breath. "*Ainchis, moileen.*"

"What is it?" she asked.

"You canna know what you do to me," he said.

Her mouth began to quiver, and she put the fingers of one hand against it. "You must go, Brendan . . . Mr. Locke."

"Aye. Well I know it."

Chapter 13

Two of Ridley's business associates, Edmund Harris and Joshua Howard, arrived from London. 'Twas noontime, and Brendan Locke had visited the library and left again, without returning to the kitchen.

Sarah felt weightless with dismay, as though there were too much air in her lungs, putting an uncomfortable pressure on her heart. If only she could exhale, she might feel grounded again. Her heart might beat normally once more.

Brendan would soon be leaving. She'd known it the moment she'd told him to leave the kitchen to pursue his search of a book in the library. She could feel it.

The bell on the library desk rang, and Maud put down her sewing. "Go and get the girls for lunch while I see what the master wants. Everything is ready."

The girls were not in the garden, so Sarah

walked over to the ruins where Jane liked to have her tea parties. She walked through the stone arch and stopped short when she saw Jane and Margaret sitting at the small table, with Brendan beside them, perched on a large rock that he must have dragged close to the table. A thick, leather-bound book lay discarded upon the stone wall.

Margaret was pouring.

That odd weightlessness in Sarah's chest intensified.

"Miss Granger!" Jane cried, and they all looked up at her.

"Luncheon is ready, children."

"Oh, but we've just started our tea," Margaret said.

"Lasses, you must do as Miss Granger bids."

"Will you come with us, Mr. Locke?" asked Jane, taking hold of his big hand. "Maud will have made plenty."

He looked up at Sarah, his eyes hooded, expressionless. And Sarah could not resist asking him to share their table. "Of course you must come."

They returned to the kitchen together and took their seats around the table. Maud had not yet returned, and Sarah went to the door to see if their housekeeper was anywhere in sight. She was not, so Sarah assumed she was still in the library.

"There has been much to do since Mr. Ridley's

associates arrived," Sarah said as she began to serve the meal. "I'm sure she'll join us shortly."

"Miss Granger made me the prettiest ball gown," Jane said to Brendan.

"'Tis not a ball gown," Margaret corrected her sister, "but a party frock."

"It's beautiful," Jane said dreamily. "Just like the princess in Miss Granger's story."

"Will you take us to Mrs. Pruitt's house, Mr. Locke?" Margaret asked in a pleading voice. "Please?"

Maud pushed open the door and sat down heavily in the chair beside Margaret. She looked ill.

"Maud?" Sarah asked. "What is it?"

"I've been sacked," she replied, and Sarah's heart dropped to the pit of her stomach. Margaret started to cry, but Maud hugged her to her breast.

"Sacked?"

At the desolate expression on Sarah's face, Brogan was ready to charge into the library to challenge Ridley when Jane asked, "What does that mean?"

"Given my leave," Maud replied, gathering Jane into her arms. The color returned to her face, and she smiled sadly. "For the first time in my life, I'm not wanted."

Brogan relaxed now that he understood the word.

"The master will be hiring a whole new staff, and they'll need a different kind of cook," said Maud.

"What kind?" asked Jane. "Won't they eat food like we do?"

"Oh yes, of course they will," Maud replied. "But much more than I'm accustomed to cooking. So now 'tis time for me to go down to my sister's."

"No!" cried Margaret, turning to plead with Sarah. "Can you persuade Mr. Ridley to keep Maud? What will we ever do without Maud!"

Sarah took Margaret onto her lap, and Brogan could see that she was trying to mask her own distress from the children. "We must think of Maud in this, love. She has been wanting to retire to Ulverston for months. She only stayed on to help us over the winter."

Margaret pressed her face to Sarah's breast and sniffled. "Will someone else come to cook for us?"

Maud exchanged a glance with Sarah, then gave the lass a tremulous smile. "Of course. Tomorrow."

The child began weeping anew. "You're leaving us tomorrow?"

"Have no worry, my sweet," said Maud. "I'll stay long enough to see you off to your party."

Margaret looked at him then. "Mr. Locke? Will you take us?"

"Margaret—"

"Aye, lass," he said, cutting Sarah off. "I'll escort you."

Silence met his statement. He should never have committed to staying another day, not when it was possible that this very day he might find the one key clue and locate the stone. But when Jane suddenly threw her arms 'round his neck and Meglet pushed away from Sarah to hug his waist, he could not regret it.

His heart swelled with an unfamiliar sensation at the affection and gratitude of these wee lasses, and he closed his eyes to relish it for a moment. For 'twas something he was unlikely to experience again, once he returned to Coruain.

Sarah blinked, unable to believe her ears. Only a few days before, he'd said he could not stay. Or *would* not . . . Sarah could not remember which. She hardly dared hope she and the girls had engaged his affections, and she guarded against reading more into his decision than he intended.

Loncrief still hung over their heads, and Sarah still had to approach Mr. Ridley about it.

Their joy over Mr. Locke's decision to escort them was dampened by the knowledge that Maud would soon be leaving. They finished the meal and Brendan stood, saying that he would return for them the following evening, with a carriage.

"Oh, and doona go near the ruins or the castle when I leave," he said, picking up the book and heading for the door.

"Why? What—?"

"There are signs that someone besides me has been poking 'round."

"Who?" Margaret demanded.

"Weel, that I doona know. But whoever it is willna bother you if you stay clear of the site."

Sarah looked out the window as Brendan left, but saw nothing that concerned her.

"Will you be giving Mr. Ridley his luncheon, Maud?" Jane asked.

"A bit later, my sweet," said Maud as she got up to clear the table. "He will not hesitate to ring when he wants it."

Sarah and the girls went up to the nursery for their afternoon lessons, and Maud soon served Mr. Ridley and the other men. The voices of the new master and his guests wafted up from the dining room to the nursery, making the girls nervous and jumpy. The girls had mixed emotions. They should have been happy and excited about tomorrow's soiree, but they were upset about Maud going away and unnerved by the presence of a stern stranger in the house.

Sarah had known of Maud's plan to leave as soon as Mr. Ridley had a replacement for her. But it did not ease the loss of her dear friend, the woman who had welcomed her to Ravenfield six years earlier, when she was so deeply in need of affection and a home.

"Miss Granger, are you sad that Maud is leaving?"

"Of course I am, love," Sarah replied. "But we must remember that Maud is going to live with her sister. And she has wanted to go there for a very long time."

"She only stayed because Papa died," Margaret informed her sister.

"She stayed because she loves you," Sarah corrected. "And she knew you needed her."

"Did you need her, too, Miss Granger?" Jane asked.

Sarah nodded. "Maud has been my very best friend, ever since I came to Ravenfield."

She felt lost and alone, and yearned for the man who had held her and comforted her more than once when she'd been upset. He'd shown her the kind of passion she would ever long for, and made her feel like the most appealing woman in the world. Yet the attraction had its limits. He might stay to escort them to Pruitt Hall, but he'd indicated no further change of plans.

Sarah sent the girls out to play in the garden after lessons, and returned to the main floor of the house, bolstering herself to speak to Mr. Ridley.

Straightening her collar and cuffs, she smoothed

her hair back before knocking on the library door. When the man called for her to enter, she took a deep breath and opened the door.

Ridley sat behind the desk as the two other men stood facing him, poring over the charts and maps on the desk. There was a haze of cigar smoke hanging over them, and Sarah suppressed the urge to cough. The three men looked at her, unnerving her with their intent gazes.

"Mr. Ridley?"

"What is it, Miss Granger?" His tone was harsh.

"I've come to ask your permission . . ." No, that was not what she'd intended to say. "That is, I have a request to make."

"Well? Speak up. What kind of request?"

"I would like your consent to take Margaret and Jane with me into town."

"For what purpose?"

She gritted her teeth in frustration. This was not coming out the way she'd practiced. Her phrasing was all wrong. "T-to live with me, sir," she said. "I've let rooms in Craggleton and I will be taking in students—"

"No."

He looked back at his charts, and his two visitors also turned back to their work, dismissing her.

"But sir," Sarah protested. "You would not have to worry about school fees, and since the girls are accustomed to me, they will be happy to stay with me in Craggleton."

"No, Miss Granger," Mr. Ridley said. He opened a drawer and pulled out a folded sheaf of paper, then handed it to her. "In two weeks' time, they will go to Loncrief School. See that they are prepared and have what they need."

Sarah looked down at the paper, but the words were blurred, and she realized her eyes had filled with tears. She'd so hoped that he would allow them to stay with her . . . "Mr. Ridley, I beg you to reconsider. Margaret and Jane consider me their only family."

Ridley looked at her coldly. "Or is it the other way around, Miss Granger? I understand you were a charity case before coming to Ravenfield. 'Tis likely you have more need of them than they you."

Sarah's mouth went dry. The man actually thought to turn it all around. Though she readily admitted she did not want to lose them, her primary reason for taking those expensive rooms in Craggleton was to provide a decent, caring home for them. If she were alone, she would have been satisfied with much less. She would be free to go to Scotland if Brendan Locke asked her to come. "Mr. Ridley, I have thought only of the girls' welfare in this. They will be much happier—"

"'Tis not their happiness that concerns me, Miss

Granger," he said brusquely. "They need more education than you can give them. And more discipline."

Sarah stood speechless. She realized she was wringing her hands, so she stilled them and thought of the only argument that might convince him to change his mind. "Sir, Captain Barstow would have—"

"That will be all, Miss Granger. Leave us."

It took a moment before Sarah realized there was nothing more she could say, nothing more to do. Her throat burned and tears welled in her eyes as she reached for the library door.

Wiping the moisture from her eyes, Sarah went to the back of the house and looked out the window at the girls, playing happily near the fountain, unaware of the fate that awaited them. Furious with herself for bungling the interview with Mr. Ridley, she was not going to be defeated.

She went into her bedroom and gathered her belongings into a traveling bag. Mr. Ridley was not going to send those girls to Loncrief, not when Sarah was perfectly capable of providing for them. She had good, respectable lodgings in town, and money in her pocket, enough to keep them warm and fed through the winter, at the very least.

On the momentum of her anger, she emptied her trunk, shoving her belongings into the bottom of the bag. She realized then that they could not stay in Craggleton. Ridley would just take the girls away from her. They would need to go far away, someplace where Ravenfield's master would never find them.

It would not be easy, but Sarah still had some of Brendan's money. She could pay their fare to . . . to Scotland, if necessary. And if she knew where Brendan's lands were . . .

No, she could not think of Brendan Locke, or the soiree they were going to miss, or how upset the girls would be to leave in the dead of night.

She stopped suddenly and sat heavily on her bed, holding her head in her hands. It was hopeless. She could not take the children away from their rightful guardian. It would not be possible to hide from someone as wealthy and powerful as Charles Ridley. He would find her within hours and show her no mercy once he discovered her. The law would not be sympathetic, either.

Her heart breaking, she wept freely now, aware that she had no choice but to let Ridley send them to Loncrief. She wanted to rail against him, to protest his decision, and to inform him that his cousin's children deserved better than that cold and distant institution so far from their home and everything they loved.

She wanted someone to reassure her that all would be well.

* * *

Brogan told himself that his promise to escort Sarah and the lasses to the soiree had no particular significance. He hadn't found the stone, so he could not yet return to Coruain, anyway.

With one last glance toward the house, he decided 'twould be best to spend the rest of the day at his cottage, working on the *crìoch-fàile* and poring over the old book he'd found in the library. Staying near Sarah would tempt him far too much. He wanted her with every drop of his blood, and knew that if he stayed, he would find a way to entice her out to the barn or into the caves.

He would seduce her, and nothing could stop him from making love to her fully this time. His too few, too brief tastes of her had not been nearly enough, and every time he saw Sarah, he wanted her more. He wanted to breathe in her scent, taste her delectable body, and slide inside her hot, tight sheath.

She'd been beautiful in the new gown, yet she'd had no awareness of her own appeal. Brogan knew 'twas going to be pure torture to escort her to Mrs. Pruitt's, where every man at the soiree would notice her, would want her as desperately as he did.

He muttered a curse and mounted his horse, then rode to the cottage. 'Twas not a great distance away, so he arrived quickly, and let himself into the cold, dreary house. He lit a few lamps, then went into the small drawing room, where he pulled his papers from his jacket before taking it off and pulling his suspenders from his shoulders. He sat down, smoothing out the diagrams on the table beside him. Finding the stone was even more urgent now.

He could not doubt that Eilinora was searching, too. Brogan did not want to stay away from Ravenfield too long, though so far, the witch had confined her searching—and her other evil activities—to the dark hours of night.

Brogan looked at the symbols that lay before him. He hated puzzles. His brother was the thoughtful one, a man who considered every angle to every situation before making a decision. Merrick was the one who should be here, working out the *crìoch-fàile*, leaving Brogan to engage Eilinora in battle.

He glanced at his drawings in frustration. Each of the *crìoch-fàile* patterns was incomplete. He'd drawn them exactly as he'd found them on the walls of the ruins, but they made no sense.

Unless he tore the paper into sections containing one *crìoch-fàile* each. Then he might actually be able to piece them together the way they were meant to go.

Turning his full attention to the paper, he tore out the symbols he'd drawn, separating each from the others. He carefully trimmed them to make clean pieces of a puzzle. He tried fitting each open circle and dot pattern to another, but the game was ridiculously complicated, and certainly not exact. Some of the symbols overlapped and some abutted, and some seemed as though they were only close matches. Brogan could only hope he'd copied the symbols exactly.

He worked at it awhile, but a number of the patterns had no match. There was no way to get some of the circles to fit together with others. So he eliminated those, one at a time, and concentrated on finding the ones that fit well together.

It took some time, but he finally made eight solid circles, putting the dots and lines together so that they fit together sensibly. Then he searched out the runes that had been etched alongside each of these eight *crìoch-fàile* and discarded the ones that had gone with the symbols that did not fit.

He came up with eight lines that made no sense. He arranged them and rearranged them, frustrated by his lack of practice at such riddles. Finally, after trying every possible combination of lines, he came up with a short verse that was typical of an old Druzai song.

> *Seek ye daughters / with depth of sight,*
> *With blood and bone / that shimmer in light.*
> *Muscle and stone / are hers to say,*
> *And hide from all, / precious gift of the fae.*

He felt certain this was it, but now he had to sort out its hidden meaning—if it actually had one.

Depth of sight would indicate a seer, and he thought mayhap the seer in question referred to a daughter of Dubhán Ó Coileáin.

He knew that the *brìgha*-stone would shimmer a deep red light when it was held in a Druzai hand, so the second line clearly referred to the stone. The third line made no sense to him, other than referring to the stone itself, but the fourth seemed obvious. The stone had been a gift of the fairy, as ancient Tuath Druids had called the Druzai.

The thought of Druids reminded Brogan of the very valid reason for Druzai remaining separate from the Tuath. It was much too easy to dominate these people, to stir up rivalries, to meddle in their legal affairs, in their families. Eilinora was not the only vicious sorcerer who had ever risen from Druzai blood, nor would she be the last. 'Twas Brogan and his warriors who made sure they never gained the power to act.

Yet Eilinora had been the worst. Many worthy Tuath warriors had lost their lives in the terrible wars she'd orchestrated. The witch had committed murders and instigated rivalries, played on fears and weaknesses that had caused the clans to go to war. 'Twas after she and her followers had been captured that the elders had created Coruain and mandated that the Druzai remain separate from Tuath.

No matter what the circumstances.

Brogan let out a frustrated sigh and set aside thoughts of his beautiful Sarah in her burnished copper gown. He felt restless, and if he'd been at home on Coruain, he'd have challenged a few of his men to combat, honing his physical skills while he burned away his desire for the Tuath woman.

Forcing his attention back to the clues, he reminded himself he was not a man to be ruled by the demands of his cock. He had yet to be governed by his desire for a woman, and Sarah Granger was surely not the most desirable of the women he'd known.

He could not think of one who was more appealing, but certainly there had been a Druzai female in his past who'd captured his attention as intensely as Sarah had.

There must have been.

Disgruntled by the direction of his thoughts, he reconsidered the clues, going over each line of his translations. But no new thoughts came to mind. He turned to the book he'd brought from Ravenfield and began to read the only volume he'd found in Ravenfield's library that might refer to Dubhán's descendants.

The earliest entries were written in the familiar

runes. There was mention of Lord Dubhán, the hollowing of the caves and the building of the fortress over them. The author referred to warring parties that tried to overrun Ravenfield, and their persistent lack of success.

Brogan did not doubt it. There were no Druids or tribes of Tuath that would ever be able to overcome a Druzai lord. Yet the Tuath could easily be subjected to an ambitious Druzai sorcerer. He continued reading the entries, eventually locating a familiar passage. It differed only slightly from what he'd put together from the *crìoch-fàile* puzzles, and carried essentially the same message.

Seek ye daughters with depth of sight,
With blood and bone that shimmer in light.
She holds the luck within her bower,
The key to ancient Druzai power.
Muscle and stone are hers to say,
And hide from all, precious gift of the fae.

Brogan rubbed his forehead. 'Twas more than what he'd determined from the puzzle, but still no clearer. It was a disappointment. He'd been certain that the puzzle would solve the location of the stone.

Now he had to solve the riddle of the lines.

He realized the room had turned cold, so he set the book aside and went to the fireplace. Stack-

ing wood in the grate, he lit a fire to take away
the chill, considering the effort it took to survive
in the Tuath world. Naught was easy here, from
clothing and sheltering, to something as simple as
staying warm.

'Twas doubtful there was a Druzai woman in
all of Coruain who could make a life for herself
here, especially if she were all alone. Like Sarah.

She deserved a husband who would take care
of her. Someone who would see to her needs and
. . . a man who would love her.

He rubbed the back of his neck, frustrated by
. . . Of course it was due to his lack of success in
finding the blood stone. It had naught to do with
his promise to escort Sarah to the Pruitt event and
making sure that she made an impression on her
young squire.

'Twas what would be best for her. Ravenfield
would soon be secured for her and the children,
so she would never again have to worry about
losing her home.

He began to pace. Crowell could not fail to
notice her, especially in that gown Maud had
made for her. It hugged every feminine curve,
and displayed more than a hint of her enticing
qualities.

He decided it was not necessary for her to be
quite so alluring. Surely the neckline of her gown
did not need to dip quite so low, nor should her

arms be left entirely bare to every pair of male eyes at tomorrow's soiree.

Gritting his teeth at the thought of the torture he would have to endure on her behalf, he tossed a few twigs on the fire. The evenings were chilly in this place, and Sarah's gown should provide more warmth. If only one of these foolish Tuath men had bothered to notice more than her lack of property, she would have no reason to display her attributes so openly.

If they had, one of them would surely have wed her already. She and the children might have been secure in their house and home, and Sarah would not find herself in a position of begging Charles Ridley for the right to keep the lasses with her.

And if Sarah had trusted him, she would avoid the confrontation he knew she was going to have with Ridley. The man would certainly refuse her request to keep Meglet and Jane with her in Craggleton.

A furtive sound at the back of the cottage caught Brogan's attention, raising his hackles. He left the lamps in the drawing room and walked quietly to the kitchen. He had left no traces for any Odhar to follow, but he was prepared for battle. 'Twould almost be a relief to confront one of Eilinora's minions, face to face.

If they'd figured out who he was, he would be free to use his magic.

Something scratched against the door and he yanked it open. Sarah tumbled inside, breathless and disheveled, her face wet with tears. He grabbed her before she fell, holding her quivering shoulders in his hands.

"Sarah–" He quickly pulled her to his chest, looking beyond her, ready to challenge whoever had accosted her. But no one was behind her.

"*Mo oirg, moileen.* You must have run all the way. What's happened? Are you hurt? Are the children—"

She shook her head against him. "He won't let me take them. They'll g-go to Loncrief."

Brogan realized he was shaking, too. He took a deep breath and held her tightly. "I willna let that happen, Sarah. I promise you."

"H-he's their guardian."

"Aye. But you must trust me." He slid his hands down her back, and then up again, and she seemed to melt against him.

"They'll be alone, Brendan," she whispered. "With no one to care for them. They will suffer harsh p-punishments for the slightest infraction of the rules. It will be cold in winter—"

"Hush, sweet," he said, his lips against her forehead. "I can prevent it."

Her heart beat rapidly against him, and Brogan knew Sarah feared the lasses would experience the same bleak childhood she had known.

He hugged her tightly, wishing he could tell her exactly how he intended to make it right.

Wishing he could have prevented the harshness in her own life.

He inched back to look at her in the dim light, and brushed away her tears with his thumbs. Her mouth trembled in her distress, and he could not keep from touching his lips to them. To reassure her.

But when she slid her arms up his chest and 'round his neck, he could not control his reaction. The merest touch of her hands had the power to arouse him instantly. Her lips were warm and soft, and he kissed her slowly and carefully.

Yet when his cock swelled with need, his tongue boldly sought hers. He feasted on her mouth, reveling in the flavor that was Sarah's alone. He pulsed against her, his blood roiling through his veins at the cradling of her soft body, the surging of her breasts against his chest.

She tangled her fingers in his hair, burning his scalp with her touch as he deepened the kiss. Meeting every thrust of his tongue, she made a breathless whimper of arousal, and Brogan could think of naught but possessing her. He wanted her lying beneath him, her legs 'round his waist, his cock deep inside her.

With only his primal need driving him, he lifted

her into his arms. Carrying her through the house, he did not stop until he reached his bedchamber and lowered her to the floor.

A dim light shone through the curtains, illuminating Sarah's face, from her moist eyes to the small dent in her chin. Brogan lowered his mouth to hers as he felt for the knot of hair at the back of her head and released it.

Brogan never felt more alive than when she sighed into his mouth. His body burned, every nerve and vein, every muscle and sinew. Desperate for her touch, he started to unfasten his shirt, but quickly lost all patience and yanked it over his head, letting the buttons fall where they may as they tore from the cloth.

"You are so hard," she said, sliding her fingers through the hair on his chest. He growled when she touched his nipples and teased them with her fingertips.

Desperate to feel her bare skin, he opened her bodice and let her gown drop to the floor. "You wear too many layers, *moileen*." But he made quick work of them and was soon cupping her naked breasts in his hands.

"You smell as delicious as your peach pie," he said, trailing kisses down her neck. "And feel as soft as th' moss at Ravenfield. Y'are magnificent, lass." He reached her nipple and sucked it into his mouth.

Sarah arched her back and held his head in place. "Oh, please . . ."

He knew what she wanted, but he intended to make slow, perfect love to her, sending her to the peak and back as many times as she could bear.

Framing her breasts with his hands, he pressed his face between them, then lowered his mouth to her belly. He knelt and grazed her mound with the palm of one hand, then pressed a kiss to the small nub that was the center of her pleasure.

He heard her sharp intake of breath and felt her legs go weak. Easing her onto the bed, he unfastened his breeches and followed her down, his body desperate to possess her.

He kissed her again, his tongue sweeping through her mouth as he slipped his hand between her thighs, wanting her with an urgency that left him breathless. Mindless. Burning.

She was tight when he eased one finger inside her, and moist with arousal, her hips writhing, moving against his hand. When he pulled one of her hard nipples into his mouth and swirled his tongue 'round it, she whimpered and nearly came off the bed.

"You are so beautiful, *moileen*." He laved her nipples and stroked her cleft until her breathing quickened and he felt her muscles contract in pleasure. She shuddered and cried out, her features taut, her hands tightening in his hair.

She kissed him fiercely, slipping her hand into his breeches. He felt a fierce delight at her tentative caress and cupped her hand, moving with her, tutoring her as she skimmed her hand down the length of his erection. His breath quickened as she explored him, probed him gently with her fingers. He groaned aloud when she encircled his cock and stroked him.

Brogan arched into her palm before kicking away his breeches. He needed a moment's reprieve or he was not going to last, but she showed no mercy. She raised herself over him and took control, stroking him while she pressed hesitant kisses to his chest, then to his abdomen.

His entire body contracted when he felt her tongue on his belly, and he nearly climaxed when she touched it to the tip of his erection. He propped himself on his elbows to watch her tentative movements, first licking, then taking him into her mouth and sucking deeply.

Growling with need, Brogan pulled away, shifting their positions, pinning her beneath him. He thrust one of his legs between hers to spread them wide, then moved between them, positioning his cock at her entrance, whispering her name as he entered her.

Taking care to avoid hurting her, Brogan found bliss in one slow stroke. She was hot and tight, her body an exquisite match for his own.

* * *

Sarah gasped at the intrusion of his body into hers. He held perfectly still, surely to allow her to adjust to his size. In the faint light of the room, she could see a fine sheen of sweat on his brow, hear the harsh rasp of his breath.

Touched by his gentle care, Sarah knew that she loved him. She'd been right to come to him. She raised up to brush a kiss on his mouth. Whatever discomfort she might have felt was gone, and her compelling need to draw him inside returned in force.

"Sarah."

The sound of her name on his lips whispered through her, and she knew he must feel as she did. Keeping her eyes locked with his, she moved her hips, welcoming him, urging him to fill her deeply.

"You are so beautiful," he said. "Not a man on earth could resist you."

His eyes shuttered closed as he withdrew, then slipped inside again, and found a rhythm that deepened her arousal. Letting her feminine instincts rule her movements, Sarah wrapped her legs around his waist and met his every hot, slick slide, arching against him in wanton abandon. He towered over her, braced on his powerful arms, his thighs hard between her own. Sarah felt utterly female, cherished and protected as he made her his.

Fire blazed through her and she dug her nails into his shoulders as the tempo of his movements increased. Sarah felt herself spiraling toward that explosion of sensation he'd caused earlier, and their intimate bond became complete when he opened his eyes and met her gaze.

He touched her again, caressing that most sensitive place between her legs, and the low burn of her arousal burst into flame. She was consumed by sensation, pure and exquisite as he thrust one last time, then lowered his body onto hers and shuddered with his own completion.

Chapter 14

Brogan rolled to his side and pulled Sarah with him. He tucked her into his embrace, curling his body 'round hers. Smoothing her hair back from her face, he feathered soft kisses on her cheeks, her ear and nose, and realized this bed had never been as appealing or felt as comfortable as it did with Sarah in it.

He could hardly believe there had been no sorcery in their lovemaking, for it was the most magical experience of his life. He'd lost control entirely.

And he wanted her again.

"I hurt you." He considered using magic to ease her pain. But he would not draw Odhar attention to Sarah.

She gave a slight shake of her head and moved closer. "Perhaps a little at first."

Brogan tightened his arms 'round her as an unfamiliar aura of balance came over him. 'Twas an easing of the turmoil that had plagued his soul since Kieran's death.

Coherent thought fled his mind when he felt Sarah's lips on his chest. She eased her way down and touched one of his nipples with her tongue, sending arrows of fire through him. He swallowed thickly. "Sarah, *moileen*, you cannot . . .'Tis too soon for you."

He gripped the soft flesh of her buttocks as she licked each of his nipples in turn, aware that he could not make love to her again. Not until the soreness of her body subsided.

He drew her up to face him, and when their eyes met, he felt mindless once again. "Sarah, you are so . . ." He took a deep breath. "You have no idea how beautiful you are."

She glanced away in embarrassment. "You are the only one who has ever thought so."

"Then everyone else is a fool." And they would realize what they had missed when they saw her at Mrs. Pruitt's the following evening. She was everything a man could possibly want . . . intelligent, considerate, passionate . . .

An ideal bride.

He muttered under his breath and pulled her against him. Crowell did not deserve her, nor did any other Tuath he'd met. Yet Crowell was the man who'd engaged her affections for some time. If he were to return them, Sarah would be content. 'Twould never be a *céile* match, for he sensed that Crowell was too shallow a man to feel a deep connection with his mate, but there was no other course to follow.

And he had spent far too much of his attention on Sarah's problems and too little on his own. He had a riddle to solve, and it was not going to get done while lying in bed with his lovely Sarah.

Absently, he caressed her back, drowsy and full of *sòlas*, yet preoccupied by a troublesome and unfamiliar sensation that he was missing something of importance.

She sighed and let her body relax against his, and he couldn't think clearly. He only wanted to pull her closer and keep her with him forever.

Yet he knew he could not. From the deepest corner of his mind came the reminder that he could not stay with her, nor could he take her to Coruain with him.

He felt her sigh against him. "If only I could convince Mr. Ridley to allow me to keep the girls," she said quietly, "all would be perfect."

"Sarah, *moileen*, can you no' trust me to fix everything before I go?"

Sarah felt ill. Of course he still planned to leave. Nothing had changed.

Nothing, besides giving her virtue to the man

she loved, the man who did not return her feelings. She was a fool.

He tightened his arm around her, but she pushed away and slid to the edge of the bed, fighting tears. She couldn't very well blame him for taking what she'd freely offered, but her heart splintered, nonetheless.

She reached down and gathered her clothes, hurriedly dragging them on. Not even the harshness of her life in Craggleton had prepared her for this kind of hurt.

"Sarah—"

She skittered away from his touch and left the room, carrying her shoes with her. If she stayed any longer, she would surely succumb to her tears, and her earlier despair had not served her well. Yet compared to all she'd had to endure over the years, this was nothing. She would survive.

She'd gotten only partway down the hall before Brendan caught up to her and drew her into his arms, her back against his chest. She felt his breath on her cheek. "I'm . . . sorry," he said. "I should never have—"

Sarah bit her lip to keep it from trembling.

"I don't want your apology, Brendan. Just . . . just let me go." Before she could no longer control her tears.

He hesitated a moment, but soon released her, and she went down the stairs with as much dignity as she could muster. She stopped to put on her shoes, then let herself out the door at the back of the house, hardly realizing it was nearly dusk.

Her tears began to fall in earnest as she started down the path to Ravenfield. She wiped them away and reminded herself that life had seemed bleak before, but she'd managed to go on.

She'd been mistaken in coming here to Brendan's cottage, too upset to think clearly. There was no hope of a future with him. It was a bleak realization, but true. Sarah knew better than to delude herself into thinking that what had transpired between them was anything more than a brief affair. She'd been nothing but an amusing diversion for him.

And she hadn't even been particularly amusing, not when she was about to be separated from Ravenfield and the children. There had to be a solution to the situation. She just hadn't thought of it yet.

Or had Brendan figured it out for her? He'd said that John Crowell wouldn't be able to resist her. Had he wheedled the invitation to Mrs. Pruitt's for the purpose of putting her in the squire's company, then paid for her to buy cloth and make a gown that would attract him?

The notion was too appalling to consider.

She meandered back toward Ravenfield, mov-

ing carefully due to the unfamiliar soreness between her legs. Brendan had known about it and
prevented them from making love again, causing
Sarah to wonder how many other women he'd
known so intimately.

How many other women had believed he cared
for them above all others? The thought gave her
pause, but it was a question she did not want to
ask. The answer might be too painful.

It seemed forever since she'd thought John
Crowell was the embodiment of all that was worthy in a man. And Sarah had been pathetic, thinking that one polite nod from the squire, likely
given absently, had made him the most fitting
candidate for marriage.

Now she could not consider herself a fit wife
for anyone. She would attend Mrs. Pruitt's soiree
in her beautiful gown and know that the intimacies she'd shared with Brendan made her exactly
the kind of woman who was scorned in decent
society.

Aware that Maud would look after the girls,
Sarah took the long way back to Ravenfield, so it
was dark when she lifted the latch on Ravenfield's
garden gate and went inside. She walked past the
fountain and went toward the house, but her attention was caught by a light shining through one
of the gaping windows of the ruins. She craned
her neck to look at it, puzzled and annoyed to

think anyone would wander down there without permission.

Brendan had mentioned that someone else was mucking about the ruins, and Sarah felt just perturbed enough to go and confront whoever it was.

She diverted her course and headed for the castle, wondering whether one of the girls might have gone out there. Or perhaps it was Andy.

A clear warning came into her mind, cautioning her to stay away from the castle, causing her to stop in her tracks. The thought was stronger than any premonition she'd ever had, yet she could not very well allow a fire to burn on the site. It could spread to the house, endangering all who were inside.

She resumed her dash toward the ruins, gathering up her skirts to hop over the lowest wall. The light was moving toward the caves, and Sarah immediately thought of the search Brendan had been conducting ever since his arrival.

Perhaps someone else sought the same dull stone he'd described. He'd said it had no value, but if that were the case, why had someone else come for it?

There was so much she did not know about the man. He'd asked her to trust him to make everything right, but how could she do that? He spoke so little of himself and of his reason for coming to Ravenfield . . . How was she to put her faith in him?

She tamped down the tears that threatened again, and hurried down the slight incline of the old castle bailey. With only the flickering light beyond the castle wall to guide her, she headed for the steps where Brendan had fallen . . . where he'd first kissed her.

Distracted by the thought, she tripped over something in the dark, and fell to her knees.

It was Andy Ferris. "Oh dear God," Sarah whispered. She glanced up at the wall and realized he must have fallen. Surely he'd known it was dangerous to wander those ruins in the dark. She shook him. "Andy? Andy, come now. Wake up. We must get you to a—"

She let out a gasp when her hands came away wet and sticky. *Bloody*.

Her alarm deepened. Why had he gone climbing about in the dark? He had never done such a thing before, being content to sleep in the barn or one of the caves.

Before Sarah had a chance to consider what she might have done to prevent Andy's accident, she heard a sound behind her. Turning, she saw a shadowy form coming toward her. She pushed up to her feet, but before she could even gather her thoughts, the figure raised its arm. Sarah tried to shield herself from the blow, but it came, nonetheless. She felt a sharp crack at the top of her head, and saw stars swirling at the backs of her eyes. Then all went black.

Brogan knew Sarah needed some distance, so he allowed her to go on ahead without him. He berated himself in every possible way for hurting her, for taking what he'd wanted—what he'd *needed*—without thinking. He'd betrayed her innocence, drawing her to him without a thought to the consequences for a Tuath woman.

He'd waited long enough. 'Twas dark, so he was going back to Ravenfield. He'd have gone there whether the Odhar were near or not, just to be close to Sarah in the little time they had left.

He crossed the small Hartwell garden and went out to the barn to saddle the mare, but was interrupted by an intrusive thought.

"M'lord Brogan!"

Brogan stopped in his tracks at the sound of Colm's voice. He rubbed his forehead in bewilderment, unsure that the thought he'd heard actually belonged to the dragheen. He felt unsettled enough to hear voices on the wind, when the only voice he wanted to hear was Sarah's.

He must have been addle-headed when he took her to bed. There was no other explanation for his poor judgment. Yet he'd wanted her with an urgency that was unsurpassed. He wanted her still.

"Something has happened. You must come. Now!"

'Twas definitely Colm.

Brogan wasted no time, but tightened the cinch and jumped onto the mare. He headed to Ravenfield as a feeling of dread spread through him.

Sarah. Something had happened to Sarah.

He kicked his heels into the mare and increased his speed, riding dangerously fast in the dark, all the way to Ravenfield. Dismounting at the garden gate, he left the mare to wander free, and went into the garden, seeking Colm.

"What's happened?" he demanded, noting the lack of any lights in the windows of the house.

"'Tis Miss Granger, m'lord," said the dragheen, and Brogan's heart dropped to the pit of his belly.

He jumped into the fountain to face Colm, impatient with the slow-moving creature. "Where is she? What happened to her?"

"She saw a light near the caves," he said. "Interlopers. I tried to warn her away—"

"No' a sìthean, come to do mischief?"

Colm ruffled his feathers, a grating sound on Brogan's ears. "Sir, I couldna see. But I think not."

On their own power, dragheen could not move more than a few feet from their station. Brogan was aware of the guardian's limitations, yet that knowledge did not lessen his frustration. "How long ago?"

Colm hesitated. "It took some minutes for me to catch your attention, m'lord."

"*Mo oirg.*" Brogan's thoughts had been fully preoccupied with Sarah. With the way he'd hurt her. With the gaping hole in his soul since she'd left him.

He wasted no more time, but pulled his dark coat 'round him to cover his white shirt as he took off at a run toward the ruins. Stealthily, he vaulted over the low wall and went into the first chamber of the castle ruins, silently searching for whoever did not belong.

There was no torch, no lamp lit anywhere in the vicinity. He hurried through the open chambers, but saw no sign of any intruders. But in the last chamber, near the stairs where he'd first kissed Sarah, he discovered her lying unconscious in the grass.

Another body lay adjacent to her. Not a child, he realized with relief.

Brogan knelt down and took Sarah's hand in his as he touched her forehead and shifted his vision to look for magic. "Sarah . . ."

She was breathing, and he said a quick prayer of thanks. Taking a moment to light a match, he perused the body that lay nearby. 'Twas Andy Ferris. With a cursory examination, Brogan concluded there was naught to be done for him. Once again he glanced about for signs of anyone—of Eilinora or one of her followers—hovering nearby, but saw naught.

Returning his attention to Sarah, he lifted her into his arms and carried her to the house, pushing open the door that led to the kitchen. 'Twas not far to the room where he'd slept before he'd started spending his nights in the ruins, so he took her there and laid her gently on the bed. Reluctant to let go of her hand even for a moment, he quickly lit a lamp, then sat down on the bed beside her and leaned close, rubbing her hand, speaking softly, imploring her to awaken.

He was no healer, and his inadequacy frustrated him. If the Odhar had been lurking outside, he'd have risked his life doing battle for her. As it was, he could only hope and pray she'd not been too gravely hurt.

At least he knew she'd not been hurt by magic, or he'd have seen a few sparks on her.

Looking for obvious injuries, he ran his hands over her head and soon found a lump just above her hairline. 'Twas dry, so he knew it had not bled, but he did not know how serious the injury was. "Sarah. *Moileen*, wake up."

Brogan had never felt so helpless, so entirely powerless to act. He called her name repeatedly, and had gone to the door on the verge of going to wake Maud when she made a quiet whimper. At the sound of her distress, he quickly returned to the bed and knelt beside it. "Sarah?"

She opened her beautiful green eyes and looked at him, furrowing her brow with obvious confusion. He had never felt such intense relief.

"Brendan?"

"Aye. How do you feel?"

"What happened? Why am I . . . Where am I?" She turned her head to look 'round the room.

He rubbed one hand across his face, reluctant to remind her what had transpired between them.

What he could not change.

"You came back to Ravenfield. Went down to the ruins."

She closed her eyes again, as though the lamplight hurt them. "The light."

"I'll put it out." He started for the lamp, but she stopped him.

"No. Down by the cave," she said. A tear rolled from her eye to trail into the hair at her temple, and Brogan's chest constricted.

"Andy!" she cried.

"Aye. I saw him."

"H-he fell from the wall," she said tearfully. "I don't know why he would go up there. Surely he knew better . . . But someone else was there. It was too dark to see who it was, but I heard him approaching from behind." She furrowed her brow, then grimaced as though the movement hurt. "I turned to look, but he h-hit me with something. I . . . I tried . . . He came at me before I could get away. There was a peculiar odor . . . "

Brogan took her hand in his, aware that he should question her about the intruder, but he was more worried about the bump on her head and the pain he'd caused her. He tucked a stray curl behind her ear and gently brushed his knuckles against her cheek.

She turned her head, pushed herself up on her elbows, and started to climb out of the bed. "I must get upstairs and see to the girls."

"Nay," he said, alarmed by her pallor, "you need to rest here while I go back to the ruins and see if anyone is still out there."

She closed her eyes and visibly composed herself, putting distance between them. "I cannot stop you from going out to the castle, Mr. Locke," she said, keeping her voice low and detached. "But please lock the door when you leave."

He winced at the overt formality of her words.

"If you'll excuse me," she sat up stiffly, "I must see to the girls. I w-wasn't here when they went to bed, and after all that's happened . . ."

Her voice wobbled as she spoke, and Brogan would have pulled her into his arms had she not held herself quite so aloof. But it was clear she wanted naught to do with him, that she recognized the afternoon's interlude for the mistake it was.

"Please go."

He clenched his teeth and watched her stand. He reached for her when she staggered, but she refused his assistance. He could only watch helplessly as she left the room and headed unsteadily for the stairs.

No one was out there.

Brogan searched the caves and the ruins, and found naught but a few signs that someone had lurked there. A bit of rubble where he knew he'd cleaned up earlier; the torch Sarah had seen had been extinguished, but was still hot.

He returned to the yard where Andy Ferris's body lay, and knew the magistrate would certainly be called this time. Sarah had wanted to summon Crowell when Brogan had washed ashore, so he concluded it would be necessary to inform him of Andy's death.

His disgust with the Odhar was renewed. There had been no reason to kill an innocent like Andy. The man was no threat to them. With such limited intelligence and virtually no speech, he couldn't even have told anyone of their presence. But Brogan could not involve himself with it. Sarah would tell Crowell the truth—that she'd heard a noise and gone to investigate. That someone had struck her and left her on the ground.

What she told Crowell of his part in the night's events was up to her. Brogan had Odhar to pursue and a riddle to solve.

He needed to do a thorough search for magic sparks. Quickly altering his vision to do so, he scanned the caves, but he found naught. It wasn't until he sighted up the walls of the castle that he found a few sparks, directly under the shelf where he'd found one of the clues. 'Twas the spot where he'd destroyed the runes.

The only reason the Odhar would have used magic was for the purpose of reconstructing the runes. If Eilinora or her cronies had resorted to using their powers, they would soon reconstruct the verses. It meant Brogan had very little time to decipher what the words meant, and locate the stone.

He tried to follow the scent and the sparks of the magic on the walls, but he was confounded once again. Eilinora had somehow learned a method of concealing her trail. Likely her mentor—the force that had freed her—had the power to hide the sparks and had taught her. Else he'd have been able to track her.

A confrontation with the witch would be quite welcome right now. Brogan would have liked nothing better than to follow her sparks to her lair and mount a surprise attack. She and her followers would not stand a chance against him, not without the stone.

He went back to the fountain in the garden. "Colm, there are signs of Odhar in the ruins. I canna say how many were here, but they killed Andy Ferris."

The dragheen made a sound of revulsion. "'Tis ominous news, m'lord."

"I canna leave Sarah and the others unprotected. I'll stay out near the ruins, but I'll need you to keep watch as well."

The dragheen's wings flexed slightly. "Aye, m'lord. I'll alert you if I see aught."

Brogan made a quick jog to the barn and found only the Ravenfield pony inside. The other horses were gone, indicating that Ridley and his men were away. Craggleton was not far, so it was very likely they'd had business in town that had kept them late.

He saw no evidence of a groom in the small room at the back of the barn, so he climbed to the eaves of the building where there was a good vantage point for keeping watch over the grounds. He made a quick survey of the surrounding territory, then looked toward the house, to Sarah's window.

'Twas illuminated by a low light, the only light in the house. The curtains were drawn, so he could see only an occasional shadow as she prepared for bed. His whole body tensed at the thought of holding her in his arms. He wanted her again.

He wanted her always.

It wasn't possible. What he'd felt before could not have been *sòlas*. It could only have been the release he'd needed ever since he'd first touched Sarah.

He dragged the palm of his hand over his face, then across his mouth in frustration. What he'd shared with Sarah had not felt like a simple release of sexual tension. It had been so much more . . . and certainly not uncomplicated.

The moon reached its zenith by the time Ridley returned. He and two others rode ahead of a carriage manned by three men. They dismounted at the house and went inside, leaving the men in the carriage to deal with the horses.

No one took any note of Brogan in the concealed space he'd chosen, and he settled in to keep an eye on the place while he silently repeated the lines of the ancient Druzai verse, trying to decipher their hidden meaning. He had a clear sense that his time was running out.

Morning came as usual, but Sarah did not feel anything like her normal self. Everything had changed. She'd been attacked in the night, and Andy killed. She'd had disturbing dreams, images of poor Andy, besieged and terrified by some strange creatures of the night.

And she'd become Brendan Locke's mistress.

She bathed quickly before the rest of the house was astir, washing her hair and drying it by the stove in the kitchen, taking care to avoid touching the sore spot on her head. Trying to forget that Brendan would soon be leaving.

He had not given their parting even a second thought, telling her that he would make things right for the girls before he left.

As though that would ease the ache in her heart.

She had solved nothing by going to his cottage after her disastrous meeting with Mr. Ridley. If anything, she'd made matters worse. The girls were going away to Loncrief, Brendan was going to return to Scotland, and he still intended to find her a suitable husband. Even after . . .

She swallowed the sudden burning in her throat. No doubt he had come to accept Squire Crowell as the most likely candidate for her spouse, and would welcome his arrival at Ravenfield to look into Andy's death. It would give her another opportunity to show the squire what a brilliant wife she would make.

She muttered something entirely unladylike under her breath and started to brush her hair over the stove.

It was still early when Maud came down. She

put on the kettle, then made toast. "I don't suppose your talk with Mr. Ridley went so well, did it, Sarah?"

Sarah shook her head. "No. The girls will be going to Loncrief in two weeks."

Maud pressed her hand to her heart. "Oh, I hate to see the poor darlings go there. And what will you do once they're—"

"Maud."

Sarah's tone stopped the older woman from continuing. "What is it, Sarah?"

Sarah took Maud's arm. "Sit down."

"You're frightening me, my girl," Maud said as they sat at the table.

"Last night after dark . . . I heard a noise."

"Where?"

"Out near the ruins. I went to see what it was, and I found . . . I found Andy Ferris. Maud, he fell from the castle wall. He's . . . he's dead."

Maud furrowed her brow and clucked her tongue. "Oh dear. Poor Andy. Always had such a hard way of it. Ah, well, he's in a better pla—"

"Someone else was out there."

"Mr. Locke?"

"N-no. A stranger. Someone who knocked me down."

She did not want to go into so much detail that she frightened Maud, but it was important for her to take particular care.

"Well then, we shouldn't let the girls out of our sight, should we?" Maud said. "At least, not until this prowler is found."

"And we need to summon the magistrate. Andy is still . . . His body is . . . Well, I didn't move it after . . ."

"Oh dear. Yes, of course," she said, rising to make the tea. Without warning, two men from Craggleton came to the door and pushed into the kitchen.

"Who are you?" Maud demanded, startled by their appearance.

Sarah recognized the two, a couple of the boys who'd taunted her, all grown up. They were much bigger now, and looked a good deal more dangerous than they had as youths.

"I'm Jack and that's Roscoe. We're Mr. Ridley's new grooms as of last night," said the taller of the two. "And Frank Tyler will be coming up to the house in a minute. He'll be doing the cooking from now on."

Sarah's stomach clenched. Frank Tyler had been the worst of the boys, hiding in dark corners, grabbing her when she was carrying buckets of water or bushels of laundry and couldn't run or defend herself. She clenched her teeth and remembered that she was an adult now, and could deal with Frank Tyler.

Maud handed Sarah a tray with the tea, a pot

of jam, and the toast she'd just made, then took off her apron. "You are welcome to the kitchen, then," she said, handing her apron to Jack. She took Sarah by the elbow and pulled her from the room.

Stopping short, she turned back to the men. "One of you needs to run up to Corrington House and summon the squire," Maud said. "He's needed to see to the dead man out by the ruins."

Maud did not wait for their reply, but hurried Sarah up the stairs to the nursery, passing Mr. Ridley and his London gentlemen on the stairs. Sarah wondered if it had been one of them who'd struck her last night in the castle ruins. She supposed she should tell Mr. Ridley about Andy, but decided the less she spoke to him, the better.

She and Maud found the girls already up and about in the nursery. They had washed and were fully dressed, but afraid to go downstairs. "He's already down there," said Jane. "We saw him through the crack in the door."

"May we stay in the nursery all day, Miss Granger?" asked Margaret. "Please?"

Sarah put the tray on the table and sat down beside Margaret while Maud paced the room, wringing her hands. She did not speak of all the things going through her mind, but Sarah could easily guess.

Clearly, Maud did not like turning her kitchen

over to the ruffians hired by Mr. Ridley, nor did she enjoy the thought of leaving Jane and Margaret at the mercy of their cold, indifferent guardian. But she and Sarah were merely women, wholly dependent upon the whims of their employer.

Oblivious to the tension in the room, Jane started on her breakfast, and Sarah decided not to tell the girls about Andy, at least not yet. And she wasn't going to spoil the rest of the day and the Pruitt soiree by telling them about Loncrief, either. *Brendan was going to make some better arrangement for them.*

She sat down on one of the chairs and realized that she truly believed he was going to do what he'd promised. Sarah did not know how he would manage it, but she actually trusted him to make things right for the girls.

Margaret went to the window and leaned against it, gazing outside. "I miss Papa."

Sarah's heart lurched, and she went over to the little girl, taking her into her embrace. "I know, love."

"Mr. Ridley doesn't care for us," said Margaret. "Not like Papa."

"But I do," she said, hugging Margaret tightly. "And so does Maud."

She did not know exactly how much power Brendan had, or how a Scotsman could possibly have any sway over Mr. Ridley, but there was no doubt that he was not going to let the girls languish at Loncrief. Maybe there was another school . . . perhaps somewhere near his lands in Scotland.

"We'll have no lessons today," she said. She should not allow herself to hope for such a solution. How would he ever manage it? "We'll spend the morning away from the house, until it's time to get ready for the party."

"I have a bit more work to do on your gown, Miss Granger," said Maud. "Since my services are no longer needed by Mr. Ridley, I shall work contentedly here in the nursery until you come back. The light is much better in here than in my own room."

"Shall we go to my tree?" asked Margaret.

Their choices were limited. Sarah didn't want to go too far from the house, nor did she want the girls anywhere near Andy's body. "Yes, Margaret. We'll take a nice walk up to your tree."

"And will you tell us some tales while we sit in the branches?" asked Jane.

"Oh yes, please," said Margaret, brightening.

"That sounds like a perfect idea," Sarah said, forcing a tone much brighter than her mood.

"May we take the Fairy Luck with us?"

Sarah had never allowed them to take the box outside, but in light of their grim circumstances, she nodded her assent. "Only this once."

* * *

Brogan had to find out if the Barstow lasses were the descendants of Dubhán. If so, they would surely have the second sight as indicated in the first line of the verse, and mayhap know something of the gift of the fae. 'Twas the only way he could think of to pursue the clues.

He thought they might not be aware of what they knew, but with careful questioning, mayhap one or both of them would remember something of the ancient tales about Ravenfield and its history. 'Twas even possible they'd heard the term blood stone, or *brìgha*-stone.

Before dawn, Brogan had seen a light in the kitchen. From his place at the top of the barn, he had a perfect view of the kitchen. And Sarah inside, bathing.

Brogan's heart clenched in his chest as he watched her, obviously unaware that Ridley had hired some men and brought them to the estate. She moved slowly, as though she carried the weight of the world. Brogan knew that in her mind, she did.

Even with a distance between them, he could not help but notice her wince when she touched the bump on her head. He blamed himself, for he should have been more wary of the Odhar intruder. He should have given her—as well as Maud and the lasses—a much stronger warning not to wander alone on the grounds.

She slipped her gown from her shoulders as he watched, and his cock rose at the sight of her perfect skin and the swell of her breasts above her chemise. Their tryst had been ill-advised, and he knew that if anyone learned of it, her chances of a good marriage would be ruined. Yet when he thought of her making a good match, he swore viciously.

She belonged to no one but him. *She* was his *céile* mate, and no amount of denying it would change it. He was in love with a Tuath woman.

Without waking the men sleeping in the barn, Brogan climbed down from his perch and walked to the site where Andy's body lay. His skull was cracked, and it looked as though he'd fallen from the wall. Brogan had little doubt that he'd been pushed. How Eilinora had lured him up there, he did not know, nor did it matter. 'Twas the witch's sheer viciousness that appalled him.

Brogan returned to the house and took up a post outside the kitchen door. He would not frighten Sarah by appearing unannounced at this early hour, but he intended to make sure none of the men from Craggleton barged in on her, either.

Chapter 15

Margaret placed the Luck on the thick branch of the tree while Jane carried her one-armed doll and looked for Brownie. "Will you tell us the story of Ravenfield?" asked Margaret.

Sarah nodded. "The one with the Luck, or the—"

"Oh yes, please. When the fairy gives the Luck to the lady and tells her to keep it safe always."

As Sarah told stories to the girls, her mind worked toward a solution to Loncrief and how to keep them from having to go there.

Some deep and primitive part of her believed that Brendan would come up with a way out of their dilemma, but if he didn't . . . Rational thinking had convinced her that she couldn't take the girls and run away, for she had no doubt Mr. Ridley would find them. But if she hired on as a teacher at Loncrief, she and the girls could still be together, and Sarah would see to it that they were not harshly treated.

It was a solution of sorts . . . not perfect, but at least she could stay near the girls.

Once the rest of the household stirred, Brogan returned to the ruins and located the Odhar's sparks once again. He adjusted his vision and started to trace the magic, tracking the intermittent flickers that caught his awareness. He headed up to the fells where he had not looked before, but soon lost all trace of the sparks. He could find no scent of magic, either, but he was a practiced hunter. He closed down his other senses and focused inwardly, drawing on the cord of power that dwelled within him.

He stretched out the luminous strands that emanated from his body, aware that they would not be visible to anyone but Druzai hunters. The strands extended for miles in every direction, seeking sparks, seeking Druzai power.

The strands swelled and expanded as they coursed over the hills and through the forests, but he found naught. With no choice but to withdraw, Brogan began to pull back into himself, but something attacked him, dropping onto his shoulders and knocking him off balance. He rolled to the ground with it.

The weight lifted suddenly, but then he felt a jab in his ribs and a blow to the side of his head. Turning away from the next blow, Brogan quickly got up to his knees, but took a vicious kick to the jaw.

He shook himself out of his hunter's form and saw his attacker. "You dare, sìthean?"

The leathery creature came at him again, but Brogan deflected the blow. He turned quickly and shoved the sìthean to the ground, holding it down by the throat.

"Who sent you, *deamhan*?" he demanded. He'd never known a sìthean to behave so viciously. At worst, they were foozling pests, even here.

The creature kicked and squealed, but Brogan did not relent. "Where are the Odhar who sent you?"

"Gone!" the sìthean squealed.

Brogan gave it a shake.

"You hurt me, *athair*!"

"Not half as much I will, unless you tell me where they are."

"To the sea!" the sìthean cried. "It find safe places in the sea!"

Brogan yanked the creature up to its feet, holding onto the back of its neck. "Show me," he growled.

The sìthean started to whine. "I know not the place!"

"Aye, you do, and you will take me there. Now."

* * *

Somehow, they got through the day. Sarah let the girls play with the tin Luck and told them stories. When they returned to the nursery, she penned her letter to Loncrief, offering her services as a teacher. She tried not to think about the bleak future she and the girls had to look forward to if Brendan's plan was not successful.

Mr. Ridley summoned Sarah to the library to speak with Squire Crowell about Andy Ferris, and she told them how she'd found the poor man. The squire asked a number of questions, but apparently he did not wonder how she happened to be out walking after dark. Sarah was glad he did not ask.

She told them she'd been attacked when she discovered Andy's body, by someone she did not recognize. Squire Crowell had asked a few more questions, then admonished her to stay close to the house and keep the children with her until the villain could be found.

Maud managed to bring an early supper up to the nursery, which they ate before bathing and getting ready for the Pruitt soiree. The girls were anxious to attend the party, but Sarah wasn't quite so eager. No doubt Brendan would appear, as promised, to escort them. She knew he would not disappoint the girls.

But Sarah didn't know if her heart could survive seeing him again, knowing he wanted her there only to snare Squire Crowell for her husband.

"Go and change into your new gown, my dear," said Maud, sensing her reluctance to leave for the party.

"Maud, I don't think—"

"Nonsense, my girl. Do not think about it, just go. The girls are counting on you."

It was a challenge to keep Jane from ruining her clothes until it was time to go, but Maud kept track of both girls while Sarah dressed. As she slipped on the beautiful gown, her eyes filled with tears, aware that Brendan had been right about the color. It complemented her coloring perfectly.

She could not bring herself to care, not when she knew he'd chosen it to attract another man.

The lines fit her body perfectly, the neckline low and seductive. The skirt flowed from the waist just under her breasts, the copper fabric shimmering as she moved her legs. She slipped on her shoes, collected her long gloves, and returned to the nursery, where the girls squealed at the sight of her. Maud beamed happily as she fastened the buttons up the back of the gown.

"Oh my dear saints, it does you justice. But you must smile, you know!"

"Maud says that with a bit of luck, you're likely to meet a husband at Mrs. Pruitt's," said Margaret.

Sarah shook her head. "Maud jests, love. It would take all the luck in the world to bring a husband to a pauper's daughter."

"But the Fairy Luck—"

"'Tis only an old box, Margaret," said Sarah. "If it were going to bring me luck, it would have done so well before now."

Margaret's face fell and Sarah crouched down beside her. "I'm sorry, love. Perhaps there will be a man at the soiree who will declare his love for me."

Sarah bit her lip at the lie, and sat down so Maud could arrange her hair, taking care to avoid the sore spot.

Then it was time to go down the stairs to await Brendan, but Mr. Ridley was in the drawing room, pacing impatiently. "'Tis about time," he said irritably, digging his watch from his pocket. "We needed to leave five minutes ago."

Sarah pulled her shawl about her shoulders and started for the door, swallowing her disappointment. Seeing Brendan was going to hurt . . . not seeing was going to be even more painful. "Come along, girls." She knew Brendan had never really intended to escort them to the soiree, anyway, only agreeing to go when he'd seen their dismay at Maud's dismissal.

And she was a fool to have entertained the possibility that he could change Mr. Ridley's mind about Loncrief.

Roscoe opened the door from outside, and Sarah saw a plain black carriage with four horses awaiting them on the drive in front of the house. Mr. Ridley led the way to the carriage as Roscoe raked his eyes down Sarah's body, making her feel naked. She would have turned 'round and gone back inside if not for a second carriage—a beautiful, painted landau—that pulled into the drive.

It was an impressive vehicle with a lamp on each side, and two drivers. Drawn by four horses, it bypassed Mr. Ridley's carriage, and when it stopped at Ravenfield's front door, Brendan Locke emerged. Sarah's heart expanded impossibly when he jumped to the ground.

"Mr. Locke!" Jane cried. She ran to him and threw her arms around his legs.

Grinning, Brendan lifted her into his arms. "I am no' late, am I?"

He had a bruise around his left eye and his lower lip was swollen, and Sarah had to restrain herself from running to him to assure herself that there was no other damage. She could not imagine what had happened to him since last she'd seen him.

Mr. Ridley went to his own carriage and waited for Jack to open its door. He stood beside it and looked pointedly at Sarah.

* * *

"They'll be goin' with me, Ridley," said Brogan. He did not await a reaction, but handed Jane into the carriage, and then Margaret. A moment later, he took Sarah's hand and leaned toward her. He spoke quietly, so that no one else could hear. "You're lovely, lass. And you're mine. Doona forget it."

He was going to take her to Coruain with him.

He'd taken the sìthean to the beach, and the little sprite had shown him where Eilinora's Odhar had emerged from the sea. He hadn't been able to wheedle any more information out of the silly creature, but at least he knew the place where the villains would return when they tried to go back to the Astar Columns.

"We thought you weren't coming for us," Meglet said.

Brogan took his seat across from Sarah. He wanted to pull her to the bench beside him, to take her hand in his and promise her once more that all was going to be well. He could feel it.

He had decided to let the Odhar find the stone. Now that he knew where Eilinora and her sorcerers would go once they had it, Brogan intended to ambush the rogues and take the stone from them.

"I always keep my promises, little Meglet," he said, catching sight of a square of metal in her hand. "Tell me, lasses, will you be happy for Miss Granger when she weds and goes away to her husband's lands?"

"But Miss Granger says there is no man who would want a . . . a—"

"That's enough, Margaret," Sarah said, her voice quivering. She did not believe that all would be well, but that would change as soon as he explained. He was going to tell her everything about himself, about the Druzai and the Tuath, and ask her to come with him to Coruain to be his wife.

She was his *céile* mate. He wanted to take her into his arms, kiss her and assure her that he hadn't played loose with her feelings.

It would have to wait until they were alone and he could tell her about his magic and all that he intended to do for the lasses, for Ravenfield. Somehow, he was going to make her see that she belonged with him on Coruain, and ask her to go to his faraway home with him.

She took the children's hands in both of hers, noticing with uncharacteristic irritation that Meglet's hands were not empty. "Oh, Margaret, why did you bring the Luck?"

"Because you said you needed all the luck in the world—"

Brogan looked at the box in Meglet's hand and realized 'twas the same tin container that he'd seen in Sarah's trunk. He frowned. "The box will give Miss Granger luck?"

"'Tis an old, worthless heirloom from my mother," Sarah said. "'Tis nothing."

"But Miss Granger," said Jane. "'Tis your Fairy Luck."

Brendan looked as though he'd swallowed a herring, whole. He reached toward them and took the box from Margaret's hand. "May I?"

"It was a gift of the fairies," said Jane. "And Miss Granger told us stories about the fairy princess and all her troubles."

Brendan's expression changed, his eyes darkening almost imperceptibly. He looked at Sarah. "'Tis a Fairy Luck?"

She had no chance to reply when Meglet pointed to the smoothed markings on the sides. "See? The fairies carved something into the sides, only we cannot see it anymore."

"What does it say, Miss Granger?"

"'Tis just a silly rhyme my mother made up."

"What does it say, *moileen*?" he repeated.

"Be thy casket lost or broak," said Margaret.

Jane finished, *"Then Ravenfield's luck will dissolve in smoke."*

"But you see it's cracked," said Sarah, her own voice breaking. "And so is our luck."

Brogan's throat tightened as he considered

the possibility that *Sarah* was Dubhán's heir. 'Twould make her Druzai. Likely she had talents she didn't even know she possessed. "Can you open it?"

She shook her head and looked away. "No. My mother might have known how, but she said it was a puzzle box and could only be opened by a man who . . . a-a man who w-would . . ."

Meglet became as impatient as Brogan when Sarah's words drifted off. "Who would *what*, Miss Granger?" she demanded.

Sarah turned pale and looked up at him, her eyes confused and full of questions. "She said he would come from far shores."

"From Scotland?" Meglet turned to him, oblivious to Sarah's bewilderment. "Can you open it, then, Mr. Locke?"

"Aye. 'Tis very likely I can." 'Twas a *ràcain*—a riddle box. He'd seen a few of them on Coruain, but never had any interest in them, no more than he'd paid attention to the *crìoch-fàile*. But he could solve this, just as he'd solved the nested circles.

He slid his fingers over the crack in the top and realized 'twas no accidental fissure. He thought of all the *ràcains* he'd seen in houses on Coruain, and tried to remember the tricks that would open them. In a land where everything could easily be conquered by magic, the Druzai had a particular liking for problems that could be solved only through ingenuity.

There had to be a release on the surface of the box, something that had escaped the attention of all the generations of women who'd owned the thing. Yet he was certain beyond a doubt that this was where he would find the *brìgha*-stone.

"I think I've found the trick," he said, too impatient to work the puzzle. Instead, he used the energy of his mind to spring the top of the box. His magic definitely left sparks for the Odhar to find, but Brogan did not much care, not when he looked inside the Luck and saw the stone he sought. Besides, if Eilinora's sorcerer had sent a sìthean after him, his identity was no longer secret.

Sarah could not have been more shocked to see the dark red stone nested inside her Luck. To her knowledge, the box had never been opened.

"'Tis what you were looking for," she said, and the knowledge that he was now free to go weighed heavily on her. She'd known he was leaving, but this discovery made his departure imminent.

He nodded and slipped the box inside his formal black coat. "D'you mind if I hold this for safekeeping?"

Sarah shook her head. "Now that you've found it, you'll go."

He looked across at her, and Sarah felt the heat of his gaze. "No, lass. I've a few promises to keep first."

"What promises, Mr. Locke?" Margaret asked.

"Weel, first of all, I've promised to see that you two bonny lasses remain settled at Ravenfield with no Mr. Ridley to frighten you."

"Oh, Brendan, you cannot—"

"Aye. I can. And I will, before we go."

She felt tears burning the backs of her eyes, but the carriage came to a halt as they arrived at Pruitt Hall. Sarah blinked them back, glad for the diversion, else Margaret was sure to start questioning Brendan.

He should not make such promises to them, for there was nothing he could do about their circumstances. As much as she wanted to believe, her common sense had returned and was winning the battle against foolish hope.

"Come, my wee ladies," he said as he climbed out of the landau, helping each of the girls down. "And you, my lovely Sarah." He brushed away a tear from her cheek and touched her chin before taking her elbow to guide her out of the conveyance. "You must trust me."

"But Brendan, you don't understand."

"Ah, my dear Miss Granger. 'Tis you who doesna understand."

* * *

There was music playing as Brogan escorted the Ravenfield females into the hall, and it was yet fuller and more magical than what Sarah had played on the pianoforte, if that were even possible. Brogan looked over the crowd that had gathered and wondered if there were Odhar among them.

He would not mind if there were, for he was well-equipped to defeat any of them, especially now that he held the *brìgha*-stone.

Meglet and Jennie found some other children and went to play with them while Mrs. Pruitt greeted them. "Why, Miss Granger! You look . . ."

"Lovely, is she no'?" Brogan said, though Mrs. Pruitt did not appear particularly pleased to admit that Sarah was one of the most comely lasses in the room. He wanted to slip his arm 'round her waist and pull her close, but he could see by looking at the crowd that such a gesture was not done in public.

The woman showed them to a refreshment table at the far side of the room, where she tried to draw him away and abandon Sarah. Brogan managed to extricate himself from her grasping hands, but was unable to avoid her invitation to join the dancers. "I doona dance, madam." And even if he could, he would not leave Sarah, not while she was so upset. He needed to get her alone, wanted to explain everything to her.

If only he knew how.

The Pruitt woman gave a tittering laugh and tapped him lightly with a folded fan while Sarah tried to slip away, her skin flushing, but not with embarrassment. He could feel unease rolling off her body in waves. 'Twas well past time to get her alone.

"You jest, Mr. Locke," said Mrs. Pruitt. "Come."

"No, I assure you," he replied, returning to Sarah's side. "'Tis a skill I never learned."

Squire Crowell and his entourage arrived, with Charles Ridley right behind. The master of Ravenfield headed straight for Sarah, his features dark and forbidding. Sarah straightened, her face turning expressionless.

Ridley gave a brief nod to Brogan, then turned to Sarah. "Miss Granger, I see you have arrived safe and sound. We will discuss your impertinence later."

"Impertinence?" Brogan asked.

Ridley's jaw flexed once, but he did not alter his gaze, pinning Sarah with a hostile look. "I do not hold you responsible, Locke. She knew she was expected to ride with me."

Brogan laughed. "Do no' be any more a buffoon than necessary, Ridley. I invited Miss Granger and the lasses to ride with me. They kindly agreed, and so here we are."

Sarah gasped.

"Oh, and I nearly forgot . . ." Brogan withdrew a packet of papers from his coat and handed them to Ridley. "These documents were misdelivered to my cottage. They're for you."

Scowling, Ridley took the papers and made a quick exit as he broke the seal and started to read them. As soon as he'd decided it was safe to use his power, Brogan had changed the entailment and the wardship of the lasses, causing the new documents to appear. In a few moments, Ridley would discover he had no business at Ravenfield.

"Brendan," she said urgently, keeping her voice low. "He will take out his anger on the girls. He will think of something worse than Loncrief—"

"Bonny Sarah," he said, drawing her away from the crowd at the table, "tell me who would be their best guardian."

"What do you mean?"

"If you could name anyone in the world—anyone other than yourself—who would you ask to take care of the lasses?"

"Brendan, I—"

"Humor me, lass."

'Twas clear she did not take the question seriously, but Brogan had no chance to pursue it when Squire Crowell approached them. He gave a short bow, his eyes dancing over Sarah's figure.

"Hello, Miss Granger." He gestured toward

Brogan. "I don't believe I've met the gentleman . . ."

As Sarah made the introductions, Brogan
moved closer to her, clearly warning the other
man off, in an essentially male assertion. Almost
imperceptibly, Crowell moved back.

"Mr. Locke, I wonder where you were last night
after dark?"

"In my cottage," he replied, realizing that, as a
stranger to the district, he ought to be one of the
first to be suspected of the misdeed at Ravenfield.
Yet because he was well-dressed and wealthy, it
seemed that he was above suspicion. 'Twas foolish, but fortunate for Brogan.

"You'll have heard about the poor creature
who fell from the ruins, of course," said Crowell.
"'Tis all around the neighborhood. Not that poor
Andy'll be missed by anyone in these parts . . ."

"Aye. I heard."

"Well, here is Mr. Rutherford, whom Miss
Granger met the other day," the squire said, "and
his wife, Mrs. Rutherford." The couple stepped
forward, and Brogan recognized each one from
seeing them through the window at Corrington
House. They gave cursory greetings, then moved
on to Mrs. Pruitt.

It was Brogan's best opportunity to escape with
Sarah.

Seeing a doorway behind the musicians, he

took her through it and emerged in a dim and quiet hall. He seized her hand and pulled her into his arms, desperate to feel her body against his, anxious to prove that she belonged to him. He had the stone; now was the time to ask her to come to Coruain.

"Crowell has no claim on you, lass." He dipped his head and kissed her, their mouths melding together as one.

"Brendan, please . . ." Her voice trembled and she pulled back slightly to draw her fingers over his forehead and cheek where the sìthean had bruised him. "What happened to you? How were you hurt?"

"'Tis naught. Come here." He hugged her close and felt the pounding of her heart in her chest. He was unconcerned about the sìthean's attack and the fact that the Odhar knew who he was. He had the blood stone, and there were no Odhar alive who could take it from him.

"I must get back to the girls," Sarah said. "I cannot just leave them."

"Aye, this once you can, Sarah. They are dancing with the other children."

She broke away and took a step back. Biting her lower lip, she looked away from him. "Brendan, I . . . I was mistaken in coming to you last night. I should never have—"

He did not let her retreat, but followed her as

she moved away. "Sarah, you know I've found what I came for."

Her pretty throat moved as she swallowed thickly. She was trembling. "You're leaving."

"No' without you." He took her hand and meshed his fingers with hers. "I want you, Sarah Granger, for my wife."

Tears welled in her eyes and spilled over to course down her cheek. She closed her eyes and tried to turn away. But Brogan did not allow it.

"I'd thought to make things right for you as well as the lasses, showing you how to attract a man like Crowell. But I willna give you up."

Her chin trembled as she looked up into his eyes. "I-I love you, Brendan." She pressed one hand to her heart. "Dear Lord, I don't know how it happened so fast . . . but I can't leave the girls. I—"

"I will take care of the lasses. You must trust me."

"You keep saying that, but what can you possibly do? The entailment is clear, Mr. Ridley's guardianship—"

"Will change as soon as you tell me who would be a better protector."

"Brendan, I don't understand."

"I know you have no reason to believe me, *moi-leen*. But let me explain."

* * *

"Can you open your mind, Sarah, and try to understand—try to *believe*—what I'm going to tell you?"

Sarah nodded, feeling the warmth of his body as he leaned one hand against the wall beside her head.

"I am no' quite what you assumed me to be." He touched her cheek and continued. "My people are no' Scots. We are called Druzai. We are of a different race, though we used to live among you. 'Twas eons ago that we removed ourselves from this place, to protect your kind from us."

She crinkled her brow and tried to understand him. "Th-then where . . . ?"

"My home is an isle on the other side of the sea. We remain hidden from your world."

His words frightened her, made her feel as though she were falling through a black void.

"Sarah, I am a warrior of my people. My father was killed by our common enemy, and I was compelled to come here to find this *brigha*-stone. 'Tis a thing that possesses its own power."

"I-I don't understand you. *Brigha*?" she whispered.

"'Tis strange to you. Aye." He took her hand in his. "You're trembling, *moileen*. Are you afraid of me?"

A jolt of energy surged through her at his touch, and she felt drawn to him, like a sewing needle to the most powerful magnet she could imagine.

"No. Not of you." She trembled with the power of her attraction, and knew she would go with him, if only there were some way to take the girls with them.

He took a deep breath and gazed directly into her eyes. "Listen to me, lass. My home is far from here, and verra different from this place. I am a son of the high chieftain. My father was killed by a . . . a criminal . . . called Eilinora. The stone from your Fairy Luck—and its twin in another time and place—are the only weapons we have against her."

Sarah rubbed her forehead.

"I know this doesna make much sense to you, Sarah. You must believe me."

"I do," she whispered, though she did not know why. She loved him, but his story . . . it was incomprehensible.

He leaned forward and touched his forehead to hers. "Would you say Maud would be the best guardian for the lasses?"

"Yes. She loves them like her own grandchildren, but she is feeling her age, Brendan. She cannot keep up with them."

"But if she were to feel younger? If her bones didna ache and her sight was better?"

Sarah nodded. "Yes."

He reached into his coat and pulled out the violet satchel that had washed up with him. It was crushed flat, but when he opened it and reached inside, he pulled out a handful of gold coins. Then another.

Sarah nearly gasped at the sight of such a fortune.

He tossed the first handful of coins into the air and they disappeared, making quiet popping sounds as they vanished. The same thing happened with the second, and then the third handful, and Sarah could only gape at him. "You . . . you're a magician?"

"Not exactly. The coins are now in Maud's possession."

"But how—?"

"The Druzai have powers that canna be explained. Just know that Maud's joints no longer cause her any pain. Her eyes are good once again, and she is now a woman of means. She can hire a nurse of her choice to care for Meglet and Jane. She can go away to her sister's house, or remain at Ravenfield. The property will always belong to the lasses. Naught can change that."

Sarah took the satchel from him and shook it. "'Tis empty."

"Only if I want it to be," he said, his voice dark and seductive. "Reach inside it."

Sarah put her hand down to the bottom of the

satchel and felt a hard leather surface. She pulled out the two objects inside—replacements for the shoes she'd ruined the day she'd run into the sea to rescue him. "'Tis impossible. These could not have been inside."

"I was not to use any magic once I arrived here, so I had to put everything I would need into the satchel before I left my home," he said. "'Tis where I kept my clothes . . . and the money I gave you."

She could not believe it, yet she'd seen it with her own eyes. She'd forgotten to ask him about his suit, and how it had survived the sea with nary a wrinkle. He must truly be a powerful sorcerer . . . yet why would he want her?

The question went unasked when the music in the next room stopped and everything went silent.

"What is it?"

"Mayhap 'tis Eilinora, come to confront me. Stay here."

He went back toward the ballroom, but Sarah followed him. Margaret and Jane suddenly squealed and ran from the crush of people near the doorway, toward a man in a blue coat and light breeches. He walked with crutches, and Sarah saw that one of his trouser legs was empty. She staggered on her own feet at the sight of Captain Barstow, alive, but looking thin and haggard, in the center of Mrs. Pruitt's ballroom.

It was one shock too many.

Brendan took hold of her elbow to steady her. "Are you all right, Sarah?"

She pressed a hand to her heart and nodded. "'Tis the girls' father!" she whispered. "Captain Barstow is alive!"

Chapter 16

Even Brogan was shocked, though he did not know the man. A number of the women in the room began to weep as someone pulled up a chair for Barstow and he gathered his daughters into his arms. It was quite some time before the man was able to tell that he'd lost his leg in battle and had languished for months in a military hospital in Spain. He had not even been aware that his family thought him dead until he'd arrived at Ravenfield an hour before.

"So you've seen Maud?" Sarah asked, wiping her eyes.

"Yes," Barstow replied. "She sent me here."

One of the men announced a grand celebration in honor of Captain Barstow's return, and the music resumed, along with dancing and toasting. Sarah introduced Brogan to the girls' father, and the captain's friends soon drew him and his daughters to a small room away from the main party, where the festivities seemed even more jovial than before. Everyone celebrated the return of Ravenfield's true master, but Brogan knew his time was running out. He had to leave.

And he wanted Sarah with him.

He took her hand and led her out of the ballroom to a terrace, where they descended the steps and went out into the garden.

They stopped behind a tall hedge, in a circle decorated with numerous stone statues. Sarah sat on a bench near the center as Brendan went down on one knee before her and removed her Fairy Luck from his coat. He set it on the bench beside her and opened it, removing the dark red stone from it.

Sarah gasped when it turned a bright red color in his hand and started to glow, its color undulating so that it seemed to writhe in his hand.

"Sarah, *moileen*. My people are in grave danger," he said. "'Tis only this—the *brìgha*-stone—that will give us the power to vanquish Eilinora and those who follow her."

A strange, rough voice came to them from somewhere nearby. Sarah looked 'round, but all she could see was a statue.

"M'lord Brogan, someone approaches," it said.

Brendan turned to look at the gray stone figure of a maiden with a circlet of flowers in her hair and a basket of flowers draped over her arm. "Dragheen," he said to it, "Colm spoke of you."

Sarah gasped as the stone statue made a slow bow to him and spoke.

"I be Geilis, m'lord. They come. Odhar!"

Brendan's expression turned fierce. He suddenly grabbed Sarah's arm and started to push her away. "Run, Sarah! Get as far away as you—"

A loud crack rent the air, and suddenly he was lifted from the ground and thrown into the air. Sarah screamed.

"No one will hear you, Tuath," said a woman whose shrill voice rang in Sarah's ears.

Sarah looked toward the speaker, and saw that it was Mrs. Rutherford. The woman held her hand up, palm out with her fingers spread, as a visible streak of light seemed to hold Brendan in the air.

Terrified, Sarah picked up Brendan's red stone and thrust it behind her back. "Let him down!" she cried as the stone heated her hand.

Mrs. Rutherford laughed. "This Druzai prince is not worth your time, little Tuath."

"Run, Miss Sarah!" the statue ordered. "Lord Brogan canna help you now."

"Eilinora!" Brogan used his few moments in the air to draw on all the power he could muster. He took in a deep breath and blew out a scorching wind in Eilinora's direction, catching her, as well as her "husband" in the flames.

Eilinora released him and he started to fall, but caught himself before he hit the ground. He put up a wall of stone between Sarah and Eilinora, but it crumbled almost as quickly as he'd raised it. "Sarah, run! Get away from here!"

Brogan could not watch Sarah go, not while Eilinora and Rutherford recovered from the flames and launched their next attack. Brogan vaulted high into the branches of a nearby tree to avoid the daggers they threw at him.

He conjured numinous bonds, just like the ones the ancient elders had used to bind the Odhar minions, and started to circle the two of them. With a loud, rasping sound, Eilinora transformed herself into a wisp of smoke, while Rutherford became a snake and slithered away in the opposite direction.

A bolt of pain hit Brogan in the center of his back, and he fell to his knees, blinded by the agony of Eilinora's blow. Certain he could feel the blood draining from his body, he knew she would come in for the kill unless he acted. The snake took shape in front of him and held out his father's scepter, just out of reach.

More quickly than any eye could see, Brogan drew a broadsword from the air and speared Rutherford through the heart. Still reeling with the pain in his back, he tried to reach for his father's scepter, but Eilinora did not allow him to move. She drew a heavy rope 'round his neck and pulled it taut.

Sarah could not move, even though that strange, rasping voice of the statue kept ordering her to go.

Paralyzed in place, she watched as Mrs. Rutherford—Eilinora—yanked Brendan up by the hair and choked him with a thick rope. He'd killed Mr. Rutherford with a spear that had . . . She shook her head as though that could clear it . . . The spear had *flown* into his chest.

A heavy gold rod floated in the air above Mr. Rutherford's body, and Eilinora taunted Brendan with it as she choked him, pulling the rope tighter and tighter. "Your father let it go willingly, my dear Lord Brogan!" she screamed. "He released the spells that bound his scepter to him to spare your lives—yours and your brother's!"

She was killing him. Sarah could see that the woman held some extraordinary power over him, and it seemed to emanate from the rod—the scepter. It shimmered in the twilight, hovering over Brendan, somehow encasing him in its cold, vicious grip.

Frantic to help him, Sarah looked for a weapon to use, even though she knew nothing she could wield would be effective against such a bizarre and extraordinary adversary. If she'd had trouble believing Brendan's story, she knew now that he had not exaggerated.

He'd told her to run away, but she couldn't leave him here, not at the mercy of this vicious woman and that horrible scepter. Without thinking, she took hold of her skirts and ran toward them.

"Get away from him!"

Eilinora just laughed. But at least Sarah had provided a diversion, a temporary break in the witch's concentration. The scepter wavered in the air, then turned in Sarah's direction.

Without thinking, she held up her hand to ward off the sparks that shot toward her, and was surprised when they collided with the sharp red glow of the rock in her hand. It was the stone Brendan had searched for, and it was blazing painfully in her hand, making her feel dizzy and disoriented.

Eilinora screeched, and Brendan shoved away from her, turning to knock the witch to the ground. But a thousand needles pierced Sarah's skin, from the top of her head to the soles of her feet, and she wavered.

"Hold it there, Sarah!" Brendan shouted.

He grabbed Eilinora by the throat.

"You will never defeat Pakal, for the Druzai are weak," cried the witch.

"What is Pakal?" Brogan demanded. He

reached for the scepter while the stone burned Sarah's hand. She could barely hold it steady. She felt faint and light-headed, and it wobbled in her hand. "Brendan?"

"'Tis almost over, *moileen*," he said. But his voice sounded distant, as though he were calling to her over a roar of some horrible noise. "Hold on!"

It was almost as if the scepter itself was roaring like some creature she'd never heard of. It filled her ears and engulfed her mind so that she could barely think.

She could not hold it any longer. The red stone seemed to pull her soul through the palms of her hands, and with a shuddering cry, she dropped to her knees, crying out in pain. "Brendan!"

Just as Brogan wrapped his fingers 'round it, something tore the scepter from his hand. There was a sudden, complete silence, then a hiss as the air around him prickled with energy. The fleeting figure of a man appeared, but was quickly swallowed by a dark tear in the atmosphere.

Brogan's moment of distraction gave Eilinora the advantage. She pushed away and turned on Sarah.

Without hesitating, Brogan sent her a killing blast. The murderous witch faltered and fell, but Brogan did not stay to watch the dissolution of her body.

He rushed to Sarah's side, still bewildered by her control of the blood stone. She had to be Dubhán's heir. She was Druzai.

But she was barely alive.

What skills she possessed were unrefined, so she hadn't known how to wield the power of the blood stone, and the ordeal had weakened her dangerously. Brogan laid his hands over her heart and her forehead, then called forth every healing force he knew.

He prayed as he poured his own magic into her, desperate to restore her.

"Sarah, *moileen*, look at me."

He clenched his jaw and renewed his efforts, sending inadequate silvery healing threads 'round her body, rejecting the possibility that he might fail. She'd been honest and forthright with him, while he'd lied to her from the moment he first met her. She was competent and uncomplaining, caring for Meglet and Jane without a thought for her own happiness or welfare.

She was his *céile* mate, the one woman he could trust and confide in. He loved her.

"Please, Sarah, awaken. My life is worth naught without you." He wished he had his brother's healing strength, but all he could do was surround her with Druzai light and hope 'twould heal her.

Her body shimmered in the light of the threads, and he felt her quiver. Her eyes fluttered, and she groaned. Brogan took her hands in his own and pressed a kiss to each of her palms, healing the burns from the stone. "That's it, *moileen*. Come back to me."

She opened her eyes, but they did not focus at first. She drew back in fear, then saw him. "Brendan?"

"Aye ... Brogan. Call me by my rightful name."

She lifted her hand to his face and touched his cheek. "'Tis wet."

He swallowed thickly, unaware that he'd shed his first tears since he was a wee lad.

She started to push herself up, but he lifted her into his arms and carried her to the bench.

"I don't know what happened," she said. "The stone started to burn and I felt so weak."

"Doona think about it now," he said as he sat down. He pressed a kiss to her forehead, unwilling to let her out of his embrace. "You saved my life."

"The girls—where are the girls?"

"We'll go back and check on them as soon as you're stronger."

"I must look a mess."

"Aye." He smiled. "A lovely mess, but I'll put you to rights before we return."

"Bren ... Brogan?"

"Aye, lass?"

"I love you. I was so afraid that woman was going to succeed in killing you . . ."

"I am verra difficult to kill, *moileen*, but I thank you for your assistance. 'Twas quite welcome."

She swallowed and pressed her face against his chest. "I think we should go back."

"No' until you kiss me, lass."

Sarah's ordeal seemed like part of a strange, disconnected past. She could remember every detail of Eilinora's attack, but it seemed as though it had happened to someone else.

"I must return to Coruain, my love," Brogan said. "My people need the protection of the stone. No doubt my brother has found the other stone and awaits me there."

Sarah felt like the dullest of women, unable to follow even the simplest of conversations. "But Eilinora . . . is she not . . ."

"Vanquished? Aye. But some stronger power released her from her prison. I'm fairly sure 'twas he that took my father's scepter from me just now. I felt his power. 'Tis only with the *brìgha*-stone that we'll be able to defeat it."

She felt his gaze, intent on every nuance of her expression. She'd never heard of Coruain or Druzai or any of the other things he'd spoken of. But she knew that everything he'd told her was true.

And she knew that she loved him. She was his for the taking.

Captain Barstow had returned, so Mr. Ridley would leave Ravenfield, and Maud could go to Ulverston a wealthy woman. He truly *had* made things right. "Brogan, did you . . ." She frowned. "Captain Barstow . . . he was dead."

Brogan shook his head. "I had naught to do with it, love. No Druzai can raise the dead, so it must have been a mistake, just as he said."

She slipped her arms around his neck and raised her face to his. He trembled slightly when she pressed a kiss to his lips. Brogan let out a long sigh and hugged her close. "I love you, Sarah. But you havena yet consented to be my wife. Will you no' put me out of my misery?"

"Yes," she whispered, cupping his face with her hands. "I'll marry you."

She slid her fingers through the hair at his nape and he kissed her, easing his tongue through the seam of her lips, searing her with his heat. He made a low sound and covered her breast with his hand as she arched into his touch.

With a groan he broke their contact and took a deep, shuddering breath. "I would take you to the cottage and make love to you now," he said. "But we must hasten, *moileen*. Coruain needs us."

Brogan assisted her as she stood, holding her until she felt steady on her feet. Then he made a slight motion with one hand, returning her gown to the state it was in when they'd arrived. It was clean again, and even more beautiful than before, if that were possible.

"Sarah, I am going to do something that will make your parting with Ravenfield easier."

She nodded, trusting him with all her heart, but feeling startled when the statue spoke once again.

"My congratulations to you, Lord Brogan," the dragheen said. "And to your lady. 'Twas well-done."

Brogan gave a nod of acknowledgment, though he knew he had not been entirely victorious. He'd had his father's scepter in his hand, yet something—Pakal?—had taken it from him.

"Geilis, if you will," Brogan said to the dragheen. "Send a suggestion to Captain Barstow—tell him to take his daughters home to Ravenfield. Now."

"Aye, m'lord. 'Twill be my pleasure to serve you."

He felt Sarah gaping at him, and he slipped his hand 'round her waist. "I'll teach you about my world—our world—in time, *moileen*. For now, we must hasten to say our farewells."

The Barstow family was gone when they returned to the soiree, and Brogan and Sarah followed close behind, arriving at Ravenfield shortly after the captain and his daughters. The lasses were happy, but tearful when they heard the explanation that Sarah was going to elope with Mr. Locke and go to his lands in Scotland, for that was the only account they could give.

"It was the Luck, wasn't it?" Meglet asked.

"It worked, Miss Granger!" Jane cried. "It brought you a husband!"

Sarah nodded and looked to him, her love glowing brightly in her eyes. Brogan felt his heart tighten in his chest at the sight of her, his *céile* mate, the woman who would bear his children, who would feel his love for all time. The power of his passion for her staggered him.

They soon took their leave of those she loved at Ravenfield, but before they started down the path to the beach where Sarah had discovered Brogan half drowned, he stopped her. "One last thing," he said.

He reached down to the ground, and Sarah saw a small bundle of fur appear in his hand. "A kitten!" she whispered. "'Tis black and brown striped, just like Brownie."

Brogan set the small creature on the ground, and as he sent it toward the house, he caused the door to open just wide enough for the kitten to fit through.

When it was safely inside, they hastened to the beach. "I am not m-much of a swimmer," Sarah said, shivering in the cool evening air.

Brogan drew her against his body and held her close, reassuring her, warming her.

"Then 'tis fortunate you willna be required to swim, my love. I'll protect you. My magic will take us to the columns where we will pass through to my time, to my place."

"Kiss me first."

Drawing her into his arms, he pulled a luminous shield 'round them. And as he kissed her, they plunged into the sea toward the life they would share together.

Avon Romantic Treasures

Unforgettable, enthralling love stories, sparkling with passion and adventure from Romance's bestselling authors

Avon Romances
the best in
exceptional authors and unforgettable novels!